Mike Nemeth

A Tissue of Lies

a novel

This is a work of fiction. All characters, locations and events in the narrative – other than those clearly in the public domain – are products of the author's imagination and are used fictitiously. Any resemblance to real persons, living or dead, is entirely coincidental and not intended by the author. Where real historical figures, locations and events appear, these have been depicted in a fictional context.

For more information:

www.mikenemethauthor.com

Interior book design by White Rabbit Arts

at The Historical Fiction Company

Cover design by Peter Telep at www.bespokebookcovers.com

ISBN (paperback) 978-1-962465-37-3

ISBN (eBook) 978-1-962465-38-0

Acclaim for *A Tissue of Lies*

"An engrossing story of a kid deciphering the fine line between right and wrong. Eddie is a complex anti-hero: not as holy as he thinks, but capable of deep feeling, rendered in lyrical prose. Readers will root for his crooked search for a compromised goodness." - Kirkus Indie Reviews

"*A Tissue of Lies* is a compelling work with a fantastic narrative power and style … The book is a poignant coming-of-age tale that captures the essence of a generation marked by rebellion, sacrifice, and the pursuit of identity … Nemeth's storytelling prowess brings a period in history to life through a rich tapestry of characters and events, leaving a lasting impact on the reader …" - K. C. Finn for Reader's Favorites

For Elizabeth Adeline Weiss Kamke

My emotional refuge and protector.

Rest in peace.

Table of Contents

“The last temptation is the greatest treason:
to do the right deed for the wrong reason.”
- T. S. Eliot

1970

Prologue

I'm as good as dead.

On July first, in a shameful, and shameless, televised event, a bloodless bureaucrat from the Defense Department turned the crank on a translucent drum filled with 365 plastic balls, each inscribed with a day of the year. With the indifference of a bored bingo caller at a nursing home, he plucked balls from the drum and called out the dates. In living rooms across the country, nervous families waited in anticipation to hear their nineteen-year-old sons' birthdates and draft order.

The forty-second ball bore my birthday, June fourth, a draft number so low it left no room for hope or optimism. But I continued to watch, drawn to the drama like a rubbernecker passing a car wreck. I tried to imagine at what point in the drawings boys barely old enough to shave would feel safe. Signing off the program, the bureaucrat left no doubt. Like tuna snagged in a net, nineteen-year-olds with the first one hundred twenty-five birthdays drawn would be conscripted to fight a war in a third-world country few can find on a map.

Four days later, a terse draft notice—when and where to report—landed in my mailbox.

What had been a grassfire in 1966, when my brother was drafted, has become an inextinguishable conflagration now that I'm in the government's crosshairs. Nearly two million Americans have served in Vietnam and some fifty thousand have returned from the war in body bags, and yet more troops are needed because we are losing the war.

Vietnamization is a political PR stunt but not a reality in the jungles and valleys where more than 335,000 U.S. troops continue to fight. Nixon promised to withdraw 150,000 troops over the course of twelve months, which stoked some optimism among draft-aged men, then reversed himself a month later and terminated deferments for fatherhood, agriculture, and critical occupations, tightening the noose around young men's necks. In Paris, Kissinger conducts a futile negotiation with the North Vietnamese who refuse to bend to our will. I hope Henry enjoys the croissants and foie gras while America's innocent youth eat C-rations.

I had no money of my own for college and qualified for a mere pittance in financial aid as my family had the means to fund my education. Mom said Dad had mellowed, and encouraged me to ask for college tuition, but I refused to give him the satisfaction of denying me.

Desperate, I traipsed from one military recruiting office to another seeking a way to avoid the dehumanizing Army, jungle rot, and Viet Cong bullets. But the smart draft-dodgers had beaten me to the punch. The allotments for the National Guard, the Coast Guard, and the Navy were full for months to come. Thoughts of defecting to Canada crossed my mind, but I had neither the courage nor the conviction to become a political refugee.

My last hope for a reprieve was the Air Force, which I heard was still taking recruits. I arrived early and was second in line with no one behind me when the door opened. Accustomed to the routine, I filled out the application while the recruiter huddled with the other boy behind a cubicle privacy wall. Posters depicting smiling airmen lined the walls, and scale models of airplanes hung from the ceiling. When the boy left with a look of disappointment on his face, I took his seat across the gray metal desk from the Air Force recruiter.

In his sky-blue uniform, this recruiter appeared less formal and less pompous than the other recruiters, but like them, his job had become as easy as selling ice cubes in Hell.

"Look," he said, hands folded on my application papers stacked in front of him, "the only way you can avoid the Army, Eddie, is to be on active duty in another branch of service before your reporting date. That isn't going to happen in any routine way."

I wondered what he meant by "in any routine way." Was he looking for a bribe? I had some knowledge of bribes.

"I always intended to join the Air Force after high school, but I waited too long. This next semester I was set to enroll in a college and join the Air Force ROTC program." That was a lie.

Sighing, he reluctantly lifted my application off his desk and perused it.

"High school grades were great. You should be in college."

"Long story." With a hand gesture I urged the recruiter to keep reading.

He glanced at more pages and whistled. "Your IQ score of 143 is impressive. That's genius territory."

A genius wouldn't make the mistakes I've made.

Dad once told me wealthy men found substitutes to fight in the

American Revolution. “Is there any way you could swap my entry date with one of your other enlistees who has more time?”

The recruiter leaned back and blew air, like a whale breaching. “No, everyone is in a crunch to get on active duty.” He tapped my application and raised his eyes to the ceiling. After a moment, he rose and peeked around the cubicle barrier to see if anyone else was in the office. Then he looked back at me as though he were sizing me up to marry his daughter. “I do have one trick up my sleeve, and you may be the first guy who is smart enough to make it work. It’s simple and yet the guys who’ve tried it, screwed it up.”

I slid forward in my chair, willing to listen to any scheme that could keep me from carrying a rifle.

The recruiter explained that there are 120 questions on the Armed Forces Qualification Test, and I would need a score between thirty-one and forty to be a Cat IV, a category of marginal draftees who get spread around the four branches of service. “The Army will take some Cat IVs and dump the rest on the Marines unless the Navy or Air Force wants a particular draftee.” He promised to pick me off the pile if I was willing to engage in a little subterfuge.

“I should be able to find forty questions I can answer.”

“Good luck.”

No trick, no ruse, no lie is too shameful or unpatriotic a tactic to avoid this war. I’ll try the recruiter’s scheme to wiggle out of Nixon’s noose—I call it the do-or-die gambit—but, after arriving at the Armed Forces Entrance and Examining Station in Milwaukee today, doubt, fear, and anxiety have returned in full force. There are no identifying markings on this foreboding, low-slung brick building, and the windows are darkly tinted so the public can’t witness what’s done to boys as they become fungible government assets.

I should be at a college studying English Literature but instead, I’m standing in formation, naked, among twenty-odd white Wisconsin farm boys and a couple dozen Black city kids. The Black kids are defiant, slouching, eyes challenging, certain they’re subjects of discrimination. The farm boys are stoic, shoulders back, eyes unblinking. I’m merely scared.

The white-coated medical staff measured our height and weight, checked our eyesight and hearing, listened to our hearts and lungs. Now a man I presume is a doctor makes his way down my line, cupping the genitals of each draftee in his latex-gloved hand, asking him to cough. Sometimes twice. The doctor spins each kid around, bends him over, and probes his anus. Like a blacksmith checking a horse's hoofs, the doctor lifts each leg and examines the arches of each foot.

A few kids are excused on the spot.

My heart races as I gulp air in anticipation of my turn. The one consolation is that it happens to all of us. After I'm prodded and poked, the doctor moves on with a grunt and a sigh. I'm healthy enough to die in combat.

An Army sergeant orders us to put our street clothes back on, then herds us into a large auditorium like cattle going to slaughter. We are told to sit at grammar school desks and ordered not to touch the written exam or the No. 2 pencils that have been positioned on each desktop. My co-conspirator, the Air Force recruiter, is in the room as promised.

If my gambit to evade the Army doesn't work, Dad will be relieved that I'll be sent far away, no longer a ghostly specter preening on the moral high ground, silently condemning his transgressions. When Dad heard of my draft notice, he called it karma, poetic justice for what I did to him and my brother in 1966.

More eloquently, T. S. Eliot said, "The last temptation is the greatest treason: to do the right deed for the wrong reason."

1966

Chapter One

"How do I look?" Mom spun around in the kitchen like a runway model. Tall and shapely, with dishwater blonde hair in a bouffant style, she wore a navy dress with large white buttons down the front, matching heels, and a coquettish smile.

Carla, my baby sister, jumped out of her chair and squealed with delight. Her blue eyes lit up as she lunged toward Mom with her gangly arms outstretched for a hug.

Mom held her away with both hands. "Don't crush me. Just tell me how I look."

Abashed, Carla stopped. "You're pretty, Mama." She sat back at the table where we'd been playing Fish because Carla had to be entertained twenty-four by seven.

"Eddie?" Mom cocked her head waiting for my assessment.

"Stunning, Mom. Dazzling. Absolutely ravishing."

"I love being ravishing." She chortled. "You always use big, sophisticated words. The best your father can say is 'nice.' Where's Danny?"

As though she had conjured a rabbit from a hat, Danny burst into the kitchen and dodged Mom, heading for the back door. At six foot two, with an athletic build and curly black hair, Danny was a lady killer. In his Navy pictures, Dad's hair had been curly. Mine was straight and flat as a ironing board. Everything about Danny was carelessly, casually perfect from his hair to his teeth to his smile to his cheekbones and dimples. When Mom and Dad made Danny, they got it right, like a tastefully decorated room or an artfully arranged flower garden. They did well with Carla, too. She was cute now and later would be pretty. I was plain as white bread.

"Where are you going?" Mom asked Danny.

He stopped, a dumbfounded look on his face, no excuse on the tip of his tongue. It took him a minute to come up with, "Jimmy is picking me up on the corner."

"On the corner? He can't come to our house?"

"Faster this way." He reached for the back door handle.

"Can you at least comment on how I look?"

Turning back, he said, "You look nice, Mom." He dashed out the door.

Mom sighed. "Oh, well, I'll knock 'em dead tonight."

Dad emerged from the bathroom with his black hair slicked back like Jimmy Cagney. His cardigan sweater and dress shirt made him look friendly and casually superior. In her heels, Mom stood a bit taller than Dad. My siblings and I got our height from Mom's side of the family.

Dad grabbed Mom's elbow and shepherded her toward the back door. "We're running late, Kat." Mom's full name was Abigail Katherine Jaeger Kovacs but Dad called her "Kat" when he was feeling lovey-dovey. Or irritated. Otherwise, he and everyone else called her "Gail."

Two Saturdays a month, Dad and Mom went barhopping at the places where mill workers did their drinking. He called it a date night. Mom complained that Dad ignored her as he discussed union politics and contracts to win the workers' votes. But the nights on the town gave Mom a chance to primp and flirt and drink as much as she could get away with. Dad's Saturday night campaigning had propelled him from union secretary to vice president and then to president of the union. I wondered how many drinks he bought to get the votes.

As they left by the backdoor, Dad shouted, "I'll drive you home when we get back, Abby."

Last I knew, my maternal grandmother was snoozing in the living room recliner. Whenever my parents were away, Gram—that's what Carla and I called her—stayed with us. She could have played Mrs. Santa Claus in TV commercials. Pleasingly plump with permed gray hair, a round face and a jolly disposition, she was my favorite person on earth. I didn't need babysitting, but Carla was only eight and a handful. Gram spent those nights getting up to change the television channels for Carla, adjusting the rabbit ears for Carla, refilling Carla's soda, and prodding Carla to take a bath. Mom spoiled Carla so she was a silly little brat.

After finishing my favorite Saturday night dinner of hotdogs and potato chips that Gram always prepared, I retreated to my bedroom. Originally, our house was a two-bedroom, one-bath house, in a tract of cheap starter homes built on farmland south of the Fox River. Over the years Dad finished both the upstairs and the basement, walling off a den and a space for a pool table in the basement, and installing a Jack-and-Jill bathroom between two bedrooms upstairs in what had been intended to be an attic. I had the first bedroom at the top of the stairs, so I could always hear Danny tromping past my room after a night out with friends who had cars.

I grabbed *To Kill a Mockingbird* off my bedside table and sat in my ratty easy chair under a photo of John, Paul, George, and Ringo. The novel was required reading for my advanced English class. If my book report knocked the socks off Sister Mary Clare, I could finish first in the program, ahead of the weird girl in the other eighth-grade classroom.

Our house was set deep in our lot, back from the street, so the window beside my chair offered a view of half-a-dozen neighboring backyards. As the sun set, shadows grew behind the houses and the neighbors headed indoors.

To get in the mood to read, I tuned my transistor radio to WOKY in Milwaukee to listen to the British rock bands that dominated the Billboard charts. I loved growing up in Appleton, a city big enough to have one of everything, yet small enough to be navigated by teenagers on bicycles. But when Gram gave me the radio for my tenth birthday, I was introduced to a huge and vibrant new world that someday I wanted to experience firsthand. I adjusted the antenna and set the radio on the windowsill for better reception. While Dad read the local newspaper to keep up with the news, I listened to far-flung radio stations to learn the happenings in the rest of the world. Most nights I fell asleep with the radio pinned between my ear and the pillow.

Now I was ready to dig into the assignment. I'm a fast reader, so I quickly devoured the first half of *To Kill a Mockingbird*. We weren't rich like some people on the north side of our town; we were on the dividing line between poor and middle-class, like the Finch family in the novel. Jem was about my age and his sister, Scout, was close to Carla's age, but I identified with Scout and thought she was a lot like me. I admired Atticus. If I hadn't planned to be a priest, I'd have wanted to be a lawyer.

I stood and stretched and moved around my room to get the circulation going. I had a lot left to read in a book Mom thought offensive.

"I can't believe they make you read a book with the word "nigger" on every page. In a Catholic school, for Christ's sake."

"That's the way they talk down there," Dad had said. "You saw the demonstrations in Selma on the news."

"They attacked the Negroes with dogs and fire hoses. What kind of animals are those Southerners? We should have let those states secede."

I stifled a laugh at Mom's simplistic solution; had the states seceded the plight of the Negro would be even worse. "Sister Mary Clare says her advanced class is mature enough to read classic literature." I was proud to be trusted with a book that had been banned in some schools. I shouldn't have bragged about it to my parents.

"We should control what the teachers assign," Dad said.

"They're not real teachers," Mom snapped. "They're just nuns."

I was accustomed to my parents' occasional railing against the Catholic school. They felt the tuition they paid was both exorbitant and a license to criticize the school.

I sat back down in my chair and picked up where I left off. As I read the part where Tom the Negro was to be put on trial, I feared his predictable conviction. I laid my head back and imagined the various ways in which this story might end. I liked to do that—guess the ending before the author unveiled it—and I was often right.

In my peripheral vision I sensed motion, something outside in the dark. I switched off the lamp for better night vision and waited for my eyes to adjust. There! A man crept through the nearest neighbor's backyard. Comically bent at the waist, he took long, slow strides toward our house, bobbing up and down like an overgrown insect. He stopped and peeked around the side of the neighbor's house, then broke into a run and leaped over the hedges lining our driveway. I lost sight of him as he moved toward the house and then I heard the screen door squeak. No longer a laughing matter, I grabbed a baseball bat and moved to the top of the stairs.

My heart pounding in my chest, I was ready to dash down the stairs to protect Gram.

"You're home early," Gram said.

"Not much going on tonight." I recognized Danny's voice and relief washed over me. Danny was the giant insect.

"How did you get home?"

"Jimmy dropped me off."

He's lying, I wanted to yell.

"I didn't hear a car."

"Been sayin' it for a while, Gram. You're losin' it. Jimmy's car is noisy as hell."

Danny hadn't been out with Jimmy. As Danny hurried up the stairs, I hustled back into my room. Soon, I heard the water run in our shared bathroom, Danny washing away the evidence of his secret activities.

***

Danny slept in most Sunday mornings, so I had the bathroom to myself. After showering, I worked Brylcream into my hair—a little dab'll do ya —and styled it. I wanted to imitate the lead singer of Jay and the

Americans, so I parted my hair on the left, built a small pompadour in front, and swept both sides back. A square face with high cheekbones and a slight Asian tilt to the eyes nodded its approval in the mirror. Danny and I inherited Dad's brown eyes and facial features while Mom had blessed Carla with an egg-shaped face and blue eyes. We could have been mistaken for two different families.

I slipped into my gray flannel dress slacks, a checked shirt, and black penny loafers. I was ready for church. Dad was ready for church, too. He owned two suits and wore them on alternating Sundays. This Sunday he wore the charcoal gray tweed over a white shirt and a flashy red tie that looked like an impressionist painting. He handed Carla the two pancakes he had cooked for her and passed her the Aunt Jemima syrup.

"I'm running late," Dad said to me. "You'll have to fend for yourself."

"Don't worry about me, Dad. I'm self-sufficient."

"Don't burn the house down."

He grabbed his black fedora, the one with the red feather in the band, and left through the back door.

I moved to the front room and watched him prance down the street, head high, a proud grin on his face. He wanted the neighbors to know he was somebody important but his black, grease-encrusted nail beds belied his social status. His desperate, almost pathetic hunger for admiration made me feel sorry for him.

Dad was an usher who escorted the elderly and the infirm to their pews, and later, at the designated time during the Mass, he and the other ushers prowled the aisles and stretched their long-handled wicker baskets down each row collecting the parishioners' contributions. The peer pressure to place hard-earned cash in the basket caused everyone to cough up a couple of bucks. The money piled up fast since St. Catherine's Catholic Church conducted six Sunday Masses, standing room only.

There were four Catholic parishes in Appleton and more in the surrounding towns of Menasha and Little Chute so I had the impression that most everyone was Catholic. When John F. Kennedy ran for President, I was surprised to learn that Catholics were a minority in America and regarded as strange and perhaps dangerous. Nixon supporters warned voters the Pope would rule America if JFK were elected. That's funny. I never once heard the Pope mentioned in our house. I doubt Mom and Dad knew the Pope's name was Paul VI. That was my responsibility in the family; I kept up with such things.

In the kitchen Carla was eating a frosted doughnut from the dozen Mom had bought on Saturday. She hadn't eaten the pancakes Dad made for her. "You're going to get fat," I chided her.

"Like you?"

I sucked in my stomach. "I'm not a shrimp like you. Where's Mom?"

Her mouth full, Carla jerked a thumb toward the window that overlooked the backyard.

Mom was at the picnic table, still in her bathrobe, drinking coffee and smoking a Winston. "I don't suppose Mom would go to church with me."

"She never goes the morning after date night." Carla had the insight of a precocious child.

"You should come to church with me."

"I only go when Mom goes. You know that."

Carla attended the public grammar school rather than the Catholic school where I was a student so she was in danger of growing up without any religious training at all.

"We can only afford one privileged child," Mom had said about my Catholic schooling.

Out the back door I walked around the stacks of Sunday newspapers, tied with twine, lying in our driveway. Usually, I delivered papers before serving as an altar boy at a later Mass, but this Sunday I had a special role to play in an earlier Mass. The papers would have to wait.

After months of frigid temperatures and calf-deep snow, I basked in the gentle sunshine as I paused in front of our house. In a neighborhood of wood frame houses, our faux brick exterior, accented by brown and yellow shutters, was distinctive, but not as impressive as the eggshell white, two-story home beside us. That house sat on Danny's side of our house and blocked the view from his single window and provided the seclusion he wanted in the back bedroom. That house marked the boundary of my parents' neighborhood. They did not associate with the Lutherans who lived farther north.

Five blocks later, I passed the elementary school with its black-topped playground, the rectory where the priests lived, and the wood-frame convent that housed our nuns. Around the corner, I reached the front of the church. Like the rectory and the school, the church was constructed of near-white limestone bricks, and stood two stories tall, topped by a masonry cross. Beneath the cross, four large stained-glass windows rose above two massive brown oaken doors that might have dated to Medieval times. I went into the vestibule and up to a marble font. I pressed my fingers to a sponge to release holy water and made the sign of the cross.

The 8:45 Mass was nearly over. The choir in the loft above me was singing a final hymn. To the right, I entered a small office.

"You're not allowed in here." Dad sat at a table, covered in collection money. He stacked the coins and bills according to denomination and recorded the amounts on a white tablet. As the parish treasurer, Dad collected, counted, recorded, and eventually deposited the Sunday collections. The Sunday collections were the lifeblood of the church.

"Sorry, just wanted to let you know I'm playing a special part in the next Mass. In case you want to watch."

"I know what altar boys do." He didn't look up as he tossed bills onto their proper stacks, like a Blackjack dealer distributing cards.

"Today is different, I'm giving the sermon." I waited for some sign of pride in his son.

His head jerked up in surprise. "You're giving a sermon?"

My face flushed with heat. I had overstated my role. "I'm reading a script. Only about five minutes long."

"Doesn't sound like a big deal." He shooed me away with a backhanded wave.

I'll bet he'd drop everything and drive a hundred miles to watch Danny take one swing at a baseball.

Like a salmon swimming upstream, I wound my way up the broad center aisle, against the flow of modestly dressed neighbors who had done their Sunday duty. I marveled at the beauty of our stained-glass windows, the stations of the cross down the outside aisles, the hand-carved wooden doors on the confessionals, and the twenty-foot-tall sculpture of Christ on a cross above our altar. I felt at home in my church.

I took the steps up to the sacristy where the priests and altar boys dressed in their vestments. The two altar boys from the previous Mass smiled as they scurried out the side door. Monsignor Muller, a grumpy old man, and the senior pastor for our parish, was disrobing. *Good,* I thought, *I won't have to deal with that curmudgeon.* A sixth grader named Kenny filled wine cruets. He would be my assistant altar boy.

"After you take those cruets out to the sanctuary, you can light the altar candles," I told Kenny. He nodded and went about his business.

As I dressed in a red cassock and white surplice, Sister Mary Alice and Father Ronald Bauer entered the sacristy.

"Ready for your big day?" The priest's cheeks were rosy-red, as though he'd just run a mile.

"Yes, Father."

He handed me three typed pages. "That's what you'll read for the sermon today. I'll introduce you and then let you have the pulpit."

I was excited about speaking to the audience but butterflies stirred in my stomach. "Thanks, Father." I moved out of his way and had a look at what I would read.

Sister Mary Alice helped Father Bauer into a white and gold chasuble and stole. I had never seen a nun help a priest before, and Father Bauer certainly didn't need help. He was the youngest and "coolest" of our priests, blond and blue-eyed with the body of a football running back, and Sister Mary Alice, who taught second grade, was the youngest and "coolest" of our nuns. My friends and I often speculated about what Sister Mary Alice looked like under her black tunic and veil. All we could see were laughing green eyes and smooth, clear skin, but she was often the subject of young boys' fantasies.

While Father Bauer polished the bejeweled, gold chalice, and loaded a silver platter with round, white wafers, I read the speech I was to give. The point of the sermon was clear—the church needed more money to fund the food bank. Every Tuesday, poor parishioners stood in line to get a box of food.

At precisely 10:00, Kenny and I led Father Bauer to the altar and Mass began. At the point where the priest normally spoke to the congregants, Father Bauer escorted me to the pulpit.

"Today, the sermon will be given by our senior altar boy, Eddie Kovacs. This is good practice for Eddie as he is going to the seminary this fall to start his journey to become a priest."

Murmurs rose from the crowd; welcoming smiles and positive nods greeted me. Father Bauer had advised me to look directly at the clock above the rear doors of the church rather than at the parishioners, to keep from getting nervous. I didn't look at the clock. I searched the crowd for Dad but he was nowhere in sight.

Bennie, the biggest boy in my class, and his sidekick, scrawny Jerry, stood behind the last pew. Jerry stuck out his tongue at me. Bennie stuck his thumbs in his ears and waggled his fingers.

After the "sermon," I bowed my head. "Let us pray." The parishioners bowed their heads as I read a preprinted prayer. Leading six hundred people in prayer produced a powerful jolt of pride within me. "Stick to praying, Eddie. It's what you're good at," Dad had said. For thirty seconds I felt as important as him.

Back in the sacristy, Father Bauer patted Kenny and me on our shoulders. "Good job, boys."

I told Kenny he could go. I returned to the sanctuary to extinguish the altar candles and saw that Bennie and Jerry were loitering in the vestibule.

As Father Bauer and I disrobed, he said, "Monsignor Muller wants to see you once a week until you leave for the seminary. His idea is sort of a class to prepare you for the priesthood."

Oh, no. "Thank you, Father. How will I know when he wants to see me?"

"We'll let your father know."

Two more altar boys and Father MacMillan entered the sacristy to dress for the next Mass, and Father Bauer hurried away. I made sure these boys knew their roles and that everything was set for the next Mass. To evade Bennie and Jerry, I left through the side door that led to a path between the convent and the rectory. In the garden behind the convent, Father Bauer and Sister Mary Alice strolled shoulder-to-shoulder, deep in conversation. When I stepped into view, they separated in haste and their clasped hands, hidden by the folds of her habit and his cassock, parted in midair. Sister Mary Alice looked like a doe caught unawares in the forest, ready to bolt for cover. Father Bauer sheepishly waved.

Chapter Two

At home, I changed into jeans and a sweatshirt while Gram cut the twine and loaded the papers onto Carla's red wagon. I pulled the wagon up the hill to the south and past the sixteen homes of the families we considered our friends. Two vacant lots served as playgrounds for family badminton, softball, and touch football games.

My paper route started two blocks farther away in a neighborhood where we didn't know the people well. Some kid whose father had influential connections owned the route in our neighborhood. On the route, Gram pulled the wagon and I schlepped the thick, folded bundles to front steps or porches. "Schlepped" was a word I had learned from Gram, not from school. We received scowls from several subscribers as the papers should have been delivered earlier, but the timing of my special Mass had thrown us off-schedule. In response, Gram uttered some words in German that I recognized as curses.

Dad stopped my allowance when I got the paper route, saying it was a good lesson in working for a living, but the money I made didn't cover the cost of all the books and plastic models I wanted. Danny was the caddy master at the country club, and I expected him to hire me as soon as the school year was over. Then I'd make big money.

When our wagon was empty, Gram wandered away in the wrong direction.

"Our house is this way, Gram," I hollered and pointed in the right direction.

She stopped, turned, and furrowed her brow. "Are you sure?"

"I'm sure." I went up to her and reached for the long black handle. "Let me pull the wagon."

She stopped several times to get her bearings. "Trust me, Gram, I know the way." I pulled the wagon to be a gentleman; Gram was as healthy and sturdy as a farm mule. Fifteen minutes later we were back home.

Gram kicked off the blocky black shoes she bought where the nuns shop, put on a brightly flowered apron, and set to work cooking our Sunday dinner. She cooked every Sunday because Mom wasn't interested in cooking, although she was proud of how her kitchen looked. The refrigerator, stove and dishwasher were all a green color Mom called avocado, a high-class color. Looked to me like the green-around-the-gills color people turned when they were sick.

On alternating Sundays, Gram prepared baked chicken or beef roast, always with the same sides. Today it would be the roast. Gram preheated the oven and began chopping a head of cabbage.

Dad sat in his usual spot at the kitchen table with his back to the window that overlooked the backyard, like a king sitting on his throne. But today he wasn't eating a donut or reading the newspaper. An ever present toothpick in the corner of his mouth, he was transcribing numbers from the white tablet on which he had made notes at church, to an official ledger on which he accounted for the day's collections. Next to him, a canvas bank bag bulged with coins and paper money. I peered over his shoulder as he added columns.

"What are you doing?"

From the living room, Mom said, "Don't bother him. He needs to get it right." She had showered and dressed as though she was going to church but she hadn't. Carla, wearing a dress, sat cross-legged on the floor. Something was up. Mom shot me a severe look over readers low on her nose, then shook out her newspaper and went back to reading.

I turned back to Dad and lowered my voice. "Why are you doing the accounts at home? Why did you bring the money bag home?"

Mom yelled, "Eddie!"

The toothpick rolled to the other corner of his mouth and bounced as he explained. "It's a new procedure so the money gets into the bank faster." Dad's chest swelled with pride. "I'll deposit it on the way to work instead of picking it up after work and driving back downtown. Some days when I work overtime, the deposit doesn't get made until Tuesday. This is more efficient."

Dad didn't often give me detailed explanations for things he did. "Did Monsignor Muller tell you to get it deposited faster?"

"No, I came up with the idea. It's my job to take care of their money." He made that shooing motion again and focused on the ledger.

"You'll have to move so I can set the table, Frank," Gram said.

"Wait for Danny to get home."

Dad called Sunday dinner a command performance, and everyone had to be present, no excuses.

"Where is he?"

Dad flipped his pencil in the air as though exasperated. "He went to the last Mass."

I glanced at the fake cuckoo clock above the sink. "That's been over a while." Danny always seemed to be off somewhere without a good explanation.

"I can't concentrate with all the interruptions." Dad pulled the toothpick from his mouth and stuck it behind his ear. Then he hoisted the money bag and headed for my parents' bedroom. We weren't allowed in there. While he put the money away, I glanced at Gram. She paid me no attention as she adjusted burners on the stove.

I snuck a peek at the ledger. The total for six Masses was six thousand dollars. That was $24,000 a month, more money than Dad made in a year, and who knew how much more from the dozens of churches in the Archdiocese of Green Bay. Religion was a big business.

Dad came back, set the ledger aside, stuck the toothpick in his mouth, and opened the Sunday newspaper. Page after page, he found coupons, clipped them, and stacked them in piles according to the stores at which they could be redeemed. I knew Dad would drive to four grocery stores using the coupons to buy bargain food, brands that weren't even advertised on TV. I had been to friends' homes where they had polished wooden dining tables but I didn't see the point. The coupons slid smoothly across the Formica tabletop and Formica was easier to clean.

"Hand me the cabbage, Eddie," Gram said.

I always helped by retrieving what she needed from the refrigerator or the cupboards. She would turn the cabbage into German-style sauerkraut. I handed her the cutting board.

Danny burst into the kitchen and gave me a hip check. "Heard you were a show-off today, Chubby." He sat at the table next to Dad.

"I just read a letter the Monsignor had written to the parishioners. The priest read the letter at the other Masses." I shrugged like it wasn't a big deal.

Gram stirred a pot with a wooden spoon. "And led the prayer," she said over her shoulder. "He's better than the priests."

"You saw me?" Gram typically went to the earliest Mass so she could get home to help me deliver the papers and cook dinner.

"Of course, I saw you." She pinched my cheek. "I went to that Mass just to see you."

"You're spoiling him, Abby," Dad said.

"Poor little baby just wants a pat on the head," Danny chirped.

"Honey, I'm home!" The back screen door slammed, and the neighbor lady, Shirley, barged into the kitchen and walked up to the table beside Danny. We didn't lock our doors when we were home, not that a locked door would have deterred Shirley. She was lanky with bleached blonde hair, sequined glasses, and a loud grating voice.

"Is Gail ready?" Her gum smacked as she chewed.

Mom and Carla came from the living room. "I need some money," Mom said to Dad.

"What for?" Dad didn't look up as he shuffled his stack of coupons.

"Shirley is taking us shopping. Carla needs summer clothes."

"It's not summer yet."

"I need shoes," Carla whimpered.

"Nothing open on Sunday." He continued to sort his coupons.

"Lotta stores don't care that it's Sunday." Shirley smacked her gum.

"We don't shop at those stores. They have no respect for the day of rest."

"You're like an ostrich with its head in the sand," Mom said. "More stores are opening on Sunday every week."

"We don't have any money to spend." He didn't look at her.

Her face flushed with color. "You have thousands under the bed. They won't miss a couple of bucks."

"I'm going to pretend you didn't say that." Dad clipped another coupon.

In our home, money was the center of the universe, not a casual or occasional topic, but a serious and constant concern, like a current in a river. Our lives revolved around whether we had the money to do something or buy something or eat something.

Shirley's red-lacquered nails caught my eye as she nervously smoothed her leopard-print top and tight brown peddle-pushers. "We could just ride around town if you want. Get out of the house." Get away from Dad is what she meant.

"Where's Doug?" Dad must have wondered why Shirley's husband wasn't controlling his wife.

"On the road again. Long haul. Won't be back for few days."

"There's no time before supper," Dad said.

"The roast will take another hour," Gram countered.

Dad snapped the toothpick in half and gave Gram a testy, forbidding stare.

"Maybe some other day." Mom always caved-in to Dad.

Shirley reached to Danny's head and ruffled his curls. "I'm available every day." Shirley looked directly into Danny's puppy dog brown eyes as she said it. *I knew it! Danny came from Shirley's backyard last night.* Her strapless heels clacked as she walked back out the door.

"Don't embarrass me in front of my friends, Frank." Mom's face scrunched up like she was about to cry.

"We don't have shopping money," Dad said.

"Why not? You have money to schmooze with your friends."

"That has a purpose and you know it."

Mom walked away to her bedroom.

Gram had been lurking near the table glowering at Dad.

He pointed to the stove. "Just finish the supper, Abby."

I hated it when my parents referred to the main meal of the day as "supper." That was such a low-class term. I had learned from friends that the middle-class term was "dinner."

Gram wiped her hands on her apron and mumbled some German under her breath. "Now I need the hamburger buns, Eddie."

I handed her the buns and she formed them into doughy dumplings. Next came the milk for the thick dark gravy and then the leftover hotdogs from last night. Gram sliced the hotdogs and tossed them into the sauerkraut where they marinated and became tangy, like a pickle. For me, they were the best part of the meal.

Preparations completed, I headed upstairs to finish reading *To Kill a Mockingbird* and write my report.

I wasn't surprised Tom was found guilty at trial—injustice was the point of the story, right?—but I was shocked when the jail guards riddled Tom's body with seventeen bullets. Obviously, Tom was the good person who didn't deserve to die, the symbolic Mockingbird, and that's what Harper Lee meant by the title. But I couldn't get Boo out of my head. When Boo Radley saved Jem and Scout from Bob Ewell, another idea formed in my mind—the sheriff, Heck Tate, decided that Boo didn't kill Bob Ewell, which he certainly had, because arresting Boo would be like killing a Mockingbird. Boo was a Mockingbird, too, a Mockingbird who could have gone to prison for murder. I changed my report to say Tom was the Mockingbird who was killed and Boo was the Mockingbird who was saved.

Writing my report became easy then. I was sure I'd finish first in the advanced English class.

***

Back in the kitchen I inhaled the comforting aroma of the roast while Gram checked to see if it was ready.

"I need a beer," Dad said.

"Me, too." Danny was allowed one beer a day with Dad, but I was sure he took advantage of the quirky Wisconsin law that allowed eighteen-year-olds to drink beer at bars established solely for the use of teenagers.

I asked Mom if she wanted one.

"I can't drink that cheap shit your father buys."

I knew my job. I served two beers from the refrigerator then walked down to the basement to get replacements. Dad kept cases of beer and cases of quart bottle soft drinks under the stairs. The basement was dark and dank and infested with spiders. I went there only when necessary. The soft drink bottles had no labels but the flavor was printed on the bottle cap. We had orange, grape, black cherry, root beer, and cream soda. My friends called our drinks "pop," but I liked the more sophisticated word "soda." I chose the orange-flavored soda.

I replenished the beer supply in the frig and poured my soda. Mom had mixed a gin gimlet. Either her hangover had subsided or she was having "the hair of the dog that bit her."

When we got settled with our drinks, I asked Danny what he did last night.

"The usual. We cruised the drive-ins on Wisconsin Avenue, caught up with all our friends."

Liar. "You must have been bored, got home early."

"I was tired, played a big-boy baseball game yesterday. Went three for four."

"What took you so long to get home after church?"

"None of your business. You're an annoying little snot, you know that?"

"Stop bugging your brother," Mom said.

"You always pick on people," Carla added.

The food was exceptional but the dinner conversation was virtually nonexistent as everyone had been offended by someone else at the table. After dinner, Gram walked the two blocks to her house and Mom, Dad, and Carla retired to the living room to watch TV. Danny grabbed our yellow phone handset off its cradle on the kitchen wall and stretched the coiled cord around the corner to the basement stairs. He closed the basement door so no one could hear his conversation. He would sit on those stairs and talk all night long. I figured the girls were ugly since he never brought them home to meet us.

Dad sat on the far end of the couch, his transistor radio glued to his ear, listening to a Chicago Cubs baseball game. I would have joined the others to watch TV if they had watched *Paladin—Have Gun, Will Travel* —but Carla wanted to watch Walt Disney. Cartoons are for kids.

"You can watch whatever you want in the basement." Mom was proud that we owned two televisions.

Underground and surrounded by cement blocks, the basement TV rabbit ears couldn't pick up a clear signal. There was so much static that every show looked like it was happening in a blizzard. Besides, Danny was talking to girls on the basement steps.

I retreated to my bedroom, tuned my radio to WBZ, Boston, and grabbed a new book—*Of Mice and Men*. Sister Mary Clare said it wasn't suitable for young minds. That's why I stole it from Danny. He never read it when assigned in school, so he'd never miss it.

Chapter Three

Midmorning, a dozen of us left our eighth-grade home rooms and gathered in Sister Mary Clare's classroom for the last advanced English class of the school year. The nun read each book report aloud, commented on its insights, and assigned a grade. Every report included the parallel between the overt prejudice of whites against blacks and the fear-instilled bias Jem and Scout and Dill felt toward Boo Radley. A couple of students pointed out that Atticus believed bias was the result of not knowing or understanding the people you look down upon, the old walk-a-mile-in-their-shoes bromide. That seemed too simple to me and not always right. What if you got to know someone and your negative feelings were confirmed—they were bad people, like Bob Ewell.

The nun moved on and I got the idea she had sequenced the readings from weakest to strongest. One other boy proposed, like I had, that Tom was the mockingbird who got killed, but he didn't mention the connection to the title.

Only two reports were left to be read, mine and that of the weird girl. One student groaned. Another mumbled "Mr. Goody-Two-Shoes and Psycho Girl as usual."

"Teacher's pets," someone said loud enough for the nun to hear.

Sister Mary Clare rapped her ruler on her desk with a resounding crack and everyone jerked alert in their desk seats. "Listen up, heathens, and learn something."

It bothered me to be lumped together with the weird girl. She came to school with blue eyeshadow and black mascara. Most days, the nuns made her wash it off. Today the makeup was defiantly in place. Maybe the nuns had grown tired of correcting her; it was the last week of classes before graduation and next year Marcy would be out of their hair. Speaking of which, I saw a purple streak in Marcy's chopped-off, pitch black hair when she ran a hand through it.

I braced myself.

Sister Mary Clare took a sip of water and began. "Mockingbird report by Eddie—"

My heart sank. My report was second best. I barely listened as she announced that identifying Boo as another Mockingbird earned an A. I felt a tightness in my temples and a cold chill in my chest. I was an also-ran, a loser like all the other kids.

"The winning report was written by Marcy," the nun announced. I listened for the difference that made her report better. Then I heard it: Marcy theorized that the characters, and all of us, are a mixture of good and evil.

"How perceptive of you, Marcy." Sister Mary Clare was like a cat lapping up a bowl of milk. She gave Marcy an A+ which meant Marcy won the prize for best reader, and I was devastated.

***

In the cafeteria, Marcy sat alone at a table with eight chairs. No one liked Marcy. She was too smart and too different, but being ostracized didn't seem to affect her. She didn't creep around like other kids and beg to join popular tables. A forkful of macaroni and cheese waited in front of her mouth as she read a page in her book. I couldn't resist the opportunity to confront her about the way I'd been robbed of the prize. I carried my tray to her table and looked down at her.

I figured I should act friendly at first. "What are you reading?"

She started as though a ghost had jumped out at her and shouted, "Boo!" No one ever talked to her.

She showed me the cover—*The Catcher in the Rye*.

"Sister Mary Clare banned that book."

"You going to tell on me? I don't care if I get caught."

There it was! Nothing the nuns did to her had any effect at all. I swayed from one foot to the other and looked around the cafeteria. Several kids had their eyes on me.

"Congratulations for winning the English award." No one could blame me for saying that. "But I don't agree that the characters were a mix of good and evil. The good characters never did anything evil and the evil characters never did anything good. Where was the good in Bob Ewell?"

She shrugged. "I just told her what she wanted to hear."

I had read the book and done my own thinking. "How did you know what she wanted to hear?"

"Cliff's Notes."

"You used someone's notes?"

"No, dummy. They're cheat sheets the college kids use so they don't have to read boring books."

Dummy? "So you cheated."

"I played it smart and won. You could have argued your point in class."

I should have but I had been afraid Sister Mary Clare would embarrass me with some smart reasoning and I guess I was right.

"You beat me with a trick."

She laughed out loud. "I'm good at tricks."

My cheeks burned. Then I laughed with her.

"Your food is getting cold."

I motioned with my tray to the seat across from her. She nodded. Hoots from a few students could be heard over the usual clamor but I didn't care who was watching. Under the makeup, Marcy was cute, her face round, her skin pale, her eyes the color of seawater, her bangs sawed off short. She wore a strange combination of clothes—orange slacks, a tie-dyed t-shirt, a brown suede vest with long fringes at the bottom, and black Doc Martens. No one else dressed that way. It wasn't just her looks and dress that fascinated me; I was intrigued by how she behaved and how her mind worked.

***

Like a moth drawn to a flame, I sought her out at lunch on Tuesday and asked if I could read *The Catcher in the Rye* when she was done.

"Waste of time," she said. "He wanders around New York City criticizing adults while doing stupid things himself. The ending hints at his love for his sister and wanting to protect young children, but I think he'll just go to another rich kids' school and get kicked out again. There's no character arc; he's the same loser he was at the beginning of the day. I don't know what the fuss is all about."

"Why is it banned?"

"Too many curse words, I guess. And one of his teachers is a homo who wanted to do things to the kid, Holden."

Her casual attitude toward homosexuality made me uncomfortable. "Well, that explains it."

"Sorry I called you a dummy. I know you're going to the seminary."

"You know that?"

"I watched you give the sermon on Sunday."

I tried to look humble. "I wish we had waited until school was out."

"You were good. No need to be ashamed of it."

"I'm not ashamed or embarrassed. I just don't want the attention." That wasn't true. I loved the attention of adults but not of my classmates who weren't mature enough to appreciate my vocation.

"Made me wonder if you like girls." She gave me a taunting smile.

I felt the heat of embarrassment rise from my shirt collar to my face. "Priests like girls but they devote themselves to God."

"Father Bauer likes girls. The others are queer as a two-dollar bill."

This girl knew how to offend people. "You're wrong; they're just kind and gentle men."

"You'll see when you get to the seminary."

She couldn't possibly be right. "I'm going to be a Jesuit, not a parish priest. Jesuits are academics mostly, the intellectual backbone of the church. I don't know yet if they'll accept me."

"What if you don't get in?"

Her eyes challenged me, but I had thought through my choices. "Then I want to be a missionary and travel the world helping the poor."

"I'd like to see the world, but I'm not going to be a nun to do it."

***

The weather turned foul on Wednesday, so I had to walk to school rather than ride my bike, but I didn't care how wet I got. I was excited about seeing Marcy and I had never felt that way about anyone other than Gram. By lunch time I was dry and had ducked into the lavatory to comb my hair. I carried my tray to what had become *our* table.

What makes a person want to tell another person about their family? I had been taught by my parents to never talk about what went on inside our house, but Marcy was an exception to that rule. Today, I told her about Mom and Dad and Danny and Carla and Gram. She said we sound normal. There was a sadness in the way she said it. I didn't tell her everything about us and I felt I had cheated her when she told me about her mother, Judy, and her older brother, Ray.

"Mom works at Woolworth's downtown. Ray quit school and took a job at the lumber supply store so we can make ends meet. I'll work this summer to help out." She said her father came around once in a while, stayed a couple of nights, and then went missing for a month or two. "In between, other men come around to see Mom."

My cheeks burned and my throat went dry. My priestly instincts wanted desperately to save this girl. But I thought better of it. She wasn't looking for pity. "You didn't pick your parents."

By Thursday, the other kids had noticed that we laughed a lot and it attracted attention. Timmy and Allen, my baseball teammates, stopped by the table to listen to the conversation but they weren't brave enough to take seats. Marcy and I were outcasts and that made us a good pair.

The class bullies, Bennie and Jerry, cruised by the table and Bennie tapped me on the shoulder. "Your girlfriend gets her clothes at the St. Vincent DePaul store."

Marcy ignored them. She knew who she was and wasn't afraid to flaunt it. That must be nice.

"You don't care," Jerry said, "because you're a sissy altar boy in love with a weirdo Polack."

Marcy's last name was Jablonski. I started to get up because I couldn't let them make fun of Marcy and I couldn't let them tease me in front of Marcy.

Marcy held me down. "You're brainless creeps who'll be digging ditches your whole life," Marcy snapped.

"Chicken," Bennie sneered. The bullies walked away, hooting and howling.

"Why do you let them get away with it?"

"I'm used to it. The Dutch look down on us Polacks and the Germans feel superior to everyone. If we had some Irish or Italians here, Polacks wouldn't be the bottom of the barrel."

Everyone seemed to need someone to look down upon. The pecking order in our town also applied to Catholics who felt superior to the Lutheran minority. At an altar boy meeting, Monsignor Muller had told us that only Catholics can get into heaven, so we were blessed to be born into Catholic families.

I wasn't as tolerant as Marcy. I didn't like following the Biblical admonition to turn the other cheek and I promised myself I'd get revenge on Bennie and Jerry.

***

On Friday, I was depressed. The school year was over, so there would be no more lunches with Marcy.

"What are you going to do this summer?" I hoped to find a way to see Marcy.

"My mother has houses lined up for me to clean. I don't have to be a grownup to do it. What about you? Besides all the Masses and praying."

"I'm playing Youth League baseball, and my brother is going to hire me to caddy at the country club, but I'll have free time. Will you have some free time?"

A shy smile. She knew where I was headed with these questions. "I'll go to the library or hide in my bedroom to read."

"Banned books."

A big smile. "Of course. They're the best."

I admired her gumption. "How do you get them?"

"The library is full of them. The old lady there thinks I'm older. And Mom takes me to the bookstore and buys books for me."

"She lets you read banned books?"

"I don't have to hide anything from Mom."

That must be nice. If she was going to hang out at the library then that's where I could see her. "Do you have a bike? Do you have a telephone?"

"Sure, we're not *that* poor."

Well, she walked to school so I couldn't be sure she had a bike. "Maybe we could go to the library together."

"I'd like that."

I grinned. My summer would be fun. We traded phone numbers.

"If my brother answers, hang up," Marcy said.

"Same here. In fact, hang up on all of them."

Chapter Four

Danny's graduation and my graduation were scheduled at the same time on the same Saturday. Danny was graduating from the public high school, as Mom had done many years ago, while I was graduating from St. Catherine's Elementary, so it wasn't surprising the schools hadn't coordinated their events. Danny's graduation was obviously a bigger deal than mine so Mom, Dad, and Carla were going to watch him "walk."

"We'll come to your high school graduation or whatever they call it in the seminary," Mom said.

In a joyful mood, my smartly-dressed family piled into the car and left me waving goodbye from the porch steps.

I met Gram at her house and we walked together, arm in arm, to my school gym. She was all dolled up in a floral dress and low heels, with a handbag hooked over her arm. There was no one I'd rather have had at my graduation than Gram. I found her a good seat from which to watch the ceremony and then joined my classmates in the front rows.

On the stage, our three priests and a dozen nuns sat on folding chairs, like a royal court. After a prayer by the Monsignor and a dull speech by our principal, Sister Mary Frances, awards were presented for honor roll, Beta Society, the math advanced class, the science fair, band, and the choir. When Marcy received her Advanced English Class award, the boys from her lunch table stood and applauded, provoking scowls from the Monsignor and Sister Mary Frances, who waved us back in our seats. Their disapproval had more to do with how Marcy looked and dressed than it did with our disruption. Marcy's eyes were painted and her hair was streaked red and white, our school colors. A blouse and skirt that didn't match and tall black boots, like the girls wore on Hullabaloo, completed her ensemble. Bennie was right; her style was thrift-shop eclectic.

She flashed the plaque at me and smiled. There was no prize for second place in Advanced English but I received an Honor Roll certificate and a Beta Society pin, so I was happy enough. Fifty of us graduates walked onto the stage and received rolled-up paper diplomas tied with a red ribbon. Then we prayed again.

Afterward, kids and their parents milled about on the playground outside the gym, congratulating one another. Gram and I said hello to Timmy and Allen and their parents, then I spotted Marcy walking away by herself. I yelled her name. She stopped and waited as I dragged Gram in her direction.

"Marcy, I'd like you to meet my grandmother, Abby. Gram, this is Marcy, the girl who beat me at reading."

"Nice to meet you," Marcy said. "I've heard a lot about you."

My heart stopped.

Gram canted her head and examined Marcy. "You must be smart to win the award. Congratulations."

My heart started beating.

"I had to work hard to beat Eddie," Marcy said. She winked at me. Working hard had been using a cheat sheet.

"Is your mom here?" I peered over her shoulder.

"No, she had to work."

Marcy said it matter-of-factly. It was her reality, always alone.

"We're going to Woolworth's for lunch. Want to come?"

Marcy looked from me to Gram and back again. "I can't, I have chores and errands."

"Okay. I'll see you around."

"You know where I'll be."

Gram linked her arm through mine. We walked north and Marcy went east. As we crossed the Oneida Street bridge over the Fox River, Gram said, "Is good to have a girlfriend, Eddie."

"Priests don't have girlfriends, Gram."

"You're not a priest yet."

We headed to the Woolworth's dime store on College Avenue. My graduation present was lunch at the counter. We sat on round padded stools that swiveled. Two waitresses wore white aprons over a pink and white striped dress, the Woolworth's lunch counter uniform. I ordered ham salad on toast and a strawberry soda from our waitress. The waitress at the far end of the counter turned in our direction. Her nametag read "Judy." Marcy had told me her mother was at work and I hadn't put two and two together. Some people look poor and used up and that's how she looked. She had the narrow face, long, straight black hair, and the slender shape of someone who should have been tall but wasn't. I decided not to introduce myself. Marcy didn't come along because she didn't want to be present when I met her mother, either because she was ashamed of her mother, or because she was ashamed of me.

Between bites of my sandwich, I watched Judy serve her customers.

They joked with her and appreciated her quick service. I hoped she was making big tips. After forty minutes, Gram paid the bill and we were outside in the heat of the day.

Gram turned to me. "Eddie, would you mind if we go by my house first? I'd like to change clothes." She only lived around the corner from us, so it wasn't a big deal. A huge lilac bush grew beside her front door and I inhaled the fragrance that always reminded me of Gram. We entered a narrow living room that led to the kitchen at the back of the house. To our right were two small bedrooms. The kitchen was small, too. According to my Timex, her wall clock was thirty-four minutes fast. I took the clock down and reset the time.

She caught me replacing it. "I told you not to touch my stuff, Frank."

Frank? Frank is my dad. "Sorry, Gram, it was wrong. I didn't mean anything by it."

Her face went blank for a second and then light returned to her eyes, as though someone had flicked a switch. "Sorry." She blinked. "I got confused. That clock has a glitch but I know what time it is."

"I'll bet Dad drove you nuts when he lived with you."

After Dad was discharged from the Navy, he and Mom lived in this small house with Gram. When Danny was born, Dad used the G.I. Bill to buy our house on Jackson Street. Their time in this house was never discussed. If I brought it up, my parents changed the subject.

She chuckled. "Frank is a schlemiel, but a good carpenter. He hated the outhouse so he put in a toilet and tub."

Dad installed the makeshift bathroom in the only space available—the attic. I could see the commode from the bottom of the stairs. I had used it a few times, so I knew that another room upstairs contained a bed and little else. It amazed me that her life had been so primitive just a few years ago. I poured a glass of orange juice and sat at her tiny kitchen table.

"I'll bet you were happy when they moved out so you could have some privacy and space of your own."

Gram didn't sit. "No, I was lonely. Always I have people here. Mother and Father lived with me and I took care of them until they died."

"This was your father's house?"

"No. Mine." She sounded fierce.

I feared I might upset her, but this was history I had never heard before. "Where did you live before this?"

She hesitated and seemed to decide how much to say. "I grew up on a farm in the country. Vater worked with the cows and Mutter cooked and cleaned house, but I talked for them. They didn't speak English."

"You spoke German growing up?"

"Yes. They let me go to school to learn English, but I quit after eighth grade and went to work in the paper mill so I could save money to buy this house. Then Mutter and Vater didn't have to work anymore." She was proud of her accomplishment. She picked up her purse, ready to leave.

"Why didn't your father get a job in the city to help you?"

Gram looked as though I should have been able to figure that out myself. "He didn't speak English. I couldn't go to work with him in the city."

What I figured out was that her mother and father had come from the "old country." *Poor Gram, caring for immigrant parents.* "Why did they come to America?"

I knew by the look on her face that I had pressed too hard. She started for the door.

"A story for another time. We better go," she said. "They'll be worried about us."

I doubted it, but I got up to leave. A look of relief appeared on Gram's face, as though she had survived an interrogation.

At our house, a two-seater convertible sports car with headlights tacked onto the hood instead of embedded in the fenders, sat in the driveway. Its tomato-colored finish was like a photograph smudged by an oily thumb.

We stepped into the kitchen, where Dad and Danny were drinking beer and Mom held a gin gimlet in a martini glass. They were still dressed in their Sunday best and they appeared to be in good cheer. A decorated cake was on the table. Carla comically licked her lips as she waited for the cake to be cut.

"Did you see it?" Danny grinned from ear to ear.

I knew immediately what he was talking about. "Is it yours?"

"My graduation present, a 1959 Austin Healey bug-eye Sprite."

"It needs some work and a paint job," Dad said, "but Danny and I will fix it up."

"It's fast as hell and takes ninety-degree corners." Danny shook with excitement.

I was speechless. Where did Dad get the money for a car?

"Now it's my turn." Mom had wanted a car for years.

"Eddie won honor roll and that other thing." Gram looked at me for help.

"Beta club." I flashed two gold-star-embossed certificates at my parents.

"We bought you a cake." Mom's grin was lopsided. The drink she held wasn't her first.

I edged closer to the kitchen table. The white-frosted cake had red lettering on top: *Congratulations, Eddie!*

I wanted to hurt someone. "Did you win any academic awards?" I asked Danny.

Danny smacked the table and shot me an evil look. "You mean pieces of paper?"

Dad threw up his hands, trying to restore peace. "Danny won letters for basketball and baseball."

"Ten years from now no one will remember that you were on the honor roll," Danny said, "but the whole town will still talk about what I did in baseball and basketball games."

***

It seemed like just another Sunday, each of us following our routines: I served at an early Mass; Dad ushered at the last Mass; Danny went to church with Dad but Mom begged off. "Mass is for good Catholics," she said.

I couldn't let the Monsignor know Mom was less than a good Catholic. Gram and I delivered the papers, starting at the far end of the route. She knew the rest of the way home when we finished. Like last Sunday, Dad brought home the collected money and the accounting ledger.

Mom mentioned again how odd it felt to have thousands of dollars hidden under her bed. "You'd have to work for months to make that much, Frank," she said.

"I'd make all we need if it weren't for Eddie's seminary," Dad snapped. "It's going to cost me an arm and a leg and it's nothing but a glorified high school."

Mom slunk away to the living room, and Carla followed her. Gram cooked dinner.

An undercurrent of resentment spoiled the day, mostly my fault, I suppose. Demarcation lines had been drawn—Dad and Danny versus Mom and Carla versus Gram and me. Bring it on and we'll crush you.

Chapter Five

When I came down for breakfast, Dad was about to leave for work. I peered out the back door. The tomato-colored car was not in the driveway. "Where's Danny?"

"Left early to go to the courthouse and register for the draft."

"The draft? The Army?"

"He's eighteen and out of high school so it's compulsory."

"Can you drop me at the club? I'm supposed to start caddying for Danny today."

Dad closed his black metal lunch box and picked up his car keys. "Talk to him when he gets home tonight. Today, I want you to cut the lawn, front and back, trim the hedges, and pull the weeds in the garden."

He left. My first day of summer vacation and I had to work for free. I cursed in the German I learned from Gram.

We had a push mower that left a trail of clippings in its wake. After cutting the front lawn, I raked the clippings, bagged them, and placed the bag on the curb. I was cutting the back lawn when Dickie showed up carrying a baseball glove and bat. He was a year younger than me and lived up the street.

Dickie tossed a ball in the air and caught it. "How much work you got to do?"

I wiped sweat from my forehead. "After this I have to trim the shrubs and weed the garden."

"Dang, your dad's a slave driver. Bunch of us are going to the club for pickup games. Come over when you're done."

The club is the Southside Athletic Club, one street over, where three baseball fields offer plenty of opportunity to get into a game. "Sure, I'll catch you later."

Dickie headed across the street and cut through yards to get to the club.

After I finished the back lawn, I found the hedge clippers in the garage, essentially a large pair of scissors, and gave the hedges a quick once-over. Mom wanted them flat on top and square on the sides, something she had seen in magazine pictures of millionaires' homes.

Dad grew up on a farm in Iowa and never lost his love of dirt and fresh vegetables. He had tilled an area fifteen feet by thirty feet at the very back of our property where he grew an assortment of vegetables and lots of weeds.

I was working in the lettuce patch when Shirley's shrill voice blared as she barged through our back door. Shirley and Mom settled at the picnic table with mugs of coffee and packs of cigarettes. I stood as though to stretch my back and tried to hear what they were saying, but they leaned close across the table and spoke in low tones. They were either gossiping about neighbors or complaining about their husbands. After two cups of coffee and several cigarettes, Mom yelled, "We're going downtown."

"I'm going to the athletic club to play with Dickie," I lied.

I dawdled in the garden while Mom prepared for her adventure. She seemed to take forever. They took Carla with them in Shirley's beat-up Buick.

Their absence was a gift from God. I washed away the dirt and sweat in the shower and dressed in school clothes. My hands and arms tingled as I dialed Marcy's number. My finger poised above the hook so I could hang up if Marcy's mom answered, I listened to ring tone after ring tone. Buzz, buzz, buzz. No one answered, and my heartbeat slowed to normal.

I was allowed to ride my bike anywhere I wanted to go in Appleton, a safe place populated by law abiding, hard-working, mostly middle-class citizens. To my eyes, the town was attractive without being quaint, bustling without being overcrowded. I grabbed my camera, hopped on my bike and headed across the Fox River bridge to the intersection of Oneida and College Avenue. The square stone building on the corner housed the public library on the first floor and city hall on the second.

An old woman behind the counter, perhaps the woman who lets Marcy checkout restricted books, helped me with an application for a library card. Until Marcy mentioned the adult library, I had only used the school library or read assigned books.

I roamed the stacks of books, looking for Marcy. I bypassed romance, mystery, and sci-fi and ducked into literature where the banned books hide. She wasn't there. I walked through the section to a row of tables at the back of the floor. No Marcy. A few people were spread around the tables, notepads and open books in front of them. They appeared to be students at Lawrence College which was only steps away. *Marcy must be cleaning houses.*

Inspired by Marcy, I decided to sample some books I'd been told not to read. Fitzgerald and Faulkner were there and Hemingway. One book I was sure we weren't allowed to read was *The Sun Also Rises,* because of all the sex, or maybe because the main character had his dingy shot off in a war. George Orwell looked interesting because I'd heard the debates about his books. I pulled *1984* and *Animal Farm* from the shelf, then moved to the Action and Adventure row where I grabbed several James Bond books to stack in front of me to hide what I was reading. I sat at an unoccupied table and laid my camera atop my book-castle, ever watchful for adults who might rip *1984* away from me.

"That's a good one."

Today Marcy was swallowed up by an oversized sweatshirt that could only belong to her big brother, and her hair was pink. I raised my camera and clicked a snapshot. Don't ask me why I did that. She didn't seem to mind.

"I thought you might be cleaning a house," I said.

"I clean houses in the mornings but I'm always here in the afternoons. My father came home last night so I had to get out."

"Is that one banned?" I indicated the book she held, *The Grapes of Wrath*.

"Yeah and I want to find out why. Have you read *Crime and Punishment* by Dostoevsky?"

"No. Ah, not yet."

"Well, this guy commits the perfect crime but he can't let himself get away with it."

"He has a conscience."

"No, um, it's not something he was born with, it's his religious training. There's a conflict between what he's been taught and his free will. He says religion is like a straitjacket that prevents us from thinking for ourselves."

"Well, civilization is based upon rules and laws and religious commandments. Otherwise, we'd have chaos."

"Well, Dostoevsky has a different opinion. After I work my way through banned novels I'm going to read about the history of the Catholic Church. Lots of disturbing stuff."

A cold chill ran through me. "Be careful, Marcy. Reading books that accuse the church of wrongdoing is dangerous."

She gave me a dismissive look. "History isn't dangerous, Eddie. I want to know what I believe in."

My stomach felt queasy. My entire belief system rested upon the infallibility of the church's teachings. The words in *1984* swam before my eyes but went undigested.

"I think I'd better shove off," I said.

"Me, too. I have to cook supper or my father will throw a fit. I'll be back tomorrow afternoon. How about you?"

"I hope I'll be caddying but otherwise, sure. Tomorrow afternoon." I didn't think I was lying but I wasn't sure about tomorrow. Or any other day. "I'll put these books back."

"Take the Bond books back and I'll put the Orwell away for you." She picked up my books and headed away.

I returned the books and stepped outside to the bike rack. She joined me with a huge grin on her face. She pulled a book from under her sweatshirt and handed it to me—*1984*.

"Did you check this out for me?"

"No, they wouldn't let a kid check it out."

"We can't steal it!"

"We aren't stealing it. When you're done, we'll return it. We just borrowed it. Get it? Borrowed it from a lending library. I'll return this one, too."

The Grapes of Wrath materialized from under the big sweatshirt she had worn so she could steal books. Was I going to walk back in and tell the old lady that Marcy took them? I should have but I didn't. My religious training was in conflict with my free will, just like the guy in *Crime and Punishment*. We'd return them like Marcy said. And then I'd admit my sin the next time I went to confession.

***

Our driveway overflowed with cars—Dad's, Danny's and one I didn't recognize. I walked my bike to the garage. In the backyard, Dad, Danny, and Danny's baseball coach sat at the picnic table. They drank beer but didn't look happy. I leaned my bike against Dad's workbench and started into the backyard. Dad held up a one-handed stop sign.

I was too angry to control myself. "Why'd you leave me behind this morning," I yelled at Danny. "You promised I could be a caddy."

"I didn't promise you anything, chubby."

"Now is not the time," Dad said. "Get in the house."

"Tomorrow, Danny, or else." I knew about his secret romance with Shirley and I'd broadcast it to the world if I had to.

I turned on my heel and went into the downstairs bathroom. I closed the door and locked it, stepped in the tub and slowly, quietly raised the window. I was only ten feet from the picnic table so I'd be able to hear the men talk.

"Midlands College scouted him a lot, but they won't offer him a scholarship," the coach said. "I've tried a bunch of other schools and they've all turned me down."

"Midlands would have been perfect. Why won't they take him?" Dad asked.

The coach rolled his head around, like he was thinking up the best way to answer. He took a drink of his beer, stalling.

"Come on, Jake," Dad said.

The coach relented. "His grades don't predict college success. They're not sure he can stay academically eligible. They can't waste a scholarship on a guy who's not eligible."

Danny's head was in his hands. Danny wasn't stupid; he just didn't care about school and only wanted to get by. Danny threw his head back and opened his mouth as though to let the bitter taste of regret fly away. I felt bad for him as I knew what it meant to me to have my dream come true.

The bathroom door handle jiggled.

"Occupied."

"I've gotta go." Carla whined.

"Pee in your pants, Shrimp."

She knocked on the door and screamed, "Mom, Eddie won't let me in."

"I've got diarrhea so bad I couldn't make it upstairs. You don't want to come in here."

"Ugh, boys are disgusting."

She seemed to go away. Outside, the men were discussing other options.

"Lawrence is too small and too uppity about grades," Dad said. "How about bigger schools, schools with more money, schools that care more about baseball than about grades?"

"Now you're talking about teams with major league talent," the coach said. "Danny doesn't hit breaking balls well enough to go to a big school."

"That's crap, Jake. I've seen him hit curves."

"A few, but too many strikeouts between home runs."

"Then what are we supposed to do?"

"Best chance is to get a tryout with a minor league team, see if they can teach him what I couldn't."

Danny came back to life, leaned toward the older men. "I'm already working on that. I know a guy who had major league tryouts and still knows some scouts and coaches."

"Who's that?" Dad asked.

"Joe Morada, up the street."

"That strange guy up the street was a baseball player?"

"Yeah, a good one. He played in the Cardinals' minor league system."

"That's your best bet," the Coach said. He drained his beer, pushed himself up from the bench, and pulled his legs out from under the picnic table.

I closed the window and walked into the living room.

"Did you spray in there?" Mom asked. She was watching the CBS Evening News.

"Fresh as a daisy in there."

She studied me with inquisitive eyes. "Why are you dressed up? I thought you were playing ball."

"I was but then I ran to church to talk to the priests."

"I should have known. You're there more than you're home. Next time you have to poop, catch it sooner and use your own bathroom."

"Sure, Mom. Listen, when Danny comes in, tell him to make me a caddy at the club."

She gave me the sad look moms use when they're about to tell you what you don't want to hear. "Danny doesn't want you to caddy at the club, dear."

My heart sank and my eyes burned. I sat on the edge of the couch cushion. "Why not? I'm big for my age. I can carry clubs."

"It's not that. He doesn't need his little brother hanging around him while he works. And he doesn't want to be responsible if you screw up."

Screw up? What about Mr. I-can't-hit-a-breaking-ball and his swell high school grades? "How am I supposed to make money this summer?"

"I'll talk to your Dad about your allowance, but you'll have to work for it."

"I work for it—the lawn, the garden, the shrubs, the dishes, the trash. Danny and Carla never lift a finger around here."

"They have other things to do. I'm not happy with the shrubs. They're not square and they have Indian feathers sticking out the top. Dad says the garden still has weeds. Try again tomorrow to get it right."

I can't wait to get out of here and off to the seminary. "I can't do it tomorrow. I have my first baseball game."

"Then the day after but don't forget or you'll never get an allowance."

Dad and Danny came in the back door and I heard Dad shake the toothpick dispenser to get a fresh one.. Dad sat on the other end of the couch but Danny went straight to his room.

"That coach is an idiot," Dad said. "I'll find Danny a school."

I waited for Mom to say something about my allowance but she ignored my problem.

"Since Danny's not playing anymore, you could come to my game, Dad."

"When?"

"Tomorrow." I told him where. "I'll be playing center field." I sounded and felt as obsequious as a Royal butler.

Dad shook his head. "I'll be busy finding Danny a school."

"Sure. Danny's more important."

Dad ignored my gripe.

I slumped back onto the couch to lick my wounds. On TV, Walter Cronkite reported on the conflict in Vietnam, using that calm, steady voice that engendered absolute trust.

"General Westmoreland now has presidential permission to involve U.S. combat troops in the conflict in Vietnam. The General wants forty-four battalions to increase the U.S. presence to 117,000 troops by November first."

We seemed always to be at war with someone and since World War II, it hadn't gone well for us. "Why are we fighting in Vietnam?" I asked Dad.

He was surprised I would seek his wisdom so he put on an air authority. "We have to stop the spread of Communism, give the people of South Vietnam a democratic government."

I wanted to ask why the Vietnamese had to be like us, but I didn't want to expose my ignorance. I imagined spreading democracy was a lot like missionaries spreading the word of God. "They don't seem to want a democracy."

"What they want doesn't matter." Dad scoffed. "We'll bomb them into submission."

I headed to my room and pulled an atlas off the shelf. When I found Vietnam, I was shocked by how small and insignificant it appeared.

Chapter Six

At the crack of the bat, I turned and ran for the outfield fence. Over my left shoulder, the ball climbed over the sun and hesitated at its apex before hurtling toward the warning track far ahead of me.

I pumped my arms and dug my spikes into the soft field but I wouldn't reach the fence in time. After three long strides, I pivoted to face home plate and located the ball falling from the sky like a meteor crashing through earth's atmosphere. Fear froze the blood in my veins. I stretched my glove hand toward the heavens and jumped as high as my legs could propel me, but I caught only a handful of spring air. Ten feet behind me the ball collided with the outfield wall, bounced once on the warning track, and caromed off my shin.

Ignoring the sting of the ball, I scuttled on hands and knees to retrieve the ball, watched the batter round third base and head for home. I rose and fired the ball in one fluid motion. The ball sailed over the cutoff man, ricocheted off the pitcher's mound, and bounded toward the catcher. He left his position and smothered the ball on the infield grass as the batter slid across the plate behind him.

Game over.

I blew it.

I rested on my haunches, holding my breath to stave off tears of shame. After several minutes of self-pity, I chanced a glance around the field and spotted Dad standing on the third base line. I hadn't expected him to show up. Now I wished he hadn't.

I joined my teammates, their faces long and sad, in a line, congratulating the ebullient winners like we'd been taught by our coach. When Allen, our pitcher, passed the kid who hit the home run, he spat, "It was just a stupid fly ball."

A stupid fly ball I didn't catch. *My teammates blame me for losing the game.* It's the first game of the season, on the first Saturday of summer, and I was already a failure.

The batter shoved Allen and a scuffle ensued, but coaches quickly separated the two teams and the players dispersed. I shuffled toward Dad and my coach who waited for me with their arms folded across their chests. I tried to read Dad's mood. *How bad will this be?*

When I was within earshot, Dad said, "You run too long in one place."

I wondered if that was a professional opinion. After all, he was an engineer.

"He shouldn't have looked back," the coach said. "It slowed him down. We teach 'em to run to the spot, then pick up the ball 'cause you run faster looking straight ahead."

Dad nodded in full agreement. "He didn't read the ball off the bat. Didn't get a good jump."

I stopped in front of Dad. "I knew it was over my head. Way over."

I turned to my coach. "You had me playing too shallow."

Dad smacked the back of my head hard enough to knock off my cap.

"You'll play where the coach tells you to play, young man."

"Frank, not all boys are cut out for center field." The coach picked my cap out of the dirt, dusted it off, and set it on my head. "Eddie doesn't have the speed to cover center field no matter where I position him."

I shuffled my feet, not sure if I should interlope again or catch up to my teammates. Fear of their ridicule paralyzed me. I wanted to play organized baseball because it was Dad's favorite sport. The mistake I made was wanting to be a center fielder because Mickey Mantle was Dad's favorite player. The mistake the coach made was giving me a try.

"Wouldn't surprise me if you cut him," Dad said to the coach. "Struck out twice today."

The coach shrugged. "He got a walk, scored a run."

"He didn't hit a lick in Little League so don't expect him to hit for you, either. His brother, Danny, is the baseball player in our family."

"Sure. I remember Danny from his Youth League days. That boy was a homer just waiting to happen."

"He was a star in high school ball. He's sure to get a scholarship to play in college."

That's a lie.

"Well, Eddie here has one skill that will keep him on my team." The coach gripped my shoulder in a fatherly way. "Did you see that throw? All the way from the warning track? Your kid's got a cannon for an arm."

Dad scoffed. "You're not going to try to make him a pitcher, are you?"

The coach spat out his chewing tobacco. "Nah, but I need a catcher." He cupped a hand to his mouth and leaned toward Dad as though whispering a secret. "Our catcher should have waited for the throw and blocked the plate." He straightened. "And I'd like to have a catcher with a gun." The coach gave me an appraising look. "If he ain't afraid of the ball that is."

Catcher! The position is reserved for kids who can't run and can't hit but are willing to demean themselves by chasing wild pitches around the backstop. But it's either play catcher or get cut from the team.

"I'm not afraid of the ball, sir." I puffed out my chest, mimicking Dad's confidence.

"That's what I want to hear." The coach flashed a mouthful of brown tobacco-stained teeth and gave my shoulder an encouraging smack.

"Then I guess you're a damn catcher. You should stick to praying. It's what you're good at." Dad shook his head and walked away.

The coach shrugged. "Somebody's gotta do the dirty work. Let's get your equipment."

I followed him to the dugout where he filled a canvas bat bag with shin guards, chest protector, face mask, and a padded catcher's mitt. The equipment was old, the seams frayed and torn, the straps stretched and no longer elastic, the edges worn smooth. But they were my ticket to play Youth League baseball. I walked home alone with the "tools of ignorance" slung over my shoulder.

As I lugged the equipment to my room, Danny stuck his head out his bedroom door. "You must be the chubbiest kid on the team. They always make the chubby kid play catcher."

"Keep it up, Danny, and I'll tell Mom where you hide the *Playboy* and *Penthouse* magazines."

Something like confusion flickered in Danny's eyes. He had a disconcerting habit of tossing my room and pawing my things and now he worried that I did the same thing to him. "You'll never find them, chubby."

***

I intended to drop the "borrowed" book in the outdoor return slot and run away before Marcy saw me, but she was waiting at the bike rack, wearing that same huge sweatshirt.

"If you drop the book in the return box, they'll know it was taken without permission and they'll be on the lookout for who did it." She stretched out her hand. "Give me the book and I'll put it back on the shelf."

She slid the book under the sweatshirt and I followed her into the library. While she put the book in its proper space, I waited at a table. I should have left, but I didn't. She was like an addiction I couldn't shake.

I asked myself if I was waiting because I wanted to save this girl or because I wanted a girlfriend one time before I became a priest. She came out of the stacks with another armload of history books.

"Did you read *1984*?"

"Yes. Orwell is whacko, a paranoid nut job."

She looked at me the way nuns do when you've missed the point of the lesson. "We have less than twenty years to learn the truth before Big Brother starts brainwashing us."

"You're off the deep end, Marcy. Maybe you should read *Little Women* or *Pride and Prejudice* instead of banned books."

"That junk?" She slid *Animal Farm* across the table. "See what you think of this one."

"I'm not going to let you steal another book."

"Wake up, Eddie. This is the stuff they don't want you to know."

She dropped three books onto the table. I reached over to see what she had chosen. *Rabbit Run* by John Updike, *The Last Exit to Brooklyn* by Hubert Selby, Jr. and *Naked Lunch* by William S. Burroughs made a contraband pile I shrank away from as though they were a nest of Black Widow spiders.

"They're all banned because of sex."

She huffed and puffed like a cartoon dragon. "There's more sex in the Bible than in these books combined."

She "borrowed" *Rabbit Run* for herself and *Animal Farm* for me. I knew I was on a slippery slope but I couldn't help myself.

***

I tried to square the hedges off by clipping a branch here and there but I didn't see much difference. At dinner I bugged Dad about my allowance.

"You're going to be too busy with this priesthood stuff to earn an allowance. Monsignor Muller wants to interview you this evening."

Dad had a Finance Committee meeting at the Rectory that night so I asked if I could ride to church with him. He said I should ride my bike because there was a lot to cover in the meeting and he'd get home late.

I parked my bike beside the three black Pontiac sedans that crouched in the Rectory driveway. The priests didn't buy the cars. Dad arranged for a local GM dealership to donate the cars for a tax write-off.

I didn't know if I was important enough to use the front entrance of the Rectory, but I did have an appointment so I rang the bell.

The kindly old housekeeper swung the door open for me. She led me to a small office and asked me to wait. Cheerful chatter arose down the hall as Dad and a couple of other Finance Committee members arrived. After ten long minutes, Father MacMillan entered the room. He was short and slight and looked smaller and somehow younger in his black cassock and distinctive collar.

"Good evening, Father. I have an appointment with Monsignor Muller."

"The Monsignor asked me to have this chat." He didn't sit behind the desk. He pulled up a side chair and we sat knees-to-knees for the interview.

"Let's begin with your confession so you'll be free of sin as we talk."

I wasn't prepared for this. It was bad enough to disclose sins when the priest was hidden by the screen in the confessional. "You mean right now, out in the open?"

"This is the way it will be for you from now on, Eddie. You'll have a regular confessor at the Seminary and after you become a priest, you'll confess your sins face-to-face to a superior." His watery blue eyes looked at me with anticipation. His callow cheeks and sparse brown hair gave him an unappealing, unhealthy look.

I was trapped. But I forced the words from my mouth, "Forgive me, Father, for I have sinned." I told him I stole two books from the library but returned them. The lies were beginning to pile up and I knew it was because of the time I spent with Marcy.

"Did you tell the librarian what you did?"

I swallowed hard. "No. I just returned the books. I didn't mean to keep them."

"Which books did you take?"

This is a terrible trap, like the holes the Viet Cong dig so our soldiers fall onto poisoned stakes. "Two James Bond books."

He chuckled. "Those books are okay for you to read. Why steal them?"

I gave him a one-shoulder shrug. "I haven't received my library card yet."

He laughed. "Is that all you have to confess?"

I acted like I was thinking. "That's about it."

A sly look formed on the priest's nondescript features. "Do you masturbate, Eddie?"

A flash of heat enveloped my head and my vision blurred. A Playboy centerfold flashed through my brain.

"You know it's a sin." He raised his eyebrows. "Don't hide anything from me, Eddie. God will know."

"I'm not hiding anything, Father." I resolved to stop looking at Danny's girlie magazines.

The priest gave me absolution. "For your penance, go back to the library and tell the librarian what you've done. On your way home, stop in the church and say five Hail Marys."

"Yes, Father."

"You can call me Father Mac or just Mac."

I hoped we were done. He clasped my hands in his and looked deep into my eyes. "Do you like girls, Eddie?"

We weren't done. Possible answers flashed in my mind like messages on a revolving billboard. "I'm not crazy about them. I don't have a girlfriend or anything like that." *How would Marcy have answered?*

"That's good, Eddie. It will be easier for you if you're not attracted to girls. It's a long road to the priesthood."

He dropped my hands and moved his to my knees. It made me very uncomfortable. I remembered Marcy saying the priests are queer as a two-dollar bill.

"I know about the vow of celibacy, Father."

"Of course, you do. I hear you want to be a Jesuit but you're more suited to working in a parish, like I do. You'd be a great addition to our Diocese."

I didn't know how Father Mac would know what I was suited to do. He didn't know me at all. But getting into the Jesuits was as hard as getting into Harvard. "There's nothing final yet."

"I want you to serve at my Mass each morning and get together for chats maybe once a week. See if I can change your mind. How does that sound?"

Like torture. "I'd be happy to do that, Father Mac."

"Go do your penance." He blessed me with the sign of the cross. "Bless you, my son."

Since I was supposed to say my penance in the church, he led me to the backdoor of the Rectory which opened onto the school's main hallway and the sacristy. We passed the open door of a large room where the other priests and committee members sat at two round tables. They weren't discussing church finances. They were playing cards. Bottles of beer stood before the men, including Monsignor Muller and Father Bauer. The air was redolent with cigarette and cigar smoke. Dad had his back to me so he didn't see Father MacMillan push me past the doorway, but Father Bauer gave me a friendly nod.

"See you in the morning, Eddie."

I walked through the sacristy and down the steps to the transept but I didn't go into the nave to say my penance. I waited five minutes and then crept out the side door, down the path beside the convent, and around to where I left my bike. I pedaled hard all the way home.

***

I ran up the stairs and barged into Danny's bedroom to plead with him to let me caddy so I didn't have to serve at Father MacMillan's Masses every day. Although Danny's car was in the driveway, he wasn't in the house. Neither were Mom and Carla. My twisted mind immediately jumped to the conclusion that Danny was next door at Shirley's house, having a good time. If I caught him, he'd have to let me caddy.

To get into character as a stalker, I slipped on a black sweatshirt and pulled the hood over my head. Down the stairs and out the back door, I rushed into a light rain shower. Undeterred, I crept around our garage and into Shirley's backyard. I moved into the darkness beside her garage and waited, getting soaked by the steady downpour. It seemed a long time but it was probably less than fifteen minutes before the back door opened and out stepped … Doug, Shirley's husband. I slid along the side to the rear of the garage and plastered myself against the back wall. I heard Doug doing something in the garage and it scared me. I wanted to run home—since Doug was home, Danny wasn't with Shirley—but I feared he'd see me. I ran the other way, up the street, through two more backyards and waited in the rain for Doug to go back into the house. When he did, more people emerged from the house and I identified the voices as Mom and Shirley and noisy Carla. Shocked by the sudden downpour, they hustled to our house.

I was about to trail them home when the door of the house I was behind opened and startled me. Out stepped Danny and Joe Morada, the guy Dad called "strange." The neighborhood women called Morada a "confirmed bachelor"—a man who had reached the age of forty without ever having been married.

I had forgotten I was looking for Danny. I had heard, when the coach was at our house, that Joe could get Danny a baseball tryout. Finding Danny at Joe's house wasn't going to get me a caddying job. Now I'd have to wait in the rain for Danny to go home.

The two men huddled under Joe's small portico and spoke in low tones so I couldn't hear words distinctly, but their body language was that of close friends. They patted shoulders and squeezed biceps and then they hugged. They clung to one another and Joe leaned in and kissed Danny! On the lips! A real kiss, like a husband and wife. The scene sucked the breath from my body. The world spun around my head. I became dizzy and felt I might pass out, so I sat in the wet grass to keep from toppling over. My big, strong, athletic brother was … a homo? A fag? That couldn't be true.

When they parted, they seemed joyful, as though Joe had given Danny good news. Then Danny loped with the long, graceful strides of the natural athlete, through the backyards, toward our house. Joe went back inside and the lights went out in the windows facing the backyard. I needed time to calm myself so I waited for Danny to get into the house before jogging home. My only excuse for being out in the rain was that I was returning from the Rectory, but I didn't have to use it. Dad wasn't home yet and everyone else was in their rooms, changing into dry clothes. I hurried to my room and did the same.

I sat on my bed and shook my head but the scene at Joe's house was stuck in my brain, burning like a red-hot cinder.

Chapter Seven

Dad stood in the kitchen, munching on a strip of bacon. "You're up early."

"Have to serve Mass every morning from now on." A 6:15 a.m. Mass catered to day shift workers, whereas a 7:30 Mass was convenient for night shift workers on their way home from the paper mills. The church didn't schedule a midnight Mass for the 3:00 to 11:00 p.m. crowd because praying couldn't compete with drinking at the all-night bars.

"Did you hear that Joe Morada is arranging a minor league tryout for Danny?"

I had to muzzle myself to keep from blurting that Joe and Danny were doing a lot more than arranging a tryout. I hadn't decided what I would do with my unwanted knowledge: confront Danny, seek advice from a priest, tell my parents? If Danny had been fooling around with Shirley, I'd have blackmailed him to get a caddy job and stopped him from committing a sin. "Thou shall not covet thy neighbor's wife." What Danny was doing with Morada was so repugnant, the Ten Commandments didn't even mention it.

"Oh, good for Danny," I said.

Dad went to work in his car and I walked to the church, a jumble of partially formed thoughts competing for space in my brain. A couple dozen people watched from the pews as Father MacMillan conducted Mass. Some were day workers but many were elderly men and women, thanking God for another day of life. I was the lone altar boy as this was what's known as a "low" Mass, a quickie. In the sacristy after Mass, Father MacMillan wrapped an arm around my shoulders and blew wine-breath in my face.

"Would you like to make a confession before you leave?"

Does witnessing a sin merit a confession? "No, Father, I haven't stolen any more books."

He laughed. "Want to talk about the Jesuits and how to find your niche in the priesthood?"

Not with you. "Sorry, I have to get to the golf course for my caddy job."

"Sure. We can talk any day you like."

"Hello." Father Bauer stood in the doorway. Father MacMillan dropped his arm to his side as though he'd touched something hot, and Father Bauer's eyebrows climbed up his forehead. He told Father MacMillan he had been assigned duties that required them to swap Masses from now on.

This was my out. "Sorry, Father Mac. I have to be at work at the golf course at 7:30 so I can't serve at your 7:30 Mass."

"You can serve at my Mass and then go to work," Father Bauer said.

Father MacMillan's mouth opened and closed like a beached fish sucking air. My mouth hung open, too. At least Father Bauer liked girls and wouldn't be pawing me like a stuffed teddy bear.

"Sure, Father. I'll see you tomorrow."

***

I went home and told Mom that if anyone came looking for me, she was to say I'm still at church.

"Who are you hiding from?" She dropped two slices of bread into the toaster.

"No one. I have to go back this afternoon to have another talk with the priests."

"You'll be a saint before you ever get to the seminary." A hint of pride seeped into her voice, moderating the vague discomfort she often exhibited when discussing my peculiar vocation.

I hustled upstairs to finish reading *Animal Farm* so Marcy could return the book. When I got to the library, she was waiting for me, wearing a form-fitting blouse, maybe her mother's, and not the oversized sweatshirt that concealed our borrowed books.

I wore a school t-shirt that wouldn't hide anything. "How are we going to return this book?"

"Simple." Marcy snaked her slender arm through the return slot and rummaged around until she grasped a book that was thin enough to pull out of the slot. She moved the check-out card from the pocket of that book to *Animal Farm.* She grinned at me and dropped them both through the slot.

"What did you think of the story?"

"It's depressing. No matter who's in charge, the animals are mistreated."

"That's the point; the people in power always exploit the masses."

"That can't happen in a democracy."

"You're being exploited right now but they bombard you with

propaganda so you think you've got a great life."

I thought Marcy was finally wrong about something. "America is the land of opportunity where you get what you work for."

She scoffed. "You're just competing with a lot of other people who won't get anywhere. Your family will never be more than lower middle class."

While I struggled to come up with a convincing argument, her facial expression softened. "It's okay, Eddie, you'll be a priest. Want to go to the movies with me?"

The abrupt change in direction stunned me for a moment, but as though to make her argument, I turned my empty pants pockets inside out to show that I had no money.

She smiled. "Did you learn that from Charlie Chaplin? I have money."

"What's playing?"

"*Dr. Strangelove or: How I Learned to Stop Worrying and Love the Bomb.* It's playing at the Grande Theater."

The ratty old Grande Theater wasn't in the downtown district. It played second-run flicks, cult movies, and movies no one's ever heard of. "They won't let kids into that show."

"I look old enough to buy the tickets."

With her fully made-up face, two rings on each hand, and three bracelets on each arm, Marcy could easily pass for sixteen. Maybe eighteen. I must have looked like her kid brother. We rode five miles to Wisconsin Avenue, on Appleton's far north side. Getting into the movie was a breeze. Marcy was very good at acting as though she belonged in the adult world. Maybe that's why she seemed so weird in school—she was more mature than the rest of us.

We shared a small popcorn and an orange soda through a single straw. We laughed at Peter Sellers but the movie left me terrified of nuclear weapons and the people who controlled them. In the dark, Marcy's hand found mine and interlaced its fingers with mine. I was glad she couldn't see the flush in my cheeks. At a particularly funny moment on the screen, she squeezed my hand and I squeezed back. It made me feel funny. I was relieved when the pilot rode the bomb like a rodeo bull and the movie ended. I had heard my classmates talk about what they did with their girlfriends at the movies.

Outside, I shielded my eyes from the sun until they adjusted to daylight. I examined Marcy's face for a reaction to what we did in the theater, but she acted as if holding hands with a candidate for the priesthood was perfectly natural.

"Stand in front of the ticket window." I lifted the camera from around my neck.

She smiled and posed, one hand on a cocked hip. I snapped the picture. I was losing my sense of who I was. Did I think I could use the photo as a bookmark in my Bible when I became a priest?

"Let's get an ice cream float," she said.

When I gave her a look, she said, "My treat."

Money wasn't the reason for my hesitation. Marcy had declined our invitation to have lunch at Woolworth's the day we graduated and I had supposed it was because she didn't want her mother to see us together.

"At Kresge's?"

"Dummy! My mom will make us a good one."

She's made some sort of decision about us.

We rode back downtown and pulled up outside Woolworth's. She skipped through the door like a happy kid at a carnival. All the workers knew her and they gave me the once-over. The lunch counter was crowded and the only pair of side-by-side seats were at the far end. As we made our way to the seats Marcy caught her mother's eye and signaled that she should join us. Her mother gave me a big smile.

Under her mother's heavy makeup there was a faint discoloration along her left jawline, an apparent result of the return of Marcy's dad. Marcy performed the introductions.

"Marcy has told me all about you, Eddie. We'll have to have you over for supper." Her voice had the breathless quality Marilyn Monroe had made famous.

"That would be nice, Mrs. Jablonski." I was being courteous. I wasn't ready to admit that I wanted to be Marcy's boyfriend.

"Call me Judy, please. Now, what can I get you kids?"

We ordered root beer floats and Judy hurried away to fix them. Conversation at the counter was loud and lively, like a bar without alcohol, so we could talk without being overheard. The vision of Joe and Danny kissing was a lump in my throat, perilously close to bursting forth. I needed to share my problems with someone, and Marcy was my safest listener, but I told her about my interview with Father MacMillan first.

"Told you they're all queer," she said.

"It's a sin and he's doing it in the Rectory of all places."

"He's safe there and he's safe with altar boys and future priests who won't tell on him. That's why he picked you."

I wasn't about to accuse Father Mac of molesting an altar boy, but Father Bauer seemed to suspect something and felt he had to protect me.

Judy came over with our floats. If she hadn't looked so tired and worn out, she'd have been pretty. Without makeup and purple hair, Marcy would have looked like her mother.

"Anything else for you two?"

We shook our heads and she went back to her station.

I pulled from my straw. "Father Mac told me it will be easier to be a priest if I don't like girls."

"I guess so, but God made boys to like girls." She made a slurping sound as she sucked melted ice cream and soda through her straw.

Did God make all boys the same way? Father Mac had temptations one way and I now realized I had temptations the other way. Is one way better than the other for a priest? Yes. Liking girls isn't a sin.

Marcy tipped her soda glass on its end, and like a baby bird being fed by its mother, she opened her mouth and let the last dollop of ice cream drop into her mouth. I felt comfortable with her because she had seen and endured every terrible thing in her family life. I could tell her anything, couldn't I?

Before I could talk myself out of it, I leaned close and I whispered, "I think my brother plays for the other team."

"Hunh?" She furrowed her brow in confusion.

"Or he might be a switch hitter."

"I don't know anything about baseball, Eddie."

I grimaced and let out a breath. "Not baseball. I think he likes men. Ah, better than women."

She nearly choked on her soda. "He's a poof? A queer?"

She was too loud. This wasn't the right place for this discussion. "Keep it down. The whole town doesn't have to know."

She sucked the last of the soda through her straw and set her glass on the counter. "The star athlete, Daddy's favorite. Whaddaya know?"

"Shh. We can talk about it later."

She swiveled to face me. "How do you know?"

I checked to make sure Judy wasn't watching, leaned in, and whispered in her ear. "I saw him kiss Joe Morada, a neighbor man."

She shrugged and looked doubtful. "A real kiss, or just a peck on the cheek?"

She was still too loud. I touched my lips with a finger. "Right there."

Her mouth made an O. "That must throw your dad for a loop."

The heat rose again from my neck to my cheeks. How could I hear confessions if everything embarrassed me? "He doesn't know. What do I do now? Do I tell my parents? Do I tell Danny what I saw?"

She shrugged again. "Why do you have to do anything?"

"I don't want him to get caught by … other people. Maybe he can be fixed."

"How do you fix it?"

"With prayer, I guess. God can fix anything."

"Hasn't worked for me."

***

As we were leaving, Bennie and Jerry entered. We had to pass close by them.

"The weirdo and the sissy," Bennie sneered.

"She's got cooties." Jerry laughed and headed for the back of the store.

Marcy flipped them the bird and we pushed through the door to the street. I recognized Bennie's bike, a red and white Schwinn, leaning against the storefront.

"You have a nickel I can borrow?"

Marcy dug in her little beaded purse and handed me the coin.

"Hold up his back wheel."

Marcy looked confused but did it. I pressed the nickel between the chain and the teeth on the bottom of the rear chain wheel and carefully turned the crank until the nickel was lodged. Hidden by the frame, Bennie wouldn't notice the coin until it was too late.

"What's that going to do?"

"When he starts pedaling the nickel will pop the chain off the rotor. He'll need a wrench and some skill to get it back on."

"He'll know you did it."

"I don't care." Marcy's feistiness was rubbing off on me.

Chapter Eight

I leaned on the kitchen counter, helping Gram cook dinner. Giggles came from Carla's bedroom where she and Mom were doing girl things. From the living room came the sounds of Dad shaking out his newspaper as he moved from section to section. We could have been mistaken for a normal family, but Danny wasn't home yet.

"Whoa, Gram!" I grabbed her arm before she could dump a can of peas into the skillet. "Don't you have to drain the peas first?"

Gram blinked twice. "I forgot." She moved to the sink and drained the juice from the can. She was making something she called slumgullion, a skillet dish with ground beef and any vegetable in the pantry—peas, carrots, sliced potatoes, green peppers if we had some. She dumped the peas into the skillet and went to the cupboard to get a can of soup. She cranked the can open with practiced dexterity and dumped the contents into the skillet. When she set the can down next to the stove, I saw that it was Cream of Chicken soup. She should have let me get the soup.

"Gram, it's supposed to be Cream of Mushroom soup."

Gram fished her glasses out of a pocket, the ones with the black plastic frames, and examined the label as though it had changed since she got it out of the cupboard. "Jesus, Mary, and Joseph, I'm such a klutz."

I tossed the can into the trash and led Gram to a seat at the table. "Let me finish this." I stirred the food and scooped a sample with a spatula. As though it might bite me, I lifted it to my lips and stabbed it with the tip of my tongue. "It's okay," I whispered. I put a finger to my lips—it's our little secret—and yelled, "Dinner is ready."

Mom, Carla, and Dad wandered into the kitchen. Mom had applied blush to Carla's cheeks, mascara to her eyelashes, and a dab of lipstick to her mouth.

"Isn't she cute?" Mom asked.

Dad and I made noncommittal sounds. An eight-year-old in Mom's makeup was cute, but Marcy in makeup was condemned as too sexy for a fourteen-year-old. It seemed a paradox to me.

Carla sniffed the air like a bird dog. "Euw! Let's order pizza."

The screen door slammed and the five of us jerked alert.

Danny leaned into the kitchen and said, "I'm going to see if Joe's made any progress on a tryout."

"Eat dinner first." Mom directed Carla to set the table.

"I want pizza," Carla said.

"Do what your mother tells you," Dad said.

As Carla passed out plates, silverware, and napkins, I patted Gram's hand. She removed her glasses and wiped her eyes with a handkerchief.

Apprehension built in my gut as my family took their first bites of the food. They wrinkled their noses and furrowed their brows as they tried to figure out why the food tasted different.

"What did you do to the slumgullion, Abby?" Dad asked.

Before Gram could confess her mistake, I defended her. "She made it just like always. I helped."

Mom took a tiny bite. "It's different, but not terrible."

"I can't eat it." Danny dropped his fork onto the plate and stood.

"It won't kill you," Mom said. "Sit down."

He huffed but sat.

"I want pizza." Carla banged two fists on the table.

"Good thing we didn't have company tonight," Dad said.

"We never have company." Mom shrugged. "You don't like company."

"Is that why we never get to meet Danny's girlfriend?" I'm not sure if I was trying to expose him, or just embarrass him.

"I don't have a steady, chubby. I play the field."

"All the girls he talks to all night long." Dad gave Danny a proud smile.

If Danny's a queer, who is he talking to all night long? "They must be ugly as sin, dingleberry. That's why we don't get to meet them."

"You're such a goober, you wouldn't know what to do with a girl."

I bit my tongue.

"What's a dingleberry? Is it like a strawberry?" Carla asked.

"It's the last piece of poop hanging off your butt after you wipe," I said.

"Euw."

"Eddie!" Mom scolded.

No one finished their meal. Mom finally realized that Gram had been in a stupor throughout this ordeal. "Want Danny to run you home, Gram?"

As though she just awoke in the morning, she lifted her head and stared at Danny. "No, Bill will come and get me."

Danny scoffed at her. "Uncle Bill's been dead for ten years."

"Who's Uncle Bill?" I didn't know I had an uncle.

"I'm going to grab a bite with Joe." Danny got up and left.

That's not all he'll grab. Although Joe had made the first move to kiss Danny, Danny hadn't been averse to the intimacy and seemed willing to return for a second helping.

"Why don't you walk Gram home?" Mom asked me.

I helped Mom clear the table while Gram gathered her things. "She's not right, Mom."

"She's just old," Mom said.

"And senile." Dad took his newspaper and a toothpick into the living room.

"I'm still hungry," Carla moaned.

"I'll fix you a sandwich." Mom went to the cupboard for a loaf of bread.

As we walked to Gram's house, I took her arm in mine to steady her, but she had no trouble physically. It was her mind that had a problem. It scared me.

By the time we reached her house, her mind seemed to have cleared. She asked me to come pick the apples off the ground under the big tree in her backyard. "Maybe you could cut the grass, too."

"Sure, Gram, happy to do that."

I settled her at her kitchen table and drew a glass of tap water. I handed her the glass and sat in the other seat.

"I didn't know we had an Uncle Bill."

She smiled. "Bill was my boyfriend." Her eyes went dreamy, apparently reliving the memory. "You boys were too young to understand so we called him Uncle Bill."

I wanted to know why Gram had a boyfriend and why no one ever spoke of my grandfather. "What happened to Grandpa?"

"Ach, that *scheisskopf* left me with two babies."

Two babies? "He just walked away?"

"Straight out the door."

I couldn't understand why anyone would leave my Gram. She was the best person in the world. And she had two babies. "Did you marry Bill? Was he my step-grandfather?"

Her face fell and I thought she was upset by my probing, but she answered me. "We couldn't get married."

"How come?"

"I was still married to Grandpa."

Mom and Dad thought young boys wouldn't have understood that

Gram was dating a man while still married. They were right.

"Why didn't you get a divorce?"

She shrugged. "The priests wouldn't let me. Catholics can't get a divorce."

The Pope frowns on it but people do get divorced sometimes. "They couldn't stop you, Gram."

"They were going to ex-whatever you call it. Kick me out."

"Excommunicate." Her husband abandoned her but the church was going to excommunicate her. How unfair. "Who said that, Gram? One of our current priests?"

"Sure, Muller."

She pronounced his name the German way.

Why would he want to control Gram's life?

"Why don't I remember Bill?"

"He died when you were very small."

That made me sad. "So, Gram, I never knew you had two children. I only knew about Mom."

Her eyes teared up and one little droplet crept down her cheek. "You're named after Edward, my little boy."

I was afraid to ask the logical next question but I'd never get a better chance. "Where is, ah, Edward?"

Gram broke down and bawled and I was sorry I had asked. She laid her head on her arms, on the table, and cried. I wrapped an arm around her and waited. She whimpered for a while before regaining her composure.

"Edward drowned in the river while I was at work. My father was supposed to watch him but he went off with another boy and fell off the railroad tracks."

I knew where that must have happened. There was a railroad trestle over the river at the bottom of the Lawe Street hill.

She dried her eyes. "I think I'll go to bed now. Thanks for bringing me home, Eddie."

I had to stop questioning Gram about her history. All I accomplished was ripping the scabs off her old wounds. It was none of my business, was it?

As I walked up our driveway, I suppressed the urge to sneak down to Joe's house. Spying on Danny made me sick, but I had to get proof of his indiscretions if I was going to stop his sinning. I wondered if Mom knew about Danny, or if women could tell when a guy was queer. Maybe that's why she defended him. But I'd been gone a long time and I didn't want

Mom or Dad looking for me. Angry voices came through the screened back door, so I stopped short of the stoop and listened.

"That Morada guy is stringing you along, pretending to be an important guy, but he'll never get you a tryout." I had never heard Dad sound so disappointed.

"It just takes time," Danny said.

Danny is worried he'll be cut off from his boyfriend. I was glad I hadn't wasted time spying on Morada's house.

"You should play semi-pro ball," Dad said. "A scout could notice you and get you a tryout."

Mom joined the fight. "You guys act like baseball is a career. It's just a game you play until you grow up, Frank."

"He's only just graduated. Give him a break."

"How long do I have to wait, Frank? You gave Danny a car, but you have me and Carla to worry about, too."

"I'm doing my best," Dad said.

There was a lull in the conversation and I visualized the three of them staring into space. I was glad my path to the future was set and not the subject of a family debate.

Danny broke the silence. "Just give me one more chance at baseball. If it doesn't work out, I'll get a stupid job."

A chair scraped across the floor.

"That's the plan. Give him one more chance, Kat."

No sounds came from the kitchen and I imagined they'd all gone to bed. I reached for the door handle and stopped with my hand in the air when Mom said, "You've really messed him up, all that stupid talk about baseball. Danny's an adult. He should get a real job and pay us rent. Or get his own place."

"Danny will be fine. Eddie was a mistake and then you had to try again for a girl. We have too many mouths to feed."

What? Mistake?

"Eddie's going away and I'll take care of Carla."

Mom made it sound like a peace offering, but Dad didn't buy it.

"Eddie will cost more away than at home. Carla's starting to cost a lot. You bought her clothes without my permission, and spent money on yourself, too."

"You get a union job at a filthy mill, buy a shoebox for a house, and a used Chevy, and they tell you that you're middle-class. What a joke."

"Factories are the backbone of our economy. You wouldn't have anything without my job."

“I have nothing with your job. I can’t take care of our kids.”

“You baby Carla, and Gram babies Eddie, and you turned them into spoiled brats.”

“You ruined Danny with your fantasies. I still have time with Carla.”

“Danny will be all right. I guess we both failed with Eddie.” Dad’s voice had lost its energy.

“You can’t relate to him because he’s smarter than the rest of us. The nuns say he’s a genius.”

“Why would a genius want to be a priest, live without women?”

“You look down on the priests but you play cards with them, drink their beer.”

“I have my reasons.”

The rapid-fire conversation skipped a beat.

“You need to take the pill so we don’t have more mistakes,” Dad said.

“The Pope says no.”

“Since when do you listen to the Pope? The Supreme Court just ruled it’s our right, so take the pill, Kat.”

“I’ll take the pill if you buy me a car and give me spending money.”

“That sounds like I’m paying for it.”

“That’s the way marriage works. You’ll get yours if I get mine.”

“You’ll get yours when I get my next raise.”

“Well, I’m not giving anything away on credit.”

I had to stifle a laugh over that zinger. Dad made no response and the kitchen fell quiet. I gave it a few minutes before breezing in through the back door as though nothing was wrong. I was surprised to find Mom sitting alone at the table.

“Is Gram okay?” She looked at me with weary eyes.

“I put her to bed but I don’t think she’s okay. Her mind isn’t working right.”

“She’s just old, Eddie.” Her voice sounded weary, too.

If Mom was right, growing old was the worst thing that could happen to a person.

Chapter Nine

Father Bauer said the workers' Mass so fast it made my head spin. I had to run around the sanctuary to keep up with him. And the Latin words? They tumbled out of his mouth like baseballs dumped out of a practice bag. Twenty-five minutes flat and we were back in the sacristy, disrobing.

"I'll see you tomorrow." I hung my robe in the cabinet.

"Only if you want to, Eddie."

I turned, confused. "I thought the Monsignor wanted me to serve every day?"

"No, that was Father Mac's idea. Give the Mass to one of the younger kids. Let them get the experience."

"Okay. What about confession?"

"What about it?"

"Do you want to hear my confession now?"

He had a puzzled expression on his face. "You have something serious to confess?"

No, but Danny does. "Not really."

"Then just use the regular confessional."

He didn't have to tell me twice. I ran out of there before Father Mac arrived for the next Mass.

I changed into play clothes and headed up the street to find Dickie and the other neighborhood boys. They were in a vacant lot, playing a miniature form of baseball within the confined space. The bases were only forty feet apart and the neighbor's fence at the back of the lot was maybe one hundred feet from the flattened cardboard box that represented home plate.

"Can I play?"

"Sure," Dickie said. "We've been looking for you. Guess you've been busy with priest stuff."

The six kids were all one or two years younger than me, so I let Dickie pick three kids and we'd play three against four. Before I took the mound, I said, "By the way, Dickie, you've got the first workers' Mass tomorrow."

"Aw, I don't wanna get up for that."

"Father Bauer asked for you."

"Really?" The kid's eyes lit up. "Does he think he can make a priest outta me?"

"Maybe you'll be the senior altar boy next year. Maybe that's why."

"Aw, seriously?" His expression was a mixture of joy and trepidation. "That early in the morning?"

As the senior altar boy this year, I was the boss of the other altar boys. "You have to do it." I almost felt bad about throwing Dickie into the snake pit at church, but he'd serve Father Bauer, not Father Mac.

These neighborhood games weren't like real baseball games. Batters either struck out or circled the bases while fielders chased ground balls.

When it was my turn to bat, Dickie said, "Bat left-handed. You're too big for this field."

That sounded fair. I stepped up to the plate and took two slow pitches that were nowhere near the plate.

"Swing at somethin'. No walks in this game." Dickie wound up like Sandy Koufax and grunted with the effort.

The pitch was only a foot off the ground but over the plate so I gave it an uppercut golf swing and met the ball perfectly. It sailed high, right over the fence at the back of the lot. My teammates cheered; Dickie's teammates jeered. I trotted around the bases and leaped the last three feet to land emphatically on home plate. "We win." I was a star in neighborhood baseball.

Dickie huffed. "Go get my ball, show off."

We walked the fence line but couldn't see the ball stuck in the shrubbery. I tested the rickety fence and it wobbled. "You're smaller than me, Dickie. You climb the fence."

"I'm not going over there," he said. "That old woman has a huge black dog."

On cue, the dog appeared, charging at us, and barking.

"Game's over." I started away.

"You owe me a ball, Eddie."

"Don't forget Mass tomorrow."

"You're a creep, you know that?"

I told myself that playing ball with the younger neighborhood kids was good for my self-confidence.

Rummaging through the fridge for a midday snack, I pushed aside Tupperware containers of leftover meatloaf, tuna casserole, chicken legs, peas and carrots, mashed potatoes, and a pork chop. "Waste not, want not," Dad often preached. Mom explained his leftover obsession came from being raised on a pig farm in Iowa during the depression. He was number eight of nine children and never had enough to eat. World War II saved him. He enlisted in the Navy and then he always had enough to eat.

I made a sandwich of cold cuts and fresh tomatoes and onions from the garden I hated to weed. I took it upstairs to eat while I finished reading *Of Mice and Men* so I'd have something to talk about with Marcy. When I reached the end, I was shocked. George killed Lennie.

The phone rang.

How could George kill the friend who depended upon him?

"You have a phone call," Mom yelled from the foot of the stairs. "It's a girl."

Oh, crap. "It's probably a nun, Mom."

I scampered down the stairs and she handed me the phone with a sly look in her eyes. Mom tried to look busy as she hung around the kitchen. I shooed her away with the back of my hand, the way Dad did. She moved to the living room but I knew she was just around the corner.

"Hello?"

"Hey, I'm done early. Are you coming?"

"Yes, Sister. I'll be there right away."

Marcy laughed so hard I was sure Mom could hear her. "You can't fake it, Eddie. Your mom knows I'm not a nun."

"The eighth-grade classroom. Yes, Sister, right away."

"Meet me at the bottom of the Lawe Street hill. There's a new bookstore I want to go to."

"I'm on my way."

Mom popped back around the corner with a big smile on her face. "The kid who's supposed to have a girlfriend doesn't, and the kid who isn't supposed to have a girlfriend does. What a screwed-up family we are."

She knows about Danny. I must have been as red as a fire truck but I wasn't giving in to her. "It's Sister Mary Frances. Wants to see me right away."

"Say hello for me." Mom smiled like a cat with a bowl of milk.

At the top of the Lawe Street hill I paused. It was a long way down the steep hill and cars whizzed by just feet away. Marcy waited at the bottom. I couldn't appear to be afraid so I pushed off and freewheeled, but kept the back pedal poised to brake. I must have been going thirty miles an hour when I streaked past her. She caught up to me on the bridge.

"You're quite the daredevil."

"You were supposed to hang up if Mom answered."

"She sounded nice. I want to meet her."

I didn't respond. I looked at the river and the railroad trestle that runs beneath the bridge. *How the hell did Uncle Edward get down there, on that trestle? And why would he do that?*

"What's the matter?"

My eyes followed the tracks to the other side of the bridge where the tracks met a paper mill, the one where Joe Morada was some kind of supervisor. Dad described the Fox River as a working river, dammed every few miles to supply hydroelectric power to the many paper mills along its route. Edward and his friend must have jumped onto the tracks from the mill landing on the other side of the road then walked the tracks under the bridge. Why? To prove they were brave? Did Edward fall, or did a train come along and knock him off?

"Hey." Marcy shook my shoulder. "Earth to Eddie."

"Gram told me that my Uncle Edward fell off the railroad tracks down there and drowned."

Marcy slipped her hand through my arm and gave me a side hug. "I'm sorry."

The river ran fast below the Oneida Street dam a mile upriver and cascaded over another dam downriver. Along the way, the current was irresistible, the roiling black water capped in white foam writhed like a venomous snake. I wondered if Edward was swept over the next dam. I wondered where they recovered his body.

"It was a long time ago." *Was it?* Gram didn't say when it happened but she called him her little boy. She said her husband left her with two babies. Mom was born in 1925 and Edward was still a baby when Gram's husband left. Then the drowning most likely happened in the 1930s.

"I have to go to the library." I had to do it.

"What for? I want to see the new bookstore."

"I want to read Edward's obituary first." I started across the bridge and Marcy pedaled fast to catch up.

On the other side of the river, we walked our bikes up the steep hill. The stone retaining wall on our left was covered in spray-painted graffiti. In yellow someone had painted, *Apathy will destroy Lawrence College.* Beneath it in white someone painted, *Who cares?* At the top of the hill the leafy Lawrence College campus stretched for two blocks to the west. People criticized the small school for imitating the Ivy League.

We rode three blocks to the library where the helpful old lady behind the counter set me up with a microfiche reader and the records of the Appleton Post-Crescent newspaper for the 1930s. Marcy wandered off as I started with 1939. It took about thirty minutes to find what I was looking for, a brief notice from July 19, 1937.

Edward Jaeger, son of Abigail Jaeger, fell off the Chicago and Northwestern railroad bridge, three hundred feet east of Lawe Street, and was swept downstream. His body was recovered by a motorcycle patrolman the following day.

He was so far from the safety of the paper mill that he couldn't outrun an oncoming locomotive. He did go over the dam and farther downstream. But the other boy didn't drown. He'd have told Gram that Edward went into the river. She'd have had a terrible night searching for her little boy.

Edward was born January 15, 1927. He was a fourth grader at McKinley Elementary School. He is survived by a sister, also named Abigail, and his grandfather, Joseph Sachs.

No mention of a father, gone sometime between Edward's birth and his death. No mention of Gram's mother, either. It seemed peculiar that he went to a public grammar school rather than St. Catherine's.

"Ten years old. How awful." Marcy read the piece over my shoulder.

I popped to my feet. "Let's go."

"Are you alright?"

"I'm named after him. I wanted to know who he was and now I know."

The new bookstore was in Kimberly so we rode east down College Avenue and over another bridge across the river. Dad's mill sat under that bridge. The new bookstore occupied two floors of a renovated building and housed more books for sale than the library had to lend. Up and down the stairs, in and out of the stacks, we cavorted like kids in Santa's workshop. Marcy pulled *Lady Chatterley's Lover* from the shelf and sat in an easy chair to skim the sexy parts. I found *Fahrenheit 451* and a chair near her.

After an hour, Marcy had books piled all around her chair. "We don't have to borrow from the library, we can come here and read better books than at the library."

"Better do it quick because the church is going to shut this place down for selling pornography, sure as the Pope is Catholic."

I got up to put my book back and thought she was doing the same but when I started for the door, Marcy walked to the cash register with one book.

The clerk at the register stuck out a hand and Marcy tried to give her cash. The woman wouldn't accept it.

"Eighteen or older." She waggled her fingers, asking for ID.

Marcy said something I couldn't hear, put her money back in her purse and joined me.

"Did you try to buy *Lady Chatterley's Lover?"*

"No, *Slaughterhouse Five.* I guess they don't want us to know what we did in the war."

"Eighteen or older, I heard her say."

"What difference does four years make? Let's get something to drink before we go all the way back home."

She led me through a connecting door to a coffee shop. Behind a counter of baked goods, clerks poured coffee for customers. More than a dozen small tables were crowded with book lovers enjoying a summer afternoon.

I had saved a couple of dollars so I was about to buy us cream puffs when she yanked my arm and pulled me out of the line, out of sight of the people at the tables.

"What are you doing?"

"Look at the table in the right-hand corner," she whispered.

I peeked between people in line. A young man and woman were sipping coffee and talking at the table. "What about it?"

"You don't recognize them?"

I peeked again and realized the young man was Father Bauer. Without his cassock and collar, I hadn't recognized him.

"So what? Priests don't have to wear their clerical robes everywhere they go."

"You, dummy, he's with Sister Mary Alice."

"What?" I moved around the line to get a better look. The young woman with short blond hair was also wearing street clothes, but there was no denying it. The cute round face and big eyes belonged to Sister Mary Alice. Now she and Father Bauer were holding hands under their table. I was gawking when the priest glanced my way. I ducked behind the line.

"Did he see you?"

"Maybe," I said breathlessly.

Bent at the waist, we hustled out the front door. We ran to our bikes and pedaled toward Appleton. I didn't look back. I didn't want to know if they had seen us.

***

"Sister Mary Frances really did call," Mom said.

"Again?"

She gave me a c'mon Eddie look. "She wants to see you tomorrow morning."

"Same place, the classroom?" I played the ruse all the way to the end.

"You're supposed to ring the bell at the convent."

Oh. "She must have forgotten to tell me something."

"If you say so."

I went upstairs to clean up and when I came down for dinner, the gang was all there. Gram had baked a meatloaf. I took a tentative forkful and it tasted like she used the right ingredients.

"Eddie has a girlfriend," Mom announced.

She just can't leave it alone.

"If the goober has a girlfriend, she's gotta be fat as him." Danny laughed at the absurdity of me having a girlfriend.

"She's better looking than your friends, dingleberry." I almost said, *boyfriend.*

"You shouldn't call people a dingleberry." Mom shook a finger at me.

"Oh, but goober is okay?" I stabbed my meatloaf.

"You both need to be nice."

"A girlfriend is good news, Eddie," Dad said, a big smile on his face. "Maybe she'll change your mind about the seminary."

"She's just a classmate who happens to be a girl," I said. "I'm committed to my vocation."

"Women have a way changing men's minds, Eddie." He gave Mom a pointed look. "You and Danny could invite your gal friends to dinner. I'll throw some burgers on the grill."

"No way I'm putting a girl on parade here," Danny said.

"Eddie's girlfriend is pretty."

Everyone turned to look at Gram.

Mom stopped her fork in midair. "You met her?"

"At the graduation. Smart girl."

"Eddie's got a girlfriend," Carla sang.

"Well, the rest of us would like to meet her," Dad said. "Any day is okay, Eddie."

"Sure, Dad." *Match that, Danny.*

"See, Eddie's not afraid of us."

"It's not a competition, Frank. Danny doesn't have a steady and Eddie's only in eighth grade. He's too young to have a girlfriend." Mom tried to end the conversation before words were said that couldn't be unsaid.

"I'm in high school, Mom. I can bring Marcy over."

"Maaarcy, Maaarcy," Carla sang.

Danny squirmed in his seat. "Well, I don't want to pick one girl over another. They get upset when you do stuff like that."

After dinner, Danny left to check in with Joe. I volunteered to walk Gram home, but first I ran upstairs to get my Kodak Instamatic camera. I hugged it under my arm so no one would notice, but no one was watching me. Gram invited me in for a soda, and I suppose, some more talk, but tonight I declined. I had a different mission.

There was no light coming through the one window in Danny's room, so I was sure he was still at Joe's house, "checking in." I snuck through the dark backyards and positioned myself beyond Joe's back door for the best camera angle if they came outside for another smooch. Then I waited. I stood for a while but they didn't emerge so I squatted and waited. My legs cramped, so I sat in the grass and leaned back against Dickie's garage. I caught myself nodding off. If I was going to do this, I could wait no longer. It was possible that Danny wasn't in there and I was on a wild goose chase.

There were lights coming from a large window at the back of Joe's house, so I crept over to get a look. Standing in Joe's flower bed, the top of my head reached only to the bottom of the window, so I jumped and peeked over the sill. That split-second revealed a sort of den with a couch and TV. Joe smiled from the couch as Danny, his shirt unbuttoned, buckled his belt.

My head spun so fast I thought I would pass out. Danny and Joe weren't just hugging and kissing. They were … I gulped and waited for my dizziness to subside, then I jumped again. They were on the couch now, cuddling.

I removed the flash attachment from my camera, lifted it over my head, pointed and clicked. I didn't know if I had gotten them in the frame, so I did it again, pointing the camera more to my right. I still couldn't be sure. I got my camera ready, holding it in front of my face so

I could aim where I looked, and I jumped. At the top of my leap, I snapped the picture that proved everything—they were kissing again. Maybe it was the shock of the scene, maybe it was my lack of coordination, but the camera banged against the windowsill when I dropped to the ground. My Kodak popped out of my hand and tumbled into a mess of geraniums. I lost my balance and trampled the flowers as I stumbled onto the grass. *Scheisse.*

I grabbed the camera and made a beeline for my house. When I heard Joe's back door slam, I cut between houses and out onto the street, hoping Joe and Danny would waste time looking in the backyards. Past two more houses, I sprinted up our driveway, and into the kitchen. I stuffed the camera under my shirt, caught my breath, and walked into the living room. Dad was asleep on the floor—that's how he napped, on his stomach, his head propped on his arms—and Mom sipped a cocktail. Carla must have been in her room. I headed straight upstairs.

"Is Gram okay?" Mom asked.

"Peachy-keen, Mom."

I closed my door and hid my camera in winter boots at the back of my closet, grabbed a book, took a seat in my chair, and waited for Danny to appear. My breathing slowed as I worked my way through the mystery. Danny hadn't been talking to girls all night long. He had been talking to his boyfriend, Joe.

Danny approached our house on the street as Joe came through the backyards. They met on our driveway and turned circles looking for whoever trampled the flower bed. They had searched toward our house, not up the street. Either Danny suspected it was me or he wanted to be sure it wasn't me. By the time Danny swept into the living room, I was calm.

"Is Eddie here?" he asked Mom.

"He took Gram home but he's back."

"How long?"

"Huh?"

"How long has he been home?"

"A while. Why?"

Danny clomped up the stairs and barged into my room.

"Get out!" I yelled.

He closed my door behind him. "You have anything to say?"

"Yeah, get out."

"What's going on up there?" Mom yelled.

Neither of us answered. Danny glared at me, hands on hips. This standoff was different than I thought it would be. Thoughts of blackmailing Danny for a job at the golf course evaporated like water in the desert. His sin was too serious to be used as blackmail. After I got the film developed, I'd force Danny to see a priest. Father Mac would understand.

I could tell Danny was thinking, too. He couldn't be sure I had made the noise at the window. He couldn't expose himself by accusing me of snooping on him. He had to pray I didn't see anything. Prayer would be good for him. He walked out the door.

Chapter Ten

I took the film out of my camera, loaded a fresh roll, and laid the camera in the top drawer of my bedside table. Easy to find if Danny thought to look for it.

My first stop was at the neighborhood drugstore where I left the exposed film to be developed in triplicate. I prayed the film was fed into some big machine that printed the pictures anonymously and stuffed them into an envelope at the end of an assembly line.

From the drugstore, it was a short ride to the convent. Sister Mary Agnes, my eighth-grade teacher, answered the bell. She directed me to a small sitting room just inside the door. "Wait here." No small talk, no *how nice to see you.*

A couch on one wall faced a wing-backed chair on the other. The furniture could have been a hundred years old. Crucifixes hung on three walls. I didn't sit, and I didn't relax. Other than the creaking of the wooden floor above me as nuns walked around upstairs, the place was quiet as a graveyard.

After a while, a habit whooshed and the wooden rosary that hung from the nuns' sashes clacked as a nun approached. Sister Mary Frances walked into the room with a grim look on her face and waved me to the couch. She sat in the armchair.

"Do you still want to be a priest, Mr. Kovacs?"

Sister Mary Frances was a foreboding presence who had been known to rap the knuckles of disobedient students with a ruler and lock them in closets for hours. She stared at me through rimless glasses.

"Yes, of course. I've always wanted to be a priest."

"You were our first choice for the seminary, smart enough, holy enough, committed enough, and we did our best to groom you. Now we're unsure about you."

Who's "we?" She and the Monsignor? Or does Father Mac have something to do with this inquisition? I suppressed an urge to rebel as the hackles rose on the back of my neck. "I've done everything Father MacMillan and Father Bauer have asked, Sister."

Her eyes were like a welding torch boring a hole through me. I pretended to be steel but I melted like wax.

"Our purpose was to add you to our cadre of Diocesan priests, not the Jesuits, Mr. Kovacs."

It seemed like the religious orders were in competition with one another. "Monsignor Muller is looking into it for me, but I'd be very happy to be a parish priest." That was a lie, but I wanted out of her suffocating presence.

"Good. There's one other problem." She paused as if to emphasize what came next. "Marcy Jablonski." She said the name as though she'd have to wash her mouth out with soap.

Huh? "Yes, Sister?"

"You've been keeping company with her this summer."

"I see her around. At the library and stuff."

"Some of our students saw you with her at that sinful movie theater, Mr. Kovacs. Don't lie to me."

Who's spying on us? Bennie and Jerry? "We just happened to be in the same place."

"She's a bad influence. You were with her when she stole a book from the new bookstore in Kimberly."

Father Bauer lied to cover his tracks. Marcy didn't steal any books, did she? "I didn't see her do it, Sister. I certainly didn't steal any books."

"If you want to be a priest, stop associating with her."

I wanted to tell this fat old witch to keep her eye on Sister Mary Alice and leave me alone. "Marcy hasn't influenced me, Sister. I'm true to my faith and my vocation."

"Keep it that way. Stay away from that little devil, Mr. Kovacs."

She rose, moved to the doorway, and waved a hand at the front door. She walked into the dark interior, and I let myself out.

I hopped on my bike and pedaled like mad straight up Fremont Street, but I had no idea where I was going. I imagined steam pouring out of my ears like exhaust from a diesel truck. How dare a nun tell me who my friends can be? Why are nuns and priests afraid of facts? I'd bet Jesuits knew how to refute, rebut, or explain all the points Marcy made.

I rode past Reid Municipal Golf Course, all the way to the dead end of Fremont Street and stopped to catch my breath. What bothered me most about my scolding by Sister Mary Frances was Father Bauer's accusation that Marcy had stolen a book. If she did steal a book, would I want to have her for a friend? Or did the priest lie to keep his rendezvous with Alice a secret?

I heard them before I saw them, and the sounds they made woke me from my reverie. Bennie and Jerry peeled around the corner from Telulah Avenue and raced straight toward me whooping like Indians attacking a wagon train. *Scheisse!* I screamed down Schaefer Street, made the corner on Bluebird Lane, and then went right, left, right, left, back and forth until I came out on Fremont again. Bennie was too fat to keep up, and Jerry, who was short and skinny, didn't have the guts to fight alone so he stayed back with Bennie. They were out of sight behind me, so I stood on the pedals and pumped hard, flying down Fremont Street toward home. Afraid they'd trail me all the way home, I turned up Lawe Street and made a right on Maple Street. I cut into Gram's driveway and dumped my bike behind her house where it wasn't visible from the street.

Gram wore a light cotton smock, and her hair was in disarray. She was surprised to see me.

"I came to pick up the apples and cut your grass," I said.

"Oh, *danke*."

"*Bitte*." I took two wooden bushel barrel baskets into the backyard and, constantly watching the street, I put the bruised and wormy apples in one basket and the good ones in the other. Afterward, I used her push mower to cut the small yard dominated by the huge apple tree. When I finished, Gram invited me in for a soda. She was in a floral dress, and she had brushed her hair.

We sat on her couch in the living room, the one with the green cushions covered in plastic, and drank in silence for a minute. She seemed tired, but I took a chance that she'd answer some more questions.

"Has Grandpa died, or do you know where he is now?"

Gram seemed ready to answer and then stopped herself. She had worry in her eyes as she considered how to answer. I leaned forward to encourage her. Finally, she said, "He's dead. Long time now."

"Oh, that's too bad."

"He was a bad man. You wouldn't like him."

"Yeah, I'm sure you're right." I wouldn't like a man who had left Gram with two small children. "Do you have any pictures of your mother and father?"

"Why do you want to see them?"

"I've seen Dad's picture of his parents, but I've never seen your parents, my great grandparents."

She removed her glasses and pinched her nose. Then she got up and walked into her bedroom. She returned with a small, framed photo. "His name was Joseph Sachs. Mother was Lottie, Charlotte Sachs."

Joseph and Lottie looked remarkably similar to Dad's parents—stern-faced, formal, austere. The difference was that Joseph Sachs was tall. That's where Danny and I got our height. "Thanks, Gram, I just wanted to know who they were."

I rode home to take a shower. Mom stopped me before I went upstairs. "Two boys were here looking for you. I told them you were at church."

"Who were they?"

"I didn't ask their names. One was chubby and the other was skinny. School friends?"

Scheisse! "Yeah, school friends."

***

I didn't give Marcy time to get off her bike at the library. "Did you steal a book the other day?"

"What's got your goat? I don't steal books."

"A store isn't a library. You can't borrow a book from a store. Did you steal a book from the Corner Book Store?"

Her face went slack and her eyes turned downward. "How did you hear about that?"

"Sister Mary Frances told me."

"I knew it! Father Bauer told on me. But I'll get him back. I'll let everyone know what he's doing with a nun."

"Sister Mary Frances said I can't become a priest if I hang around with you."

"We're not a priest and a nun having an affair. We're just kids. You're not going to let her control your life, are you?"

"I can't be with someone who steals books."

"My mother went back to the store and paid for it. I forgot I had it when we ran out of the coffee shop."

Okay, she won't going to jail for shoplifting. "What did you steal?"

She beamed. "*Lady Chatterley's Lover.*"

"Oh my God. You couldn't just steal *Slaughterhouse Five*?"

"Stop saying *steal*, please."

My feet pawed around in the dirt next to the bike rack. "Did your mother let you read it?"

"Of course. It was wicked good." She laughed. "But I won't share it with you because I don't want to corrupt a future priest."

"I think the book thing is just an excuse. They're really worried I might like girls."

"Do you hear yourself? They're worried you might be normal."

Adults talk about their children having growing spurts, but growing up now seemed to be more about learning things adults didn't want me to know. I hated the idea that a nun was telling me who my friends could be.

"If we're going to hang out together, we can't go anywhere priests and nuns go."

"Well, we're not going to hang out at hospitals or homes where people are given their last rites."

"But priests could be roaming around our neighborhoods, counseling people," I countered. "Otherwise, I never see them, do you?"

"Sometimes I see nuns at the Valley Fair mall, in a pack, like dogs. They watch each other to keep everyone in line. Like a cult."

"So, no mall." I glanced at a woman coming out of the library, a stack of books in her arms. "It's not safe here, either."

"I can borrow the books. We just need a place to read them. What about your house?"

I wasn't ready to put Marcy on display at my house. "Bennie and Jerry turned up at my house this morning, looking for me."

"Told you they'd want revenge. What about Wisconsin Avenue on the far northside? That's where the high school kids cruise the drive-ins. No reason for priests and nuns to be way out there."

Wisconsin Avenue was about four miles from our neighborhood. "What about parks? We could see people coming from far off."

For a moment she was perfectly still and stared off into the distance. She snapped her fingers. "What if we turn the tables on them?"

"Huh? How?"

"We can stalk them. Both Father Bauer and Father Mac. Catch them in the act."

"Blackmail them? I think that's a sin."

"They're the sinners. Tomorrow let's meet in the St. Elizabeth's Hospital parking lot, across from the rectory. We'll follow them and you can take pictures of them committing their sins."

Like I took pictures of Danny committing his sins. Nothing has ever made me more unhappy than recording sins. It seemed we were in a full-scale war with the religious leaders I had revered and obeyed all my life. It made me very uncomfortable, but I said, "Okay."

***

Our backyard was the scene of a party. Danny sat in the seat of honor at the picnic table surrounded by friends and neighbors—Doug and Shirley, the Wilsons from the house on the other side of us, Dickie and his parents, the Hellers from across the street, a couple of Danny's baseball teammates. And Joe Morada.

Dad had rolled the grill out of the garage onto the driveway and was flipping burgers and turning hotdogs on the grates. Everyone held beers except Mom and Shirley who had martini glasses. Carla skipped around the backyard with a sparkler although this wasn't the Fourth of July. Gram sat in a lawn chair off to the side, observing.

"What's going on?" I asked Dad.

"We're celebrating Danny's birthday."

Danny would turn nineteen on Monday. He had always been the oldest kid in his class, which made me wonder if Mom and Dad had held him back a year because he wasn't all that bright. "It's not until Monday."

"Nobody wants to celebrate on a Monday and everybody is busy on the weekend. Friday is always a good day to celebrate the end of the workweek. Grab a glass of pop and act like you're having fun."

I poured some soda, pulled a lawn chair next to Gram, and watched the lab rats interact. Joe seemed to intentionally ignore Danny, probably so no one would get the wrong—no, the right—idea about them. In a white t-shirt stretched tight across his muscular chest and bulging at his biceps, he reminded me of Marlon Brando in that boxing movie—"I coulda been a contender." His hard eyes and prominent cheekbones made him look vaguely sinister.

Joe chatted with the Wilsons. Dad and Mr. Wilson had a dispute over our backyard fence and avoided one another, but Mrs. Wilson wheedled her way into Mom's clique. When Dad called Wilson an immature idiot, I disagreed. "Dad, the man has a wife and three kids. He can't be a total idiot."

Dad said, "You'll learn that you don't have to be smart to make babies."

Although Joe left Danny to his teammates, Shirley eased up to Danny, threw an arm around him, and gave him a "birthday kiss." Doug glared at her from the other side of the picnic table but she was undeterred. I think Danny got three of her birthday kisses, and eventually Joe glared at her as well.

Carla eased up to me and whispered in my ear. "Shirley is sweet on Danny."

"Won't do her any good, Shrimp."

"Huh?"

We ate hamburgers and hotdogs, and Mom came out of the house carrying a cake with lit candles. Danny blew out the candles. “I’ll bet everyone knows what I wished for.”

I made a wish, too—I wished my brother was normal.

Chapter Eleven

I should have been excited but I was scared. Would the drug store let a kid have pictures of two men kissing? Would they call the cops on me? Would the priests find out? Or, God forbid, Sister Mary Frances? I couldn't leave the pictures at the drug store or they might call my house and say, "Hey, come pick up your kid's dirty pictures."

My heart couldn't decide whether to jump into my throat or burst from my chest as I coasted up to the drug store. I shuffled down the greeting card aisle and up the candy aisle, loitering until no one was in line at the cash register. When I approached, the middle-aged cashier seemed bored.

I cleared my throat. "I'm here to pick up pictures for the Kovacs family."

She lifted a box of envelopes containing prints onto the counter and flipped through them.

"Kovacs. Here it is." She squeezed my packet to test its thickness. "Not much in this batch," she said.

Most of the envelopes were thick with dozens of prints, but mine was slim and light as a paper airplane. It contained only photos of Danny and Marcy.

"I'm just a beginner. Most of my shots don't turn out," I babbled nervously.

"Your shots. You took these pictures?"

She saw my pictures! "Everybody uses the camera so it depends which ones turned out."

"Uh huh." She asked me for less than a dollar.

She tapped her fingers on the counter as I counted out the coins, probably wondering what kind of perverted family would send a kid to pick up dirty pictures. Maybe wondering if she should tell someone. I flew out of the store, hurried home and straight to my bedroom.

I opened the packet and slid the pictures out. A note—"You should be ashamed"—was paper-clipped to a picture of Danny and Joe kissing. Maybe it was getting caught with the picture, and maybe it was the way the picture made Danny's sin a fact, but I wished I were an innocent kid again. Once thing was certain: I couldn't go to that store to buy candy, couldn't show my face there ever again. My life was being crimped—no drugstore, no library, no bookstore, no mall, no Marcy. I crumpled up the note and stuck it in my pocket. I wasn't about to leave it in the kitchen trashcan for someone to find. I'd get rid of it later.

My fingertips burned as I separated the pictures on my bedspread, as though they were possessed by the devil. The pictures of Danny and Joe were poorly lit, but it was obvious what they were doing. I pulled a book off my shelf and hid a set of prints in it. Then I hid the pictures of Marcy in a different book. Two copies of the Danny and Joe prints and the negatives I stuffed down my pants. I grabbed my camera, rode to the parking lot at St. Elizabeth's Hospital, and waited for Marcy.

Were it not for the black Pontiac sedans in the driveway across the street, I might have thought the rectory was unoccupied. A couple of women in work clothes toiled in the garden behind the convent under the supervision of a nun. The school janitor, with little else to do during the summer, washed the priests' cars in the driveway. As cars left the hospital parking lot and were replaced by new arrivals, I changed positions to stay out of the line of sight from the rectory. Stalking, I learned quickly, was boring work, and I didn't want to do it alone.

Marcy finally rolled into the lot, the tips of her black hair colored aqua blue. "That house I cleaned was a total wreck. Food ground into the carpets, a sink full of unwashed dished dishes, piles of dirty clothes under the beds. I wouldn't have done that house except it belongs to Mom's boss."

"Well, you haven't missed anything."

"I should have brought lunch."

"I should have brought lawn chairs." I wanted to show Marcy the pictures but I procrastinated. *I'm such a wuss.* "I read *Of Mice and Men.*"

She smiled. "It's a perfect story. From a writer's point of view."

"I understand why it's banned. Steinbeck thinks it's okay for George to kill Lennie. It's not."

"It's a mercy killing." Marcy sighed. "George loved Lennie so much, he saved him from the mob."

"Mercy killing is a sin. That's all there is to it." I thought I'd won that point.

"We put our pets to sleep when they're too sick to live."

"Lennie wasn't a dog. You can't take life and death decisions away from God."

"Lennie was God's mistake, broken. He was going to harm other people without even realizing it. I think God is okay with fixing mistakes."

"You must believe in a different God."

"You believe in a church, not a God."

I was shocked into silence. Never before had I thought of God and church as separate entities, but maybe she was right. What did I know of God? What the church had taught me. I had lost another point to Marcy. How could I have lived my whole life without questioning what I was taught?

I couldn't delay any longer. I drew the picture envelope out of my pants. "I have the pictures I took of Danny and his boyfriend."

Her face lit up like a cartoon bomb. "Give 'em here."

I handed the envelope to her.

She smirked as she flipped through the packet. "What are you going to do with them?"

"I don't know. Maybe I'll show them to Danny and get him to talk to a priest."

"Lots of people are homos. It's not a big deal."

"Beatniks and jazz musicians and drug addicts and sissies. Not Danny Kovacs."

She held the pictures out to me and I said, "Those are backup copies. Keep them at your house."

She smirked again. "You're not the goody-two-shoes you pretend to be." She slid the pictures and negatives into her little beaded bag. "What about the pictures you took of me? Were they good?"

Heat crept into my cheeks. I wanted to believe that hiding Marcy's picture was different from kids hiding *Playboy* and *Penthouse* magazines, but it wasn't very different. "Yes, they're nice. I should have brought them with me."

She gave me a sly look, and the silence became uncomfortable until Father MacMillan walked out the front door of the rectory, his missile in hand, his three-cornered biretta atop his head. We tensed in anticipation of a wild chase but the priest strode across the street toward us so we scampered behind cars and watched as he navigated the parking lot and entered the hospital.

Marcy let out a breath. "Just visiting the sick."

"Or giving Extreme Unction to someone."

I gazed up at the hospital windows facing our direction and imagined what was happening in those rooms. The patients were certainly ill, some dying, right there, right now. Although I'd been taught to rejoice at the prospect of a heavenly reward for a life lived in service to God, I feared death more than anything.

"Hey!" Marcy tugged on my sleeve and woke me out of my reverie. "Look who's here."

I turned and looked where she was pointing. Bennie and Jerry came around the corner from the front of the church and slowly cruised toward the convent. I knew they were looking for me. Mom had probably told them to check the church.

"Let's get out of here," Marcy said.

"Nope. They're not going to make fun of you anymore."

"You don't have to do anything for me."

"Well, I'm tired of being bullied."

Bennie and Jerry stopped and talked to the janitor as he washed the priests' cars. The janitor shook his head.

Heedless of the probable consequences, I yelled at Bennie. "Hey! Over here."

Bennie looked my way and hesitated. He and Jerry exchanged words, then rode across the street and into the parking lot. Bennie skidded to a stop in front of me, but Jerry hung back.

"You messed up my bike." Bennie lowered his kickstand.

"Looks okay to me."

Bennie gave me a shove and I stumbled backwards.

He charged like a bull, and I sidestepped him like a matador and shoved him from the side. The shove altered his course but did nothing to halt his momentum. *Dang, Bennie must weigh two hundred pounds!*

He shoved me on my side and wedged me up against a car. "You broke my chain."

I hadn't meant to break his chain. "Your chain must have been old and rusted out."

He grabbed two fistfuls of my shirt and bent me back over the trunk of the car. "You're gonna pay for my chain or I'm gonna whup your ass."

Why did I think I should confront this behemoth?

I was about to agree to pay for Bennie's chain when I heard a growl like a tiger attacking an impala. Marcy swung her purse and struck Bennie over his ear. Bennie yelped and released me.

His mistake! I stomped on his foot. Hard. He screamed and lifted his leg to grab his hurt foot. I gave him a shove and he lost his balance, stumbled backward on one leg like he was riding a pogo stick, and flopped to the ground.

Before he could lever his fat butt off the pavement, Marcy jumped on him, straddled his chest, and pummeled his face with small pale fists.

I turned to Jerry and wagged a finger at him—don't join in or I'll punch your lights out. Jerry thought about it, then pedaled away.

Bennie began to cry as pink splotches blossomed where Marcy's fists had landed on his fleshy cheeks.

I pulled Marcy to her feet and stood over Bennie, one foot on his chest, holding him down.

"I'll pay for your chain if you apologize to Marcy for the nasty things you said. If you don't, I'll tell everyone you got beat up by a girl."

Bennie looked at me with puffy, bloodshot eyes. He wiped his blotchy face with his shirt sleeve and checked it. No blood, just snot. "Deal."

"Say it."

He didn't want to, but he mumbled, "Sorry."

I increased the pressure on his chest. "Look at her and speak up when you say it. What are you sorry for?"

He looked at Marcy. "Sorry. I'll never be mean to you again."

"Good. So how much was the chain?"

Bennie screwed up his face, thinking. He didn't seem to know the actual cost and was trying to guess how much I'd pay. "Five dollars?"

It sounded more like a question. "I'll have to save it up, but I promise to pay you."

"No, Eddie can pay me back." Marcy dug a five dollar bill out of her purse and tossed it at Bennie.

Bennie climbed to his feet and shoved the money into his pocket.

I pulled the drugstore note from my pocket, smoothed it out, and stuck it under his shirt collar. "Stay in your own neighborhood or we'll break your nose."

He got on his bike and rode away.

"What's going on here?"

We jerked and turned to the voice behind us. Father Mac walked up to us and searched our faces. He may have seen the fight.

He waited for me to say something. "Just resting a minute before heading home, Father."

He gave me a doubtful look. "Go on, then. This is no place to congregate."

We hopped on our bikes and started away.

From behind us, Father Mac said, "Remember what you were told, Eddie."

Scheisse! He was reminding me that the priests and nuns didn't want me around Marcy. If Father Mac told Sister Mary Frances, my goose was cooked.

"Go left at the corner and I'll go right so he doesn't think we're staying together."

"You're letting them control your life, Eddie."

Like Muller controlled Gram's life.

She turned left and I headed for home.

Chapter Twelve

Dad didn't waste his time watching a damn catcher play Youth League baseball. On game days I snuck away before he could make excuses for not coming to the game. He watched all of Danny's games and relived his triumphs at the dinner table. He never asked about my games.

According to Dad, the Brooklyn Dodgers had scouted him as a high school player in rural Iowa, but when Hitler invaded Poland and war was imminent, he had abandoned my grandfather's pig farm and enlisted in the Navy. It was Danny's burden to make up for Dad's sacrifice. My baseball games would never be enough.

Dad was right about my hitting, of course. However, I learned to look fierce in the batter's box and milk wild pitchers for walks. I can't count the times the coach said, "A walk is as good as a hit." I knew—all players knew—a walk was only as good as a hit for a player who couldn't hit. I hadn't gotten a hit all season and my teammates had begun to grumble. Since no one else wanted to play catcher, the coach told the grumblers to shut their yaps.

The fact that I hadn't gotten a hit was on my mind as I came to bat with two outs in the bottom of the last inning, losing by a run, with Timmy on third base. The coach couldn't pinch hit for me because if we tied the game, we'd have no one else able, or willing, to play catcher. He counted on my ability to draw a walk and keep the game alive. With the pitch count full—three balls and two strikes—the odds were good that I could draw another walk, giving the next batter in our lineup a chance to drive in the tying run. But this pitcher had alternated balls and strikes so the next pitch was just as likely to be a strike. I couldn't live with the embarrassment of a called third strike to end the game. I *had* to swing at the pitch.

And I did. For a microsecond the bat and ball shared the same space and the ball rebounded off the bat. It flew in a graceful arc, over the outstretched arm of the pitcher, between opposing infielders, beyond second base, and onto the outfield grass. The tying run came home from third base and my coach slapped me on my butt as I reached first base. Our next batter, Allen, slugged a home run and won the game for us.

When I crossed home plate my teammates were there, waiting for

Allen. I got caught up in the crowd of players congratulating our hero, and the melee gravitated toward the chain link fence behind home plate where I was crushed against it by the jubilant celebration. The sharp point of a twisted metal thread ripped my uniform and gashed my upper arm. It dripped a stream of bright red blood.

I bounced into the house with a wide grin and a bloody arm.

"Ach du lieber Gott," Gram screamed. "Let me fix it."

As she applied Mercurochrome and murmured soothing encouragement, I said, "Where's Dad? I need to tell him all about my game."

Gram looked at Mom who watched from the comfort of the La-Z-Boy recliner. Although she wasn't allowed to smoke indoors, she had a lit cigarette in one hand and a gin Gimlet in the other. Life seemed to float past her incurious eyes like dandelion fluff on a summer breeze.

Lost in her own world, Mom didn't respond, so Gram answered. "Your dad and Danny are talking in the bedroom."

"What about?"

Gram gave me a cautionary look. Mom blew smoke.

Then Mom's bedroom door burst open and Danny flew through the kitchen and out the back door.

"Stop babying him," Dad said as he took a seat on the couch. "You're turning him into a pussy."

Gram paused and gave him a nasty look. "Ach! Dieser ist guter junge."

Although Dad had been exposed to Gram's German outbursts for two decades, he knew little of her language. But I understood her. "This one is a good boy." I think she meant that Danny wasn't exactly her cup of tea. Gram covered the cut with an unnecessarily large piece of gauze and wrapped an athletic bandage around my arm far too many times.

"I drove in the tying run and scored the winning run." Technically, this was true, but I didn't reveal that the next batter hit a walk-off home run and was the object of the celebration.

"Looks more like you've been in a fight," Dad said.

"No, during the celebration I got crushed against the backstop."

"So you finally got a hit. What's the big deal?"

"I thought you'd be impressed." I choked back a cry. "Why the bad mood?"

"Something more important I have to take care of." He nodded to the tear in my sleeve. "Will we have to pay for the uniform?"

For the first time in my life, I called him a dirty name. Not out loud, of course.

Mom drained her cocktail and stood unsteadily. “We’d better get going.”

She swayed as she retired to the bedroom to dress for the evening. Dad followed.

“Is it date night again so soon?” I asked Gram.

“Dad is up for reelection so he has to kiss some babies,” Carla said.

Gram and I laughed. She must have heard that line from Dad.

Dad came out of his bedroom, nattily attired in a beige cardigan and blue checked shirt. He rapped his knuckles on the bathroom door. “Hurry up, Kat, or we won’t get a seat at the bar.”

Mumbling and banging came from behind the closed door. Minutes passed. Dad paced, tossing car keys in the air again and again. When Mom opened the door, she was barefoot and carrying her heels. She bounced off one side of the doorframe and into the other side, then gained her balance.

Dad rushed to help her walk. “Jesus, Gail, you’re already tipsy.”

“After what happened today, I deserve it.”

“I’ll take you home when we get back,” Dad said.

“No one leaves the house tonight, Abby.” Mom slurred her words. She gave me a look intended to be stern but was comical.

Did Danny ask her to lock me up?

After they left, I asked Gram, “What happened today? Mom’s drunk and Dad’s in a bad mood.”

“Bad news in the mail, I think. They took Danny in the bedroom to talk.”

More college rejections? Bad news from a minor league team?

Carla and I had the usual dinner of hotdogs and potato chips. On TV, Cronkite talked over video of Huey helicopters dropping troops in the elephant grass at the edge of the jungle and helicopters with red crosses painted on their sides carrying away the stretchered wounded, one man with a blood-soaked bandage on his head, another with frayed fatigues where his leg had been. Dead bodies in green zippered bags waited on the ground, no longer a priority. “Twenty-two thousand additional troops have landed in Vietnam and B-52 bombers are now flying missions over North Vietnam. Today, the Viet Cong executed a Prisoner of War.” The Vietnam War had escalated.

Carla changed the channel. I didn’t want to hear more anyway so I lugged an entire quart bottle of black cherry soda to my room and closed the door. Marcy hadn’t “borrowed” any more banned books for me, so I searched my bookshelves for something to re-read. Dad built the bookshelves under the canted roof in the space between the chimney and the front wall of the house. Inventive use of space. The chimney wasn't for fireplace smoke; it was an exhaust vent for our oil-burning furnace, a veritable fire-breathing dragon in the basement.

As I searched for something to read, I realized my books weren't in alphabetical order by author, the way I always stored them. I was certain I had put the books back in their correct positions after I hid the dirty pictures. I snatched the collected works of Charles Dickens and the Bible from the shelf. In a tizzy, I rifled through the pages but I already knew I wouldn't find the pictures of Danny and Joe. Danny had found them. The pictures of Marcy were still between the pages of the Bible. I was surprised he hadn't defiled them.

Was Danny too stupid to put the books back in the right order, or did he want me to know he'd found the pictures? I opened the drawer in my nightstand and checked the camera. The film had been removed. Danny was too stupid to know that the film was unexposed, but he had taken no chances. I loaded a fresh roll and decided the camera would go everywhere with me from now on.

I charged through the door of Danny's room, and I was relieved he wasn't there because I didn't know what I'd have said if he were. His bed was unmade, clothes strewn on the floor, dirty dishes piled on his built-in desk. I searched his closet, pulled open all the drawers in his chest and didn't conceal my intrusion. On all fours I looked under his bed and in the space under his desk but didn't find my pictures. I didn't find any *Penthouse* or *Playboy* magazines, either. He thought he had destroyed all the evidence.

Back on my feet, I was drawn to the corkboard above his desk. He had pinned box scores and newspaper articles about his baseball and basketball exploits on the board. He was probably right that his feats would be remembered and my pieces of paper were worthless.

I carried the Dickens collection to my chair, plugged in my headphones, and tuned my transistor radio to WOKY in Milwaukee. The station had declared this Beatles night, but I didn't rock along with the music. Dickens laid open and unread in my lap—"It was the best of times, it was the worst of times."

Long after my bedtime, I sat in the window chair, worry plaguing my mind. Joe's Corvette Stingray flashed past my window. A minute later, Danny's Sprite pulled into our driveway. *They had found somewhere else to meet.*

Danny clomped up the stairs and went straight to his room. He may have thought he'd solved his problem. I thought about confronting him, but Marcy had more copies of the pictures.

I had always thought the best part of going to heaven would be that all the world's secrets would be revealed; who shot Kennedy, did aliens land in Roswell, what happened to Amelia Earhart, who built the pyramids, when will Christ return? But the best part would be avoiding hell. Danny was destined for hell whether Dad saw the pictures or not.

I was still awake when Mom and Dad came home. Their loud voices filtered into my room like smoke curling under my door. Then Gram joined in and everyone was shouting at everyone else. I peeked out my door. Danny's door was closed. I padded over to the stairs and took a seat. The staircase was partially enclosed by a wall that concealed the top four steps so no one could see me.

"Stop it, Frank," Gram said.

"She fell off her barstool, she's so drunk. She's going to cost me the election."

Mom sobbed, and when she spoke, I could barely make out the slurred words—something about dirt under Dad's feet.

"No more drinking for you," Dad spat.

From the kitchen came the sounds of cupboard doors slamming, water running, glass shattering, and from the living room, women crying. I crept down a couple of steps so I could see into the living room. Mom sat in an easy chair with her head in her hands. Gram stood beside her, smoothing her hair.

"Get back in your room."

I jumped and nearly tumbled down the stairs. From behind me, Danny grabbed my pajama top and yanked.

I swiped his hand away. "Get off me."

"This is none of your business."

"Everything is my business. You should know that."

Danny's mouth opened and closed twice, but he found no words to say. He turned and went to his room.

From the kitchen, I heard bottles being dumped in a trash bag and the back door opening and closing.

Dad stormed back into the living room. "It's all gone now. You're going to dry out."

"I hate you," Mom slurred.

Dad's left eyelid quivered, a sure sign he was uncontrollably angry. He tugged Mom out of the chair.

Gram knew the sign. "Don't you hurt her," she warned Dad.

"Just going to put her to bed." Dad walked Mom to the bedroom. "I'll take you home when I get back, Abby."

"I can walk."

I crept down two more steps. "Psst, Gram," I whispered, wanting to help her home. She gave me a two-handed stop sign—stay up there. I said a little prayer for Gram's safety and retreated to my room.

Chapter Thirteen

No one was in the kitchen. Someone was in the bathroom. The doors to Carla's and Mom's bedrooms were closed. Gram hadn't shown up. *Daylight is so hard to face after a quarrel at night.* I skipped breakfast. I wasn't hanging around to see if the warring parties had reconciled.

I was early for my Mass so I watched Father MacMillan from the sacristy. The altar boys, kids I'd trained, did a decent job. When the Mass was over, Father Mac disrobed, nodded to me, and left without a word. Father Bauer swept into the sacristy followed by Sister Mary Alice. When the nun saw me, she turned on her heel and left. Father Bauer hesitated, then went about his business. This was turning out to be Black Sunday. I tried to act as though I didn't care.

We got through Mass without a hitch but there was no chit-chat when we finished. I spent some time with the next pair of altar boys because they'd be serving Monsignor Muller who was a stickler for proper protocol. When he arrived, I exchanged greetings, told him his boys were prepared, and then left. On the way out of the church, Dad arrived to usher at the next Mass. He didn't have anything to say. It was silent Sunday.

Marcy was waiting for me on the path between the rectory and the convent. "They're on the move. We need to follow them."

"Which ones?"

"Bauer and Alice! She walked down to the corner and he picked her up. They're at the stop light down there." She pointed to the corner of Fremont and Oneida where his black sedan waited for the light to change.

"Are they in civvies?"

"He is, she's not. Come on. Let's go."

"I can't. I have to deliver papers on time this Sunday or I'll get fired. Bunch of old nags called the office and complained about me."

"Give me your camera."

It was on a lanyard around my neck. I pulled it off and gave it to her. Without another word, she was off on the chase.

"Meet me at my grandmother's house afterward." I yelled the address.

With a twenty-five mile per hour speed limit on city streets, and with a million stop signs and traffic lights between here and anywhere, she would have no trouble tracking a wayward priest and a naïve nun.

As I walked to Gram's house, I wondered where a priest in civvies and a nun in a habit could hold hands without attracting attention.

Gram was dressed for church. "Are you on your way to Mass?"

"I went already. Is okay at home?"

"Don't know, Gram. I didn't see anyone before I left for church." I slipped past her into the kitchen. "Are you coming to cook dinner?"

"Not today, I think."

"Yeah, let the dust settle."

"I'll change and help you with the papers."

"Today I'll do the papers. I have a favor to ask. You remember the girl you met at graduation? Marcy?"

"Sure, nice girl."

"She's going to meet me here after I deliver the papers. Is that okay? Can you wait for her?"

"Of course." She pinched my cheek and tugged on the fatty chunk.

"Thanks. I'll be back in a jiffy."

At home, Mom sat at the table, shielding her eyes against the glare of the kitchen lights. Carla was eating breakfast.

"Everything okay here?" I asked.

"Peachy-keen," Carla said.

Mom gave me a slight shake of her head.

"Where's Danny?"

"I think he went to Mass with Dad." Mom was barely audible, clearly suffering from a hangover.

Danny hadn't been with Dad at church. He was sneaking around again. "I'm going to deliver the papers."

"Gram isn't here yet," Mom said.

"Yeah, I stopped by to see her. She's not feeling well so I'll deliver alone."

I changed clothes, loaded up the papers, and dragged them up the hill. I started with the farthest house on my route and worked my way toward my neighborhood. I didn't go home. I cut down Lawe Street to Gram's house. Laughter came from inside as I knocked on the door.

Gram let me in with a smile on her face.

"Want some?" Marcy asked. She indicated the scrambled eggs on her plate.

"Sure, I'm famished. We can share, no need for Gram to make

more."

Gram handed me a plate and a fork and Marcy scraped most of the eggs onto my plate. "She makes them with sour cream instead of milk."

"It's the German way." Gram poured me a glass of orange juice. "Marcy told me the priests don't want you to see her."

I gave Marcy a naughty-girl-look. "They're afraid I'll like Marcy more than the priesthood."

Marcy chuckled.

"Ach. You can't go by what the priests say," Gram said. "You can read your books here, at my house."

I saw a cocky grin on Marcy's face. She'd wrangled her way into Gram's heart and contrived to find us a place where no nuns or priests would see us. Smart girl. But I was a little chagrinned that Marcy had roped Gram into our conspiracy.

"Thanks, Gram. Let's not mention that at my house, okay?"

"Ach-ne, they don't have to know."

I gobbled up the eggs, swallowed a glass of orange juice in one gulp. "We'd better be going, Gram. Mom will wonder where I am."

"You kids can come here anytime."

I pulled the empty wagon beside Marcy as she pushed her bike down the sidewalk.

"Your grandmother is amazing, supported her parents, raised two kids without a husband."

"She told you that in one visit?"

"I told her how sorry I was about Edward and that opened the floodgates."

"Listen, we can meet here to read books, but we cannot get Gram in any trouble."

"We won't." She stopped when she was out of Gram's sight. "I caught them." She handed me my camera. "It's all on there."

More pictures to develop. More pictures to hide. I felt like a spy in a John Le Carré novel. No, Marcy was the spy and I was her handler. "Where did they go?"

"They bought a coffee and went to Sunset Point Park, found themselves a shady spot away from everyone else, under a big elm tree with a nice view of the river."

"Kimberly again, where southside Appleton people wouldn't go to a park. But Alice must have been easy to spot in her habit."

She stripped in the car, had civvies under her habit. She'll probably put the habit on before he drops her off on a street corner."

"And you took pictures."

"Yep, good ones, holding hands, hugging, kissing."

More kissing? Everyone is kissing someone they shouldn't. "Now what?"

"Get them developed. If they give us any grief, we ruin their lives."

The problem I had with her plan is that it would punish the wrong people. Bauer and Alice were nice as they could be. MacMillan and Frances were the evil twins. But Bauer and Alice were committing sins, too, violating their sacred vows. If I exempted them because I liked them, was I really priest material?

I removed the film and handed the camera back to her. "Hold on to it. Use it if there's an opportunity to catch Father Mac doing something nasty."

Chapter Fourteen

For the third Sunday in a row, Dad had brought the church money home to count and deposit. When he saw me come into the kitchen, he said, "You're just in time. We're going fishing. Abby isn't cooking today so we'll catch our dinner."

"Just you and me?"

"No, Danny is fishing, too. Put your rod in the car."

I hurried up the stairs and hid the exposed roll in the winter boots at the back of the closet.

Back in the kitchen, Dad bundled up the ledgers and the money bag and carried them into the bedroom.

When he returned, I said, "Where's Mom?"

"Crying on Shirley's shoulder. Carla's with her. Come on, let's get cracking."

I got it, it was boys against girls. Dad would solidify the boys' support by taking us fishing while Mom had only one child and a neighbor to lean on. Dad wanted to come off as the upstanding good guy.

In the garage, Danny was fiddling with his rod. On the workbench he had the tackle box and a bucket full of dirt. "What took you so long? I had to dig for worms in the garden."

"Wah, wah, wah." I grabbed my rod and Dad's rod and stowed them in the trunk.

Dad climbed into the car and we set off on a male-bonding afternoon. He drove to his mill, the Interlake Pulp Mill under the College Avenue bridge, and parked in the lot. This mill turned trees into broad wet sheets of snow-white pulp which were shipped by railcar to Kimberly-Clark mills where it was refined into Kleenex. We wouldn't have been able to blow our noses without Dad's mill.

We carried our equipment across a lawn to a thick retaining wall that corralled the river and fed it to the dam that supplied hydroelectric power to the mill. I pinched my nose against the rotten-egg smell of the sulfur that decomposed the cellulose in the logs. Although the weather was mild and sunny, the cold, fishy breath of the river crawled up my nose like a ghostly, malevolent specter. At the base of the three-foot-wide, ten-foot-high wall, the water was shallow and ran over rocky riprap. A steady current hid beneath the river's placid surface.

We baited our hooks with red wigglers, cast our lines into the water, and took a seat to wait for bites. We sat shoulder-to-shoulder, and I braced for the inevitable family chat.

Dad cleared his throat. "I guess you guys heard the ruckus last night."

Danny's glum expression never changed.

"I heard glass breaking and the back door slam," I offered.

"I threw out all the liquor bottles. Your mom needs to cut back for a while."

"Maybe you should cut back on date nights." I immediately regretted my loss of self-control.

"Date nights get me elected, little boy," Dad said. "I have to show my face to the guys and hear their gripes or they'll vote for some idiot to be president."

"Don't they appreciate the contracts you've gotten them?"

Dad shook his head. "You can never satisfy these guys. You have to be one of the guys to gain their trust and get them to believe you're getting them everything you can."

"Get drunk with them and they love you. The good old boy network is how the world works." Danny sneered.

"Yeah, bring your wife along to make friends with the other wives," Dad said. "Problem is, when your mom is tipsy, she likes to be the center of attention, disrupts my conversations."

"Maybe you should go out alone. Until after the election." I thought it a reasonable suggestion.

"No, I need her with me. She can have a couple of knocks when we're out," Dad said. "But I need your help at home. Tell me if she drinks during the day. Throw her bottles out if you find them."

"You want us to spy on Mom?" I asked, more than a little offended by the idea.

"I'm not home during the day." Danny's bad mood had carried over from yesterday.

"I can't afford to send her someplace to dry out." Dad pointed at me. "You're her best hope."

I really didn't want to hear about Mom's drinking problem. "Okay, I'll watch her." I agreed only to end the discussion.

We turned our attention to fishing.

"No one is going to get a bite if Eddie lets his line drift on top of mine," Danny said.

The current had carried our lines downstream where they nestled together in one shallow spot. All three lines were tangled so I didn't know why it was my fault.

We reeled in our twisted lines and Dad untangled them. "We have to move farther apart so we don't end up on top of each other."

I moved twenty yards upriver and Danny moved ten yards downriver so we'd have individual fishing spots. Nonetheless, our lines floated to our right, toward the dam, and we had to constantly reel them in and cast them upriver to start the drift over.

Danny caught the first fish but it was a bullhead—a small, black cousin to the catfish and not edible. Not long after, Dad had a bigger fish on his line but it was a sheepshead, a bottom-feeding fish that wasn't good to eat.

I announced that I had to pee.

"You should have peed before we left home," Dad said.

"Pee in the river, goober." Danny egged me on.

"I'm not going to pee with cars going by right over our heads."

"Afraid we're going to see your little weewee," Danny taunted.

He's asking for it now. I considered homosexuality to be not only a sin but an ailment of sort, possibly an uncontrollable compulsion. But if Danny wanted to get nasty, I could be nasty, too.

"You like looking at weewees, Danny?" I raised my eyebrows.

Danny jumped to his feet, his fists clenched. "I'm gonna punch your lights out."

"Stop it." Dad grabbed Danny's leg and held him back. "I'll take Eddie inside to pee."

We walked across the grass and through the parking lot to the massive mill that looked like several buildings tacked together by a mad scientist. I knew from previous visits that each building was a step in the pulp-making process and was shaped to accommodate specific equipment.

"We'll go in through the machine room," Dad said.

He led me through oversized double doors and down a hallway toward the loud thrumming and clacking of heavy equipment. I paused at the entry to the machine room and took it all in. The finishing machine looked like three newspaper printing presses linked together. A fifteen-foot-wide sheet of snow-white pulp entered the machine at the far end of the room, wound over a drum and under rollers that squeezed moisture out of the pulp, then onto a second drum with rollers that pressed it flat, and onto a third drum where huge blades cut the sheet—clack!—into cubic-yard squares and stacked the squares in five neat piles on a platform. A forklift driver sat idling in front of the platform waiting to move the stacks of pulp to a railway loading dock. Two of the workers approached us.

"Hey, Frank, what the hell you doin' here?" the older of the two said.

"Just brought my sons to fish. This one," he jerked a thumb at me, "needs the latrine. Name's Eddie."

Dad introduced the older, rotund man as Jake, the foreman, and the younger, tall guy as Steve. He was pointing me in the direction of the latrine when a blood-curdling scream caused him to flinch. A metallic screech pierced the air and the machine ground to a stop, its motors whining like a racing engine. A siren's wail ricocheted off the steel walls.

"Emergency stop! Emergency stop!" Jake yelled.

The man on the forklift hopped off, ran to the wall, and punched a large red button. As the machine's whirring dissipated, another agonized scream came from deep in the room.

"Call an ambulance!" Jake yelled at the forklift driver.

Jake and Steve sprinted in the direction of the screams. Dad trotted after them, around the side of the machine, and I followed. I stopped short as Steve grasped a thrashing man and held him upright while Jake heaved against a roller releasing the man's crushed arm. They gently laid the screaming man on the concrete floor.

"What happened?" Dad asked.

"Duke was clearing a jam and got his arm stuck in the machine," Jake said.

I crept closer to get a look at the man writhing in pain on the floor. Duke's mangled arm pointed backward from the elbow. Shattered bone and torn tendons stuck through ripped skin. Blood splattered in all directions as Duke swung his arm in hopeless circles.

"Hold that arm steady," Jake commanded.

Steve hesitated, then took hold of the grisly arm and held it in place.

Duke let out a ferocious scream, then went limp and silent. The redness in his cheeks faded and revealed a purple birthmark on his cheek. "Did he die?" I asked.

"Passed out from the pain," Jake said.

"Why did he stick his arm in the running machine?" Dad asked.

"The feeder mechanism has been jamming for weeks and it can't be cleared when the machine ain't running."

"You've reported it?" Dad asked.

"Every day."

"Union's got to do something about this." Angry blotches formed on

Steve's face.

Dad realized I was in the circle of men, listening and watching. He pulled me away from the injured man. "The latrine is down that hallway." He pointed and gave me a push.

When I returned, paramedics were tending to Duke. Dad and the three workers moved out of the way and I joined the gathering to watch.

"Do not start this machine until it's repaired," Dad ordered the foreman.

"The whole mill backs up if we don't keep the pulp moving," Jake said.

"When the bosses figure out that production is at a standstill, they'll come running to you and they'll order you to start it back up. Don't do it." Dad placed a hand on the foreman's shoulder. "You tell them that Frank Kovacs, the President of the damned union, has issued a union safety complaint and nothing rolls out of here until that feeder is fixed."

"Yes, sir." Jake formed a look of gratitude.

The forklift operator clapped Dad on the back.

Dad shook hands and "kissed some babies," and then we left the building.

"That was gruesome," I said.

"Mill work is dangerous." Dad placed a hand on my shoulder, a rare gesture of fatherly love. "You're going to live in a rectory wearing clean clothes and doing clean work, but we have to keep Danny from ending up in a place like this."

"That's for sure."

"You cannot talk about this with anyone, you hear? Not even Danny. That man, Duke, did a careless thing that is going to cost the mill a lot of production time and medical bills. He'll get fired if this isn't handled right."

"You're going to fix it for him?"

"Yeah, I'm going to fix it. I fix all the problems."

Back through the parking lot and across the lawn we found Danny sitting on the wall, his legs dangling over the side, casting his line into the water.

"What was the ambulance for?" Danny asked.

"Man got hurt in the machine room," Dad said.

"I thought the medics had to help Eddie find his weewee."

"You are way too interested in my weewee, Danny."

I danced out of the way of Danny's swinging arm and headed to my spot. Dad's rod lay on top of the wall where he left it, but my rod and reel were gone.

"Where's my rod, Danny?"

"How should I know?" Danny feigned innocence. "Maybe a fish got on your line and pulled it into the water."

I looked over the edge of the wall and saw the rod, underwater, wedged between rocks.

Dad came beside me and looked. "Jesus, Eddie, you should have reeled it in. You can't leave a rod unattended."

Danny sat in his spot and pretended to be innocent. "Guess you're out a fishing rod, goober."

"No," Dad said. "Let me see if I can hook it with my line and drag it up." Dad reeled in his line, which he had left unattended, and tried to snag my rod with his hook. He failed and tried again. There was just enough water above the rod and just enough current to carry Dad's hook past my rod without connecting.

"You've really screwed the pooch this time, Eddie." Frustration sharpened his voice.

"It's just a cheap fishing rod."

"I'm not made of money. You have to take care of your stuff."

"Make him go in and get it," Danny said.

"What?" *Edward drowned in this river.*

"You think he can do it?" Dad asked Danny.

"Sure, why not? The river is shallow along the wall. We can tie a rope around his waist and hold him up."

Was Danny trying to drown me so I couldn't tell on him? "No way." I backed away from the river, away from Dad and Danny.

"Don't be a pussy," Danny sneered. "This is easy."

"Then you do it. You're a better swimmer."

"I'm better at everything but it's your rod, goober."

"Danny's too heavy to pull up," Dad said. He stared at the fishing pole, tantalizingly just out of reach. "The water's not deep right there." He looked at Danny who nodded.

Was I making too much of a little wading in the river? I looked over the edge and thought, *Maybe this is a chance to impress Dad.* Nonetheless, I was mad as hell at Danny. "I'll do it."

Dad took another look at the sunken rod. "I can get a rope." He jogged to the mill.

"I know you did it," I said to Danny.

"I didn't do anything."

I wondered if he was smart enough to set this up so I'd have to wade in the river. "You're such a liar. I know everything you did."

"Stay out of my life." Danny gave me a shove and I stumbled backward.

"Knock it off, boys." Dad was back with a long, thick rope. He wrapped it around my waist and tied a knot. "That should do it."

For an engineer, his idea of how to secure the rope left a lot to be desired. The rope kept slipping up my chest to my armpits and I wasn't even in the water yet.

If these guys were going to goad me into risking my life, I wanted a fair chance to survive. "There's a better way."

I untied the knot, unbuckled my belt, and pulled it off. I snaked the short end of the rope through my belt loops and made a hangman's noose. I passed the long end through the noose and handed it to Dad. If I drowned, these men would go to hell. Maybe to prison.

"Where'd you learn those knots?" Danny asked.

"I read books, dingleberry." I looked over the edge at my rod, at the water. "How am I supposed to get down there?"

Dad led me down the wall looking for a good spot to jump in the river. Forty yards away from my rod he found a place where silt had piled to within five feet of the top of the wall. Dad gave the rope a little slack then gripped his end with both hands. "Jump in. I've got you."

No one intentionally jumps in this river. I'm coming to see you, Edward. I said a silent Hail Mary, closed my eyes, and jumped. My feet landed on the silt and I slid down the slope into the water. I climbed onto a round, slippery rock and my feet slid off to either side. I lost my balance and fell into the chilling water. Dad yanked on the rope but all that did was squeeze my waist and cause pain. I used the rope to pull myself upright, shook myself off, and began the journey to my rod. The going was difficult because the rocks were uneven and jagged and the current was running against me. It was like the river wanted to swallow me. Dad pulled too hard on the rope causing more balance problems. He kept asking if I was alright. Maybe he finally saw his folly.

"Don't pull on it, Dad. Just don't let me get swept downstream."

I reached my rod without drowning. I dislodged the rod from the rocks and reeled in the line. The worm was still on the hook. No fish had dragged my rod into the river and the rod didn't jump in the river of its own accord. I handed the rod to Danny. "See if you can hold onto it this time."

Dad tugged on the rope and I cried out in pain as my stomach was crushed again. He got Danny to grab hold of the rope and the two of them pulled as though they were in a tug-of-war. But they couldn't lift one hundred thirty pounds of dead weight. Not even an inch. The rope would slice me in half before it freed me from the grip of the murderous river.

"Maybe you can grab my arms." I found a rock that was just beneath the waterline and managed to climb atop it, my clothes heavy with river water. I lifted my arms over my head. "Pull me up." I was five-feet-seven inches tall and my outstretched arms reached to about the eight-foot level, so they could touch my hands, but they had to squat to reach me and my weight threatened to pull them into the water.

"We have to find another way." The tremor in Dad's voice betrayed his fear that this could end in disaster.

"You better call the fire department to get me out," I said.

"We can't do that!" Dad looked around to see if there were any witnesses.

No, you wouldn't want the mill workers to watch as the fire department rescues the child you forced into river. "I'll say I fell in. It's my fault."

"No, go back to where you got in and we'll try it from there."

The last thing I wanted to do was walk another forty yards in the river, but Dad's idea was my best chance to be rescued without outside help. He and Danny stood, and I eased off the jagged rock.

Dad walked above me on the wall, trying his best to keep me upright, while I slipped repeatedly, skinning knees and elbows.

I scrabbled up the silt pile and reached over the wall. Danny grabbed one arm and Dad the other and I used my feet to walk up the wall and over. I lay in the grass, drenched from head to foot, and thanked God I was alive. The air temperature was around seventy degrees but my teeth chattered and my arms were covered in gooseflesh.

"Are you okay?" Dad asked.

Hell, no, I'm not okay. "I'll be fine, Dad."

"Go lie in the sun and dry off."

I lay in the sun until I stopped shivering. I thought of Uncle Edward and how cold he must have been as he struggled against the current. Dad and Danny continued to fish and they caught a couple of small perch. When I was dry, we packed up the gear and headed for the car.

"Do not whisper a word of this to your mother," Dad warned me, his finger in my face.

I looked like I'd walked through a car wash. Mom would have to be blind not to notice.

***

"Oh my God! What happened?" Mom's eyes were big as coffee saucers.

"I tripped on the bank and fell in the river." I gave my dad a look—*this is how we're explaining it*—and he nodded. "It was right along the bank so no big deal."

"It looks like you took a bath in it."

"That's what I'm going to do right now, take a bath."

As I headed upstairs, I heard Dad say, "The fish weren't biting so I'll pick up hamburgers at the A&W stand."

That brought a smile to my lips. A&W hamburgers were a favorite. I finished my shower before Dad returned with dinner. Mom was on the phone, her brow furrowed as she listened to the caller.

"Are you sure it's her?" Mom asked.

A look of shock on her face. "Where did you find her?"

A pause as she listened. "Where was she going?"

Another pause. "Where do you have her now?'

A sigh. "My husband will come and get her as soon as he gets home."

She hung up, closed her eyes, and leaned against the wall.

"What is it, Mom?"

"It's Abby. She got lost and a neighbor found her."

"I told you she should see a doctor."

"This happens with old age, Eddie."

"You guys can't ignore this any longer. Where is she?"

"At Mr. Duncan's house. He didn't want to call the police."

"That's the old guy on Lawe Street?"

"Yes, he used to work with her."

"I'll get her."

As I rushed out the door, her voice trailed behind me. "Wait for Dad."

Mr. Duncan's house was only four blocks away and I got there in a jiffy. Gram and Mr. Duncan were sitting on his front porch, sipping what appeared to be lemonade.

"This is my favorite grandson, Eddie," Gram said to Mr. Duncan.

"Pleased to meet you, sir. Is she okay now?"

"I'm okay, Eddie."

"Seemed to be a temporary confusion," Duncan said.

"I was looking for my house." Gram seemed lucid. "I know where it is now."

"Let me walk you home."

Duncan lifted two small paper bags off the porch and handed them to me.

I recognized the bags. "You were at the little market on Fremont Street?"

"Yes. I just forgot which way to turn."

"Sure, it's tricky, Gram."

I carried the bags in one arm and pushed my bike with the other hand as we walked two blocks to Gram's house. She was steady and didn't lack energy. Inside, I put the groceries in the fridge and cupboard.

"Want something to eat?" she said.

"I've got hamburgers waiting at home. Are you going to be okay here by yourself?"

"I know my way around my own house, Eddie. No wrong turns in here."

I wasn't sure I should leave Gram alone but she seemed alright. We hugged and kissed and I rode home.

Joe Morada stepped out of our back door as I arrived. His grin faded when he saw me. Neatly trimmed black hair hugged his narrow head and a precisely trimmed mustache undulated above his thin lips like a caterpillar. He wasn't much to look at but then queers probably didn't have much to choose from. I slipped past him into the house. My family was sitting at the kitchen table, smiling at me. Paper bags, hamburger wrappers, and empty French fry boats littered the table. They had made peace over a fast food dinner.

"Danny has a tryout date," Dad said. "Joe arranged it."

"With the Foxes?" I asked, just to be nice. The Fox City Foxes were the local minor league team.

"Nah, they're a Baltimore Oriole farm team. My tryout is with the Green Bay Blue Jays. That's the Dodgers we're talking about." Danny had rediscovered his cocky attitude.

"When is it?"

"Two weeks from now," Dad said. "Joe has a pitcher lined up to throw batting practice a couple times before the tryout."

"But we need a catcher." He gave me an expectant look. "How about it?"

"Me? Now I'm good enough for you?"

"You've got the gear. I thought you might like to see what it's like to catch a professional pitcher."

"Help your brother," Dad urged.

"Sure, why not. You guys are always doing nice things for me." My sarcasm was lost in the cheerful atmosphere.

"Then it's settled," Dad said. "Day after tomorrow at the Southside Athletic Club."

"Your hamburgers are probably cold," Mom said.

"Gram is home and fine now, if you want to know."

Mom was the only one who seemed even a little embarrassed for not asking about Gram. "We knew you'd get her home, Eddie."

I tested the heat of my hamburgers and found them to be cold. I made a PB&J, poured a glass of milk, and went to my room.

Chapter Fifteen

I wanted no more encounters with the nosy and self-righteous clerk at the local drugstore, so I rode uptown to a drugstore my family didn't use and dropped off the film. I asked for two copies of each print.

"Should be ready tomorrow afternoon," the clerk said.

Everything is moving so fast. "Thank you, ma'am."

I left the store in a jiffy and rode all the way back to the rectory. It seemed my life had become a series of things I didn't want to do. The housekeeper led me to Monsignor Muller's office. I figured he must be too old to grope young boys. He sat behind a polished mahogany desk. The red piping on his cassock distinguished his rank from ordinary priests. On the wall behind him hung a picture of a handsome man with long, blond hair and a neat beard. Blood trickled from a crown of thorns on his head. I wondered why he didn't look like other Semitic Jews from the Middle East.

The monsignor waved me into a visitor's chair. "I haven't seen you at Mass this week, Kovacs."

"I had to work last week for my dad, but I'll be in church from now on, Father."

"Good. Don't stray now when you're almost there."

He sat back, drew a handkerchief from somewhere under his cassock, and blew his nose like a foghorn.

"I know you admire the Jesuits, but you're too young. They find candidates among the students at their colleges—Boston College, Georgetown, Loyola, Marquette, and so forth—and take them into a post graduate program. We'd have been proud to groom a Jesuit, like growing a rare flower, but that's not to be. You wouldn't want to wait eight years to start your journey, would you?"

I felt like a customer being sold a bill of goods—parish priesthood—by a high-pressure sales team. There was no way my parents could afford to send me to Marquette, much less an out-of-state school. But I couldn't stay home with my family. "I'm committed to my vocation, Father, and I would like to begin my journey this fall, as planned."

"Good. You've been accepted by the Diocese Seminary in De Pere which will be convenient for your parents to visit. Congratulations."

My heart sank. I tried to smile but my face refused to cooperate. The thought of becoming a parish priest was unexciting. Parish priests were exalted altar boys. “What about missionary work, Father? I’d like to try that.”

He stared at me, and I was afraid I sounded ungrateful to the crotchety old man. Lately, I’d had a bad habit of saying one sentence too many.

He leaned back. “Sounds fanciful to me. You should be happy we made this happen for you. I wouldn’t recommend just any student, you know.”

He stood, signaling that he was done with me. He came around his desk, grabbed my elbow, and ushered me out of his office. “Don’t forget Mass, Kovacs.”

I knocked on Gram’s door but there was no answer. Around the front I shaded my eyes and pressed my nose to the windows but I couldn’t see any movement. If she was lost again, I’d have to run around the neighborhood looking for her. She never locked her doors so I entered through the back and went up two steps to the kitchen. A moan came from my left and I turned. She was sitting on the stairs to the bathroom. She was in a bathrobe hiked above her knees and hanging off one shoulder.

“Are you all right, Gram?”

She looked at me with vacant eyes and didn’t say anything. A bruise on one knee had swelled into a purple and yellow balloon. Another bruise blossomed on her left arm, near her shoulder. Her sightless eyes stared straight through me.

“Do you know who I am, Gram?”

Her eyes squinted and focused. “Eddie,” she croaked.

“Yes, Eddie. What happened?”

She looked over her shoulder at the top of the stairs. “I fell.”

“Where does it hurt?”

“My head hurts.” She placed a hand gently to her head.

“Okay, stay right there.”

I used her telephone to call Mom but got no answer. Scared that she was seriously injured, I did what my parents had taught me to do—I dialed the operator and asked for an ambulance.

The response was fast. The medical people were nice and gentle with Gram. They loaded her onto a stretcher and into the ambulance. Neighbors gathered to watch the excitement.

“She fell but she’s fine,” I told them. That was a lie; I didn’t think she was fine at all.

The ambulance took Gram to St. Elizabeth's Hospital, near the Rectory, where I caught up to them and walked with her into the emergency room. The nurse behind the counter asked a bunch of questions but I had few answers—Gram's name and address, what she told me about falling down the stairs. I had no idea if she had insurance. I hadn't thought to bring her purse with me. The nurse asked who would be responsible for the bill, so I gave her Dad's name and phone number.

They took Gram to an examination room and I waited a long time before a pretty nurse brought her out in a wheelchair.

"We see no broken bones on the X-rays. She doesn't appear to have a concussion so she can take aspirin for the headache."

"So, she's done? She can go?"

"She's all yours."

All mine, but she couldn't very well ride on my bike. I explained to the nurse that I had to call my parents to come get Gram, but I had no money for the pay phone. She was kind enough to let me use a phone behind the counter to call Mom again. This time she answered. She said she'd get Shirley to drive her over. I sat next to Gram, my hand on hers. She seemed groggy and listless.

Finally, Mom and Shirley came through the glass doors and fussed over Gram for a while. Mom got an update from the nurse and sighed dramatically. Gram was no help as Mom and I loaded her into Shirley's car. She was like a heavy rag doll with no will to do anything for herself. They drove away, and I followed on my bike.

When I got to Gram's, Shirley and Mom were chatting with Marcy in the driveway, laughing like old friends. Marcy had that effect on adults.

I dropped my kickstand. "What did you do with Gram?"

Mom turned to me as though she'd been interrupted. "We gave her some aspirin and put her to bed."

"We're just going to leave her? Shouldn't someone stay with her?"

"There's nothing wrong but bruises," Mom said.

"Gram's not right," I protested.

"We'll check on her tomorrow." Mom and Shirley left for home.

"Your Mom is nice."

I rolled my eyes. "Wait till you get to know her."

"I called your house but no one answered. I thought maybe you'd be here."

"I came to check on Gram and found that she had fallen down her stairs. She was hurt and dazed," I said.

"I'll keep a watch on her. Did you drop off the film?"

"It should be ready tomorrow, but I have to help Danny with his baseball tryout. I'll call you."

"Can I watch the practice?"

"I guess so." I told her where and when.

Our parting was awkward. Should we hug? I thought we could hug, like brother and sister. Next time, I planned to hug her.

***

I was in my room when Dad got home. He slammed the door behind him.

"If it isn't one thing, it's another. Now we'll have to pay for the emergency room and an ambulance ride." Dad's voice was loud, exasperated.

"Doesn't she have insurance with her retirement?" Mom asked.

"Her insurance is crap."

"There goes all the money," Mom said.

From the foot of the stairs Dad yelled, "Get down here, Eddie."

In the living room, I stood uneasily before Dad, his eyelid twitching.

Mom waited nervously for the verbal beatdown.

"Do you know how much money you wasted?" Dad's face was red. "They took X-rays and nothing was wrong."

"How was I supposed to know that? I called Mom but she didn't answer."

"Why not?" He looked at Mom. "Where were you?"

She jutted out her chin. "Shirley took us downtown to get our hair done."

"Great. How much did that cost me?"

"Gram is not okay," I insisted. "Her brain isn't working right."

"According to the doctor she's fine," Mom said.

I was tired of the verbal finger-pointing. "Fine, huh? Next time, I'll let her die."

Dad tensed, as though he might slap me, and then he walked away, shaking his head in disgust.

Mom shrugged. "He'll get over it."

"Marcy and I will check on Gram."

"Don't get in trouble with that girl, Eddie. We don't have any room for more trouble."

"We're just friends."

"Uh huh. The sex is dripping off her. Shirley called her lipstick shade

'Slutty Scarlett.'"

I smirked. "Shirley's got a dirty mind."

"Well, that's true." Mom chuckled. "I'd better see about your dad."

She left me standing there, wondering how our predictable and orderly lives had become so confused and messy.

Carla bounced into the room, freed from her captivity, and turned on the TV. She cycled through the three network channels, but it was all national news at this hour. She stopped on CBS, scoffed, and left.

In a daze, I stood there and watched the same newscast that had been playing for several weeks now. They called it the Living Room War. Every night video of Vietnam combat filled American living rooms with a stream of atrocities in closeups and color. American troops are now in the thick of the fighting. The 173rd Airborne Brigade battled the Viet Cong today. The body counts were reported like the scores of a baseball game. Ten U.S. soldiers died in the fighting, but we killed one hundred Commies. Today we won, but the draft of teenagers has been increased from 17,000 per month to 35,000 per month, as though we need a relief pitcher to close out the game.

Chapter Sixteen

Friendly Father Bauer said the 7:30 Mass, so I took the opportunity to hang around the sacristy so he could let the Monsignor know I attended. Then I got an idea. "Do you know of any seminaries for missionaries, Father?"

He folded the chasuble and placed it in a wide, shallow drawer. "You're interested in missionary work? Like Franciscans or Benedictines?"

"I don't know the orders, but the ones who go to foreign countries to help the poor. And convert them, of course."

"The Salvatorians have a seminary in St. Nazianz, over by Manitowoc. Almost went there myself."

"You're from around here?"

"Shawano. Close enough."

"I don't want to upset the Monsignor. He's already gotten me accepted to the Diocese seminary, but I'd like to know my options."

"The official name of the Salvatorians is The Society of the Divine Savior. I can get you information and an application."

"Can we keep it between us until I know more?"

"Sure, Eddie. It can be one of our little secrets." He patted my shoulder.

Ah! He knows I saw him at the bookstore. "I'm good at keeping secrets."

***

The lady at the drug store counter gave me her what-a-nice-young-man smile. "You're quite the little photographer, aren't you?"

Scheisse, all the clerks look at the pictures. The clerks probably flipped through people's pictures to get a good laugh during their lunch break. "Yes, ma'am, it's my hobby."

"What kind of pictures do you take?"

What if she recognized Father Bauer in the pictures? I forced myself to stay calm. "Just regular ones. These are of my uncle and his girlfriend. He's going to be very surprised when I show him." In two short months, lying had become second nature.

"I'll bet." She said that as though she knew the truth.

I paid and hustled home where I hid the pictures in the snow boots at the back of the closet. I didn't even look at them. Father Bauer and I were trading secret favors. At least for the moment.

***

Danny gave me a ride to the ballfield in his sports car. We were so low to the ground I thought my butt would scrape the road. He skidded around corners just to show off. Today I saw no signs of the depression and anger that had plagued him for days. Baseball was his milieu, his comfort zone.

Joe was waiting with a kid, no older than Danny. The kid's name was Chuck, a relief pitcher for the Fox City Foxes. As I climbed into my gear, Marcy waved from her seat in the bleachers. I waved back, hoping I wouldn't make a fool of myself in front of her.

Joe and Chuck pulled me aside and told me how this was going to work. I was to use finger signals to call the pitches just like major league catchers do, so Danny wouldn't know what kind of pitch was coming. One finger was the fastball, two fingers for a curve, three fingers for the slider, and a closed fist for a changeup. "Just mix them up any way you want, but don't get into a predictable pattern."

"Got it." I lowered my face mask, ready to work.

"Let's throw you a few without a batter so you get a feel for the speed. This won't be like Youth League."

That's for sure! The pitches streaked toward me at seventy-five to ninety miles an hour. At first, most of them got past me or bounced off my shin guards, but I got the hang of it once I figured out the movement of the ball. The fastballs had a little tail to my left, the curves dropped down off the end of the table, and the sliders went sideways and to my right.

Danny stepped into the batter's box and I called a couple of fastballs to warm him up. Chuck wasn't trying to strike him out so the pitches came right down the middle, and Danny hit monstrous flyballs. Then I mixed it up, and Danny flailed wildly at the breaking balls. He fouled some off, grounded some to the infield, swung and missed often. He pounded the bat on home plate in frustration.

I gave him a couple of fastballs to get him back on track and he foul-tipped one that slammed into my face guard and knocked me on my back. Danny, Joe, and Chuck came running to see if I was okay. I blinked back tears and told them I was fine. My vision was blurry at first and I missed balls I had to chase. Marcy had her hands to her face, but I gave her a thumbs-up. My eyes cleared up and I went back to mixing up the pitches. Danny went back to struggling.

Then I got an idea. If I helped Danny, he'd get away from Joe's influence and become a part of a team of aggressively masculine baseball players. That seemed a better solution than talking to a priest.

As I signaled Chuck, I whispered to Danny what was coming and he hit every fastball, most curves, and some sliders. Joe was ecstatic. I wondered if my cheating was for a good reason.

Chuck agreed he'd throw practice pitches once more before Danny's tryout and he left with Joe.

"You didn't have to do that," Danny said.

"Yeah, I did. You have to read the ball, Danny. I thought if you knew what was coming you could watch the spin and adjust your swing."

"So now you're a damn baseball coach?"

"I don't have to be a baseball coach to know that a fastball has backspin, a curve has circular spin, and a slider has side spin that's easy to mistake for a fastball. You're blessed with hand-eye coordination, but your mind is too slow."

"Hi." Marcy had joined us and waited for an opportunity to get into the conversation.

"Who's this?" Danny looked at Marcy as though an odd creature had crept out of the bushes.

"This is my, er, friend, Marcy."

He pointed at my camera around her neck. "You get any good pictures of me at the plate?"

I tried not to jump out of my skin.

"I'm out of film." Marcy threw her hands up. "Next time."

Danny grunted, too stupid to realize the camera was mine. "You coming?" He motioned and started away.

"No. I'll walk."

"Play footsie with your girlfriend, goober." He waved over his head as walked to his car.

"He's full of himself, isn't he?" Marcy said.

"Now you know what I put up with."

"He's a good hitter, though."

"Not really. I told him what the pitcher was going to throw. Otherwise, he can't hit a breaking ball. He'll never pass his tryout."

"Everyone has dreams that don't come true."

I took off my catcher's gear and put it in a canvas bag I slung over my shoulder. We started for home.

"I checked on Gram," Marcy said. "She's sluggish and gets confused easily. Called me Gail a couple of times. I guess she thought I was your mom."

"I appreciate you doing that."

"Gram's the nice one in your family. Did you get the pictures?"

"Yeah."

"Do you have them here?"

"No, they're hidden."

"Are they good?"

"I didn't look at them."

"Why not? We have to tell on Bauer and Alice."

Marcy wasn't a sweet young thing; she was a full-blown revolutionary. "Not yet. He knows I saw him at the bookstore, so he's doing me a favor."

"He doesn't know we have pictures."

"So Father Bauer is in love. Big deal."

"He's corrupting a nun! I'll bet Alice isn't even twenty-one."

"You gonna wait till you're twenty-one to fall in love?"

That stopped Marcy in her mental tracks. She wasn't used to losing arguments.

"Father Mac may be fooling around with altar boys," I said. "He's the bigger sinner."

"Then I'll follow him."

It didn't seem like the right time to try for a hug.

***

At dinner, Dad wanted to know all about Danny's practice session. Danny told him he did okay but needed to see the spin sooner to hit breaking balls more consistently. He gave me a nod and a rare smile.

"You'll be good at it by the time of your tryout. What about Eddie? Did he have to chase every ball to the backstop?"

"No, Eddie's a good catcher."

Dad sat straight. "Really?"

"In fact, a really good catcher."

Chapter Seventeen

Rain or shine, I went to Mass every morning and made sure Father Bauer saw me in the front pew so he could report my attendance to the Monsignor. After this morning's service, he intercepted me at the side door. "I have the information you wanted on the Salvatorians." He handed me a catalog, glossy brochures, and a sheaf of loose papers.

"This is great, Father, thank you."

"Let me know if you have questions or need help with the application."

"I will."

"I'll get the Monsignor's approval and recommendation for you."

It dawned on me that we were making a deal. He'd help me get into the seminary of my choice in exchange for my silence. It would have been a straightforward deal were it not for a loose cannon named Marcy Jablonski. I held the trump cards, of course, the pictures of Bauer and Alice in the park. Without the pictures, she had no case against the priest and the nun.

"Let me talk this through with my parents. I'll let you know if they're okay with it."

"Don't take too long. The fall semester is coming up fast."

He wants to get rid of me. "Sure, Father, I'll be quick."

I left the materials on my bedside table, changed clothes, and went to the downstairs bathroom to look for bandages. The hard pitches from Danny's last practice session had left bruises on the meaty parts of my hand, at the base of my thumb and below my little finger. Today we would do it again. I pushed bottles around in the medicine cabinet and a round plastic case, like a makeup compact, dropped into the sink. The clear cover popped open to reveal small pills arranged in a circle. Several pills had been taken. I turned the case over and read the label on the back: Enovid. The last time we got haircuts, Jake the barber told Dad to invest in the pharmaceutical company.

"Now that it's legal, every woman is going to take 'the pill,'" he'd said.

And then Dad had ordered Mom to take the birth control pill. He had won that battle and possibly made money in the bargain.

I taped the palm of my hand to cushion it against Chuck's pitches and rode my bike to the athletic field. Marcy wasn't there, and I assumed she was tailing Father Mac.

Chuck warmed up, and then Danny stepped into the batter's box.

"Don't swing at the pitches." I had thought a lot about Danny's problem. Maybe if he wasn't worried about hitting the ball, he could get better and faster at identifying the pitch. "Just watch them and tell me what they are."

"I can't believe I'm being coached by my chubby baby brother."

"It's not coaching; it's logic. When you're better at seeing the spin, you'll hit the pitches. Just try it."

Danny took his normal stance, and I called the pitches. Danny called them out, and I let him know if he was right.

"You're going to wear Chuck out. Swing at something," Joe yelled. Danny told him to hold his horses.

He made a lot of wrong guesses before he began to make correct guesses. After a while, his guesses were mostly right, and I told him to start swinging. He connected with the breaking balls more often than not.

"I don't understand how you can be a good coach and a terrible player at the same time," Danny said.

"I'm not terrible anymore. You should come watch my games."

***

Flushed with pride for having taught Danny to hit breaking balls, I went home and up to my bedroom to read about the Salvatorian Seminary. The brochures were filled with pictures of schools, classrooms, orchards, and smiling Africans. I leafed through the class catalog and found the course of study to be heavy on reading, writing, math, and religion. Two things were surprising and a little disturbing: only ten percent of the students graduated and some became Brothers rather than Priests. Brothers were the manual laborers of the Church.

That only ten percent of the students graduated didn't seem to bother the Order. Their goal was to provide an elite education at a school where they separated the wheat from the chaff. There was no mention of a standard to be met to become a priest rather than a Brother.

I had been told often enough that I was an exceptional student so I psyched myself up to think of this seminary as a challenge.

When I reached the information about tuition and room and board fees, my confidence dissipated. The Salvatorian seminary cost nearly twice as much as the Diocese seminary. Ordinary priests cost far less to train apparently. Dad would blow a gasket.

Downstairs, I was surprised to find that Gram had come to cook dinner. My family sat around the table, waiting for their first good meal in days.

Dad inquired about Danny's practice session, and I told him Danny was now able to reliably hit breaking balls.

"We should thank Morada for setting it up," Dad said.

That would have been a good time for Danny to tell Dad about my idea for training Danny's eyes, but Danny chose not to mention it. Perhaps he was embarrassed that he got his coaching from his kid brother.

When dinner was over, I asked Dad if we could talk about my future.

"I thought it was settled." He didn't look interested in another conversation about me.

"There's a new option. Maybe we could go in the living room."

"I don't need to hear this," Danny said. "I'm going to see Joe, see what he thought about today." Before anyone could comment, Danny was out the back door.

"Humor him, Frank." Mom gave Dad a look and told Carla to go to her room.

Mom and Dad sat on the couch and Gram took the recliner as usual. I showed them the Salvatorian brochures and talked them through the schools they ran in the U.S. and the mission in Tanzania.

"They're all so far away," Mom said.

"Why would you want to go to Africa, for Christ's sake?" Dad asked. "Appleton is the best place in the world. We have good people, safe streets, plenty of jobs, no crime. We're never on the TV news. Why would you want to leave?"

Because I'll be far from home. "I can be a parish priest when I'm older, but while I'm young and have the energy for it, I want to spread the word of Christ."

"You're such a dreamy, impractical boy." Mom wore a dreamy look of her own.

"He always has to be different." Dad turned to me. "Where is this place again?"

I told him.

"It's not that far." Dad shrugged.

"It's just for high school," Mom said.

They seemed to be warming to the idea.

"Is it cheaper than the one Monsignor Muller wants you attend? That one costs an arm and a leg."

There was no way to avoid this moment. My mouth went dry and the muscles in my chest tensed. I pulled a number-studded sheet of paper from the brochures and handed it to Dad. In less than a second, he tossed the sheet of paper at me and it fell to the floor.

"You must be stupid to even ask me," he said.

"The Diocese seminary makes ordinary priests. This one makes special priests."

"Yeah, special." He got up and moved around the coffee table to get in my face. He grabbed my arm in his thick paw and shook me. "You think you're special."

"No, Danny is special, and Carla is special, but I'm a mistake. I heard you guys talking. That's why Mom disobeys the Pope and takes birth control pills."

With two fingers he stopped his eye from quivering. "You think we should all eat beans so you can go to a fancy school? Only queers become priests. Are you queer, Eddie?"

"You'll pay my seminary tuition or I'll tell Mom how I ended up in the river."

He slapped me, and I twirled around like a ballerina, lost my balance, and fell to my knees.

Mom shrieked.

Gram was a blur, rushing past me on thick old legs, growling like a wounded animal. She attacked Dad, shocking him with her ferocity. She clawed at his face and three rivulets of blood sprouted on his cheek.

"No, Bruno. No more, Bruno," she shouted.

Carla raced into the room, crying.

My family had disintegrated.

Dad wrapped his arms around Gram, smothered her attack, and dumped her on the couch. "Get her out of here, Kat." He pointed his meaty finger at me. "Diocese seminary, take it or leave it." He stormed to the bathroom and slammed the door.

Mom and I moved to comfort Gram.

"I'll take her home," I said to Mom. "You better calm Dad down."

I lifted Gram to her feet, grabbed her purse, and led her out the front door. I didn't want her anywhere near Dad. As we walked, her chest heaved, like she was about to have a heart attack. Once I got her inside, I settled her on her sofa, "Who's Bruno?"

Her eyes were focused. She seemed to have all her faculties. "Dead man," she said.

"Was he another boyfriend or my grandfather?"

"Ach, bad man. Gone."

"But you thought Dad was Bruno."

"I was confused. I know it was Frank. He's a gomer."

"That was the first time Dad ever hit me. It's all about money, Gram. We want too much. Mom wants nice things, Carla wants clothes, Danny might not have a job, I want to go to an expensive school."

Gram patted my hand. "It's not just money. Your father thinks his life should have been different. He wanted to make a career of the Navy, but Gail said, 'It's me or the Navy, Frank. Take your pick.' Then he wanted to move to Florida and start his own electrical contracting business, but Gail wouldn't move."

I hadn't heard about Florida. I'd have liked that. I wondered if Dad regretted his choices. "Everyone has dreams that don't come true," Marcy said. "He's the church treasurer and the union president. What more could he want?'

"He wants Danny to have the life he should have had."

Sure, Danny. Dad's dream of being a baseball player was all he had left.

"He's not a bad man, Gram. He just doesn't have enough money."

"He's why Gail drinks too much."

I had no answer for that.

In no rush to go home, I watched the evening news with Gram. As usual, the lead story was Vietnam. The entire 1st Infantry Division had been uprooted from Fort Riley, Kansas and shipped to Vietnam. Defense Secretary Robert McNamara said he needed another one hundred seventy-five thousand troops to win this war. We're fighting for democracy in Vietnam and we're fighting for civil rights in Alabama and we're sending Gemini spacecraft into the atmosphere looking for someone to fight out there. It seemed that fighting defined human nature.

I made sure Gram was okay and walked home. Slowly. I slipped through the back door without a sound. All the bedroom doors were closed. Everyone was hiding.

***

I was looking for something to read when gentle tapping on my door startled me. I cracked the door just an inch and was shocked to see Carla standing there in a nightgown. Her eyes were red-rimmed and her cheeks puffy. I let her in and she fell into my arms.

"Don't go away, Eddie," she mumbled into my shirt. "Don't leave me alone here. Please."

I wrapped my arms around her, maybe the first time ever. "I have to go, Shrimp. It's my calling."

"I don't want to get beat up like you were."

"He won't do that to you. Mom will protect you."

"She can't protect herself, Eddie."

I tried to convince myself that Dad wasn't that kind of man. "It will be better for you when Danny and I are gone. Dad will have more money."

She stood back and tried to smile. I used my handkerchief to dab her eyes.

"Can I have your room so I can hide like you do?"

"Sure, Shrimp. This is a good room."

Chapter Eighteen

Before dawn, the boom of thunder shook the house and I woke to an argument wafting up the stairs. A flash of lightning through my window lit the way as I eased to the top step and sat. Soon, Danny joined me to listen. My parents' voices were loud enough to hear but restrained, not yet a full-blown-knock-down-drag-out fight.

"She needs to be in an old folks' home," Mom said.

"Her pension and Social Security would never cover it," Dad said. "There are places where she can give up her house and income and the government will pay the rest."

"No, Frank! Those places are awful. I'm not going to put my mother in one of those places. She cared for her parents at home and we have to do the same."

"We'll have a room available upstairs one way or the other, Kat."

A lull ensued, and I thought about how an old person became a piece of furniture needing a place to be stored. Then I wondered what they meant by one way or the other. I'd be going away. That was for sure.

"Carla could move upstairs." Mom sounded as though she was thinking out loud. "Abby can take Carla's room."

Danny and I exchanged frightful looks. I tried to stand; I needed to head this off before the idea gained traction. Danny pulled me back down.

"And the crazy lady lives in the room next to us?" Dad's voice rose an octave. "Look at the marks on my face. We'd have to keep our door locked so she can't kill me in the night."

"She can't stay by herself. She falls down the stairs and gets lost in her neighborhood."

"Eddie could move in with her. She's his favorite person, and he's her little darling."

"If he goes away in the fall, what do we do?"

"We could make him stay home for high school. He can go to the seminary after he graduates."

I bounced to my feet and Danny pulled me down again. The look in his eyes told me we shared the fear that our lives were changing in disastrous ways.

"That's a solution."

"I have to get to work," Dad said. "So does Danny."

"We can talk to the kids tonight."

"I've got to shower." Danny rose and left for the bathroom.

I wasn't about to give up the fight. As Danny got ready for work, I filled out the application and registration forms for the Salvatorian Seminary. After Danny left, I showered and dressed and brought the documents downstairs. Mom was in her usual spot at the backyard picnic table, smoking and drinking coffee. I sat down across from her.

"I overheard the conversation about Gram this morning."

She took a long drag on her cigarette and let the smoke come out through her nostrils. She looked like a Disney dragon. "You shouldn't eavesdrop on us."

"Living with Gram isn't going to work. If I'm going to high school here, I'll be in classes all day and she'll be alone. Are you going to watch her all day?"

Smoke caught in her throat and she was wracked by violent coughing. Her eyes became glassy, maybe from the coughing, maybe from the thought that she'd have to spend her days at Gram's house.

I saved her from having to make excuses. "No one expects you to be at her house every day. The cheaper, easier solution is for Gram to live here. You could sell her house and use her pension and benefits to support the family."

I pushed the application in front of her. "I need your signature."

She blinked three times and took the easy way out. "Your father manages the money. You'll have to get his signature tonight."

"It won't hurt to file the application and see if it's an option. If I'm here this fall, we won't have enough rooms for everybody."

"He'll kill me if I sign it."

"There's no obligation to an application. Now that Father Bauer has gone to the effort to get the application, I don't want him and the Monsignor coming around asking questions about how I lost my vocation."

Mom's eyes popped wide open. "No, we can't have the priests around here. What with your dad being so close to them, I mean."

"If I'm not accepted, we'll never mention this. If I am accepted, we'll deal with Dad then." I handed her a pen.

She stubbed out her cigarette and sighed. "Well, someone ought to get the money they want. Don't tell Dad." She signed.

I rode straight to the rectory and asked the housekeeper to give the documents to Father Bauer. I didn't feel bad about coercing Mom. It was her duty to care for her mother as Gram had cared for her parents. It was Dad's problem to make enough money to take care of everything. It shouldn't fall on the shoulders of a fourteen-year-old boy to solve the family's problems, should it?

I pedaled to Gram's house to check on her. I needn't have worried. She and Marcy were sipping Kool-Aid in the living room.

"Everything okay here?" I sat on the couch next to Marcy.

"Gram can't go back to your house," Marcy said. "She's afraid of your dad."

"He's settled down. We're working through things."

"I don't like Bruno," Gram barked.

"It's Frank, Gram, not Bruno."

She nodded and pursed her lips. "Yah, Frank."

We had a nice visit, but I could not convince Gram to come to my house. My plan had been to have her in front of us as we discussed her fate. And mine.

Marcy promised to check on her every day.

We left and walked our bikes down the street.

I couldn't contain my excitement. "I'm going to be a missionary in Africa. Father Bauer found the seminary and submitted my application."

She stopped. "Oh, Eddie you're just running away. You think the farther you go, the better your life will be but we have problems to fix right here. These priests have to be stopped."

She climbed on her bike, ready to ride away.

"Wait. Have you learned anything new?"

"Father Mac is slick," Marcy said. "He doesn't go anywhere to meet anyone, but young boys come to see him—third- and fourth graders. I don't think you're his type. You're too old."

"He meets them in the rectory? Seems awfully dangerous."

"No, he takes them into the school. We need to get inside to take pictures."

"I know how to do that," I said.

***

When Dad got home, he called a family meeting. We all sat around the kitchen table, nerves firing, breaths shallow.

"Gram is getting old and having trouble living by herself, so we have to figure out a solution." Dad sat tall and spoke officiously, as though this were a business meeting.

I wanted to knock the officiousness right off his face. "Gram needs to see a doctor about her brain."

"It's called senility, Eddie. Happens to everyone." Mom waved a hand, dismissing my concern.

"That's right," Dad said. "We're looking into options, but for the time being, we need Eddie to stay with Gram at her house."

"I'll be traveling with the baseball team." Danny adopted a smug look and crossed his arms over his chest. "Carla can have my room and Gram can have Carla's room."

"I want Eddie's room," Carla said. She couldn't look me in the eye.

So, it's everyman for herself. I cut my eyes to Dad. "Gram won't move in here. She's afraid of you."

"Well, I'm afraid of her." Dad emitted a dry chuckle to show he was half-kidding.

"We need a place eventually where people can take care of her," Mom said.

"We'll see what we can find." Dad's voice contained no enthusiasm. "Until then, Eddie, watch your Gram and sleep in the second bedroom, okay?"

They thought they had me trapped but had played into my hands. "Next time she falls down the stairs after using that stupid bathroom, I'll be sure to wait for you guys before I call an ambulance."

"Eddie!" Dad pounded his fist on the table.

"Use your best judgment, Eddie." Mom turned to Dad. "Don't you have something else you'd like to say?"

He cleared his throat, a man who'd been blackmailed.

"Mom and I apologize for the argument last night. I'm sorry I hit you, Eddie. Won't happen again."

"You didn't hurt me. Everything's copacetic."

"There ya go." Dad patted the table with both hands.

And that's how I ended up living with Gram, ejected from my family like a seed squeezed out of a grape.

To show us how magnanimous he could be, Dad suggested we go out to eat at Tony's Wonder Bar, a real restaurant where the Friday night special was all-you-can-eat perch for Catholics who weren't allowed to eat meat on Fridays.

"It's your favorite," Dad said to me. "Consider it your birthday present. And a little reward for helping the family."

I would turn fifteen the following Wednesday. All of us kids had summer birthdays. My friends say it's because the cold weather in

October and November leaves nothing for parents to do but make babies.

Fried perch, a panfish harvested from local lakes, was even better than A&W hamburgers. We went and pretended to be happy. I asked the server for platter after platter of fish and ate until I had to loosen my belt right there at the table.

“That’s why you’re chubby,” Danny said. “You eat too much.” He reached over and squeezed my chest. “Man boobs.”

I knocked his hand away. “Only boobs you’ll ever touch.”

Danny choked on his tongue.

“He’s pleasingly plump.” Mom patted my stomach. “Priests can be plump. It’s not like they have to attract women.”

Chapter Nineteen

While Dad was at work and Mom and Carla were galivanting around town with Shirley, I raided the family freezer and pantry, loaded two cardboard boxes with food and drinks, and wheeled them to Gram's house in Carla's wagon. Most days, Gram had cooked and eaten at Dad's house, so it was only fair to appropriate our share of the goodies.

That evening, Dad called Gram's house, and I answered. He was irate that the groceries in his house had dwindled.

"You didn't expect her to feed both of us on her meager earnings, did you?"

"We'll put you on rations, stack your food to one side so you don't go stealing our food."

"How about we give you a list of what to buy for us? You'll save money because you'll only have to buy the one or two things Mom can cook for you guys."

He slammed down the receiver. That made me laugh. The man was learning about unintended consequences.

Gram cooked dinners, and Marcy often joined us. Marcy "borrowed" books from the library when she wasn't stalking Father Mac. For Marcy and me, it was like the best camping trip ever.

We taught Gram to play a card game called 7-up because games stimulate the brain, but her mental condition didn't improve, alternating between lucid and confused. I couldn't let her leave the house without me or Marcy as an escort. I limited my time away to playing baseball games or stealing things from home.

On one such foray into the castle, I found that Mom was using my closet to hide her bottles of gin. For fear of Mom finding the pictures of Bauer and Alice, I removed the packet from my winter boots and took it to Gram's house.

The following Sunday, I went home to change into dress clothes and took Gram to the Mass at which I was an altar boy. Afterwards, I dropped her at her house where Marcy kept her company while I went home and changed back into everyday clothes. Gram didn't have a closet in her second bedroom so my clothes were stacked in neat piles on the floor, but I didn't want to do that to my Sunday best.

I delivered the Sunday papers and returned to the house. Dad had just finished his accounting. He took two money bags, one large with a bank name stenciled on it, and one small, to his bedroom. I stood beside the kitchen table and glanced at Dad's paperwork as Mom opened and shut cabinets, peered into the refrigerator.

"There's nothing to cook." She sounded exasperated.

Dad's hen scratching on the yellow pad, his initial counts at the church office, didn't match the entries on the accounting ledger. Every Mass had a lower total on the ledger than on the pad. The total difference was about five hundred dollars. I presumed money was going into two different accounts. Perhaps the free food money was being held apart from parish operations. Dad had a talent for managing money. It was said he could squeeze nickels and make them bleed quarters.

"Would you like to come for dinner?" With a hopeful smile, Mom drew me away from the ledger.

"Oh, no, thanks. Gram is making a roast."

"Does she want to bring it over here?"

No pots steamed on Mom's stove, nothing baked in her oven. "It's just a small one. Sorry." I had to stifle a giggle. I remembered what Marcy had said: "You're not the goody-two-shoes you pretend to be."

"Have you found a place for Gram?" I asked.

"Ah, no not yet. Everything is so expensive."

"I guess she'll have to move in here when I go away in the fall." *If I were a nice boy, I wouldn't enjoy tormenting Mom.*

Mom's vacant stare morphed into an angry glare. "We're well aware of the situation, Eddie," she snapped.

"What's going on here?" Hands on hips, Dad stood in the doorway, looking ready to fight.

"Nothing," Mom snapped again.

"I was just asking if you've found a place for Gram," I said, feigning innocence.

"Not that great over there?" A small smile and a slow nod of the head made Dad look pleased that I was suffering, as he undoubtedly had suffered when he lived in that cramped house.

"No, it's great, but Gram needs care."

"We're taking steps to rectify the situation." He and Mom shared a conspiratorial look.

"I don't like to leave her alone too long, so I'd better be going."

***

At Monday morning Mass, Father Bauer told me to check mail because he'd received word that the Salvatorians had reached a decision on my application. Excitement and fear mingled in my chest as I rushed home.

Mom and Dad sat at the kitchen table in the middle of a workday morning, looking glum. Danny wandered around the kitchen, touching this and that. Carla stood still as a heron waiting for a fish to swim past. Mom dabbed her eyes with a soggy tissue.

"What's going on?" I asked.

"Danny's been drafted." Consternation and confusion clouded Dad's face.

"He's only nineteen," Mom wailed.

I was as confused as Dad. "It came today? The mailman hasn't been here yet."

"It came a couple of weeks ago," Dad said. "I thought it was a mistake, a mix-up with his birthday. I went to the draft board to clear it up."

I remembered the day something came in the mail and everyone was in a bad mood.

Danny stopped wandering. "The minute I turned nineteen they gobbled me up like the daily special at the Diner. It was like my birthday triggered a bomb."

"What did the draft board say?"

Dad took a breath. "They're supposed to draft single men twenty-five years old first and then come down the age ladder." Dad's hand started above his head and dropped like an elevator pausing on each floor. "They said the sudden increase in draft allotments caught them by surprise. Most draft age kids have deferments—going to college, married, working at protected occupations—so they had to take everyone they could find. Bunch of old fogies smoking cigars and manipulating paper records so their grandkids don't have to serve. It's a disgrace."

"You think they're cheating?" I asked.

"No doubt about it," Dad said.

"He's a baby," Mom wailed again.

Carla started crying too. "Is he going to die?"

As reported on the evening news, the body counts were heavily in our favor and yet, our dead and wounded numbers were ratcheting up faster than the score at a basketball game. My parents' vexation over the drafting of their barely nineteen-year-old son seemed warranted, but I wondered how many single nineteen- to twenty-five-year-olds who weren't going to college could there be in a town of forty-eight thousand? McNamara and LBJ were throwing everything at the Viet Cong but the kitchen sink and they needed an endless supply of cannon fodder to do it. Every draft-age kid needed a plan, a deferment, and that included Danny.

"What are you going to do about it?" I asked. This situation was far worse than Mom and Dad imagined: queer Danny Kovacs could not be a soldier.

Four wordless mummies sat around that table, brains and vocal cords paralyzed.

The answer seemed obvious to me. "He can register at a college, get a student deferment."

"That's a last resort," Dad said. "School would interfere with his baseball schedule. I want to see what happens at his tryout."

"Can playing baseball get him out of it?"

"It worked for Joe DiMaggio, and that was a World War."

Mom blew her nose and composed herself. "Forget baseball. Danny could get a real job and go to the community college at night."

Danny guffawed. "That's the same as high school, Mom."

"I have one more trick up my sleeve." Mixing his metaphors, Dad tapped his temple. "Let's see how that works."

With that settled, I said something stupid. "Has there been any mail for me?"

"Jesus Christ, Eddie, you're not the center of the universe," Dad shouted.

"Sorry." I backed out of the kitchen.

***

We didn't have to pay for the ripped baseball uniform. Gram stitched up the L-shaped tear, and I wore my lucky uniform to every game. I did not return to my parents' house—I no longer thought of it as my house—until I absolutely had to on the following Sunday.

The place had the heavy air and suffocating silence of a funeral home, as though Danny had already been shot or blown to bits. I dressed in silence, served at Mass, returned to change clothes in silence and delivered my newspapers.

Back at the house, Mom and Carla watched Dad finish counting the day's collections.

Dad put away his ledger and the church money—two bags again.

"We're going to your favorite place, the A&W hamburger stand to take our minds off this stuff," Mom said. "Want to come along?"

I was tempted by the gracious invitation but I wanted to solve a couple of mysteries more than I wanted a burger. "Thanks, but I better get back to Gram. She's cooking."

I didn't go to Gram's. I waited around the corner a long time before my parents' car passed, then rode back to their house. I let myself in and went straight to Mom's bedroom—it was always Mom's bedroom, never Dad's. I lifted the frilly bedspread and looked under the bed. The big bank bag was there, and next to it, the small bag lay empty. I pulled out the accounting ledger and examined the numbers. Dad's notes weren't under the bed so I couldn't see if he had fudged the ledger numbers again, but the totals added to something like five hundred dollars less than usual for a summer Sunday. I put the ledger back, sat on my haunches, and thought about it. Gram needed a place to stay, I needed a lot of money for the seminary. Both bags were empty. If Dad was stealing, where would he hide the money?

I didn't find any money in their night tables but I did find an open envelope addressed to me. The Salvatorian seminary had accepted my application to attend classes beginning in September. I fumed and stomped around their bedroom for a while but calmed down when I considered both sides of the issue. I had submitted my application behind their back and they had hidden the response because they hadn't decided how to deal with it. Then Danny's draft notice had fallen in their lap. They had more problems than they could handle. I thought about laying the letter on the kitchen table to force them to talk to me about it, but I didn't want them to know I'd been snooping around. I had more to find.

I looked in their dresser and their closet and found nothing resembling a wad of money.

I went to the basement and searched the dank, dark, spaces under the stairs, around the oil tank, under couch cushions, even in the freezer. Nothing. Maybe I was wrong. Maybe the contributions were simply off. Maybe I had the wrong idea about Dad.

The garage was the last place I'd have hidden stolen money but I wanted to be as thorough as my detective hero, Travis McGee. Dad's workbench was cluttered with tools but no hiding places for a pile of cash. I moved junk away from the walls, looked in boxes, and still found nothing. Sweating in the still air of the garage, I closed my eyes, lifted my face to the heavens, and asked God's forgiveness for having such terrible thoughts about Dad.

When I opened my eyes, I was looking at plywood planking laid on the rafters to create a sort of attic under the peaked roof. I pulled a ladder into the center of the garage floor and climbed high enough to see the shapes of unidentifiable stuff in the dark spaces. I crawled onto the plywood and hoped it could handle my weight. For a moment, I was as terrified as I had been in the river. Then I inched around and peeked under and behind all the junk up there. In an old TV, its pressed-board backing hanging loose, I found a large shopping bag, like you get at the supermarket, and in it, the biggest pile of greenbacks I'd ever seen. More than enough for my tuition; enough to pay Gram's bills.

They hadn't left immediately for the hamburger stand because Dad took the time to hide today's stolen money. One sick old lady and one boy with a dream had turned my dad into a thief. Everyone is a sinner.

Chapter Twenty

"All we need to register you for classes is the tuition money," Father Bauer said as he disrobed.

I had waited in the sacristy for him to finish Mass because I wanted him to report to the monsignor that I'd been there and because I had a question for him. "My parents are trying to figure out how to afford the Salvatorian Seminary. Does the Diocese help seminary candidates with a scholarship or financial aid for poor families?" *We're even worse off now that we have Gram's bills.*

"Normally, the Diocese subsidizes the tuition for its parish priest seminary but not for seminaries run by religious orders." He frowned and scrunched up his face. "We're short of funds right now, not getting the usual donations in our Sunday collections, so you'd have to pay full price for any seminary."

How ironic that the church would have handed us money on a silver platter if Dad hadn't stolen it. Now the priests have noticed the shortfall because the donations were as predictable as tap water flowing from a kitchen faucet.

I gave him a sad, puppy-dog look. "It would be a shame if I couldn't scrape together the money for the Salvatorian Seminary."

He detected the implied threat. "Let me see what I can do."

As I rode back to Gram's house, I wondered how I could warn Dad that the priests know money had gone missing. He needed to give it back so the church could give it to me legitimately. Maybe he could keep a little for Gram. What a sinful thought! *My sense of right and wrong isn't working properly.*

***

Marcy and I dragged Gram along with us to watch Danny's tryout and get a little Vitamin D sunshine. Gram was pale as a sheet of note paper and had trouble catching her breath as we walked to the athletic field. She said her head hurt and I wondered, not for the first time, if the hospital had missed something when they checked her out after her fall down the stairs.

Dad couldn't attend the tryout. He was needed for some mechanical changeover at the mill. Joe was there, of course, and he sat with us in the stands. I felt funny sitting beside a guy who had kissed my brother. I was glad Marcy was here to help with Gram, but still a little nervous about being seen with her in public. At least this was a place unlikely for any of the nuns or priests to be.

The tryout was more organized and more thorough than I had anticipated. The Green Bay Blue Jays had three coaches and three players present for the session, equipped with bats and balls and stopwatches. First, they timed Danny's wind sprints in the outfield. Then they timed him running from home plate to second base and from second base to home plate. With his long strides, Danny was so fast his shadow couldn't keep pace.

A Blue Jays player hit fly balls to the outfield, and Danny gracefully tracked them down and caught every one of them. They had him throw from the outfield to a cutoff man and then all the way to a catcher. Danny had an accurate cannon for an arm, something we had in common, perhaps something inherited from Dad.

When they moved Danny to the infield and rapped grounders at him, the tryout became more difficult for him. He didn't read the bounces well and let several balls get past him. While he was fast, he wasn't quick. Danny wasn't going to be an infielder. They put him at first base and threw to him from various positions around the bases. Danny caught the throws but stretching to meet the ball and shorten the runner's time to first base, was unnatural for him.

"They like a big target on the first-base bag," Joe said. "With some instruction, he could play the position."

When it was time to hit pitches, I crossed my fingers, hoping for the best. I needed Danny to get off Dad's payroll. I wanted Danny to achieve his dream, Dad's dream, so Dad could focus on my dream.

Danny hit several fastballs out of the park, and we cheered raucously. Danny hit only about half of the breaking balls; some struck well to the outfield and some weakly-hit grounders to the infield. He had done better in our last practice session, so I guessed he was nervous. Or maybe this Blue Jays pitcher was harder to hit than the one from the Foxes.

When the hitting test was over, the coaches clapped Danny on the back, packed up, and left with smiles on their faces. Had he done enough? I couldn't tell, but Joe thought so. "Nobody can hit every breaking ball."

Danny said they'd let him know their decision in a day or two. The answer had to be positive; Danny was not soldier material.

***

Marcy and I had dinner with Gram and watched the evening news. Secretary of Defense McNamara had activated the Army Reserves and the National Guard to increase his total available troops by three hundred seventy-five thousand.

He sounded like a banana republic dictator, drunk with power and blood lust. The little skirmish in the jungle had become a full-scale war. I hoped Dad would come up with a way to save Danny from the draft.

Marcy didn't want to ride her bike after dark, so she hugged Gram and took off. I thought I deserved a hug but I didn't get one. I tucked Gram into bed and then lay awake in my bed for hours. I had a mother who was an alcoholic, a father who was a thief, a brother who was a homo, a grandmother who had lost her marbles, and a dream we couldn't afford. In a span of just six weeks, my life had gone from ordered and planned and blissfully ignorant to chaotic and uncomfortable with knowledge of misbehaving priests that a fourteen-year-old boy shouldn't possess.

***

I didn't think anything of it when Gram stayed in bed while I went to yet another workers' Mass. It was just another Wednesday with no reason why she shouldn't sleep in. Her routine and habits had changed a lot over the past couple of weeks.

Father Bauer asked again about seminary tuition. I hadn't come up with a good way to broach the subject with my parents, and they hadn't revealed the hidden acceptance letter.

"We're trying to figure out the money, Father."

"You're about out of time, Kovacs. Bring me what you've got."

No, you and Alice are about out of time, Bauer. If I didn't go away to the seminary, he wouldn't have the freedom to fool around with Sister Mary Alice. My knowledge of their dalliance would hang over his head like a guillotine blade. And, if I didn't go to the Salvatorian Seminary, he would have done me no favors in trade for my silence. I didn't want this power over his life; I just wanted to go to the seminary. I slunk away without another word.

***

Gram had still not come out of her bedroom so I rapped on her door. No answer. I put my ear to her door and couldn't hear movement.

"Gram?"

No answer. My heart's pace increased and my fingers grew cold. I opened her door slowly in case she was dressing, but she was still in bed, eyes closed, mouth open.

"Gram?"

No answer. I tiptoed to the bed and nudged her shoulder. No response. I touched her hand and it was cold. *Dead!* The word flashed in my brain like a neon sign and I suppressed it, turned it off. I bent close to her face and felt her breath on my face. She made a faint sucking noise as she gasped for breath. Gram wasn't dead. Gram wasn't dead! I ran to the kitchen. I didn't care what my parents would say, I dialed 9-1-1. I told the operator that Gram was unresponsive and yes, she was breathing but barely.

The ambulance arrived in five minutes flat and the attendants wheeled her out of her house. The driver told me to meet them at the emergency entrance at St. Elizabeth's Hospital.

I called home and Mom answered. "Oh, Eddie, I hope you haven't messed up again. We haven't paid the last bill yet."

I told her the situation was serious this time and asked her to meet me at the emergency room. I pedaled to the hospital and was told that Gram had been taken to an examining room. Mom and Dad arrived ten minutes later. Dad shook his head at me like I was some incorrigible kid. They were at the reception counter when a doctor came from the back and called, "Jaeger!"

We gathered around him, and he asked us to follow him through double doors and down a corridor. I thought we were going to Gram's room, but he ushered us into a small office. Mom and Dad took seats and I was left standing. The doctor closed the door and sighed. He took his seat behind the desk. I shivered.

"I'm afraid Mrs. Jaeger didn't make it." The doctor's eyes were on Dad.

Mom wailed like a wounded animal and then went limp. Dad wrapped an arm around her or she'd have slid right out of her chair.

Didn't make it. Gram didn't make it. The strange phrase made it sound like this was Gram's fault. Maybe it was my fault for not waking her up before I went to Mass.

"What happened?" Dad said.

"Massive stroke is what it looks like. There was nothing we could do."

Nothing we could do. I burst into uncontrollable, embarrassing tears. I turned to the wall, my shoulders shook, my chest heaved, and I couldn't catch my breath. My favorite person was gone. I had never experienced loss, and I didn't think I'd ever recover from it. How can you get over someone dying?

Mom sobbed wordlessly.

"What would cause that?" Dad said.

"There were no brain waves, and without signals from the brain, her organs stopped working. That happens when blood to the brain is cutoff, usually by a blood clot in the carotid artery."

Anger overcame my shock. Gram had never been the same after hitting her head during her fall. "You know that for sure or just guessing?"

"Eddie," Dad spoke softly, respectful of my feelings, I guess.

"It's okay." The doctor removed his glasses and pinched the bridge of his nose. "We don't normally do an autopsy for a natural death, but we can do one if you want to pay for it."

"No!" Mom was suddenly alert. "We're not cutting her up."

The doctor nodded and asked where he should send the "remains."

Dad said, "Whitman Funeral Home."

I suppose that's going to cost him money, too.

We put my bike in the trunk of Dad's car and drove to Gram's house. Mom and Dad waited in the car while I went inside. I suppose they didn't want the smell of death in their lungs. Maybe they thought they could keep Gram's death from being real if they didn't walk around in her ghostly shadow. If you don't acknowledge death, it won't happen to you, right? I looked at the stairs to Gram's unusual bathroom and couldn't help thinking that her fall caused her problem and the doctors had failed to detect a head injury when I took her to the hospital. That head injury caused her death, not some random blood clot.

I collected all my clothes and things and put them in the car. Then we drove home. I carried my things to my room. Mom's gin bottles were on the floor of my closet. I was home again, and I hated it. Dad told Danny and Carla the news.

"Who's going to babysit us?" Carla asked.

"Well, she was old," Danny said.

Chapter Twenty-one

I wanted to bring the worst day of my life to an end, to turn off my mind, to numb my senses, but sleep was intermittent, like windshield wipers in light rain. I dozed and woke, dozed and woke. Sometimes I cried because I'd never see my grandmother again, and sometimes I laughed when I remembered her antics. She'd survived repeated traumatic events and nothing crushed her spirit. She loved to dance and she loved to flirt. I had watched her do both at the wedding of the girl who grew up across the street. Her memory now occupied the space her spirit had inhabited. I felt alone in the world to contend with parents and siblings I didn't particularly like and who certainly didn't like me. I was scared.

Sometime after midnight, voices woke me from a dream. I eased onto the steps and listened. They were right below me, in the living room, not fighting, just having a serious conversation.

"Her house is a pile of scrap." Dad sounded worn out. "We won't get enough to pay the hospital bills and the funeral home."

"You should have taken better care of it," Mom said. "Does she have life insurance?"

"A mill policy, next to nothing."

"You'll have to come up with the money for the burial and a headstone, a marker."

"She never liked me, and now I'm supposed to spend a bunch of money on her?"

"Yes, Frank, she was my mother. You'll spend all your money on her."

"All you ever did was eat her cooking, and now you want to act like the devoted daughter."

"We're going to do right by her."

"Simpler and cheaper to cremate her."

"She was Catholic. A viewing, a funeral, a marker. I don't care if you have to spend all the money, Frank."

"You know what that money is for."

"You know how to get more."

She knows he's stealing from the church. If it wasn't for Gram, it must have been for me. I'd probably go to hell for using stolen money to go to the Salvatorian Seminary. The money should be spent on Gram and her bills, like Mom said.

Mom's admonition to steal more money was the last I heard from downstairs. Presumably they went to bed. I snuck back to my room and reunited with dreams and sorrows.

***

Marcy hugged me tightly and hung on as she cried into my t-shirt. Then I started crying again. I tried not to drip tears into her pink hair. This wasn't the way I had imagined our first hug. I was glad my parents were inside Gram's house and not witnesses to this emotion.

"I loved that woman," Marcy mumbled into my chest. "So brave. So strong."

She let go of me and stepped back, sniveling. I gave her my handkerchief, and she wiped her eyes and blew her nose.

"The viewing is Friday evening and the funeral is Saturday," I said.

"Is it okay if I come?"

"Of course."

"Can I bring my mother?"

"Sure."

She pointed to my parents' car in the driveway. "What are they doing inside?"

"Packing up Gram's stuff. They need to sell the house as soon as possible."

"I can help."

I hadn't let Marcy anywhere near my parents, but now I felt defiant. She had been a better friend to Gram than my parents. We went inside and found Dad in the kitchen packing cookware and silverware and plates and bowls and cups into boxes.

"'Bout time you got here," Dad said to me. Then he saw Marcy and took his time looking her over. "Who's this?"

"This is my friend, Marcy. She's going to help."

"This is a family thing, Eddie."

"Gramma Abby was my favorite person," Marcy said.

"What? You knew Abby?"

"She kept Gram company when I had things to do. We took care of Gram." Because you guys ignored her was on the tip of my tongue, but my point was made. "Where's Mom?"

"Packing up Abby's clothes. We'll take them to the St. Vincent De

Paul Society. At least I'll get a tax break for a charitable contribution."

I led Marcy to Gram's bedroom where Carla sat on the floor licking an all-day sucker. The bed was covered in Gram's clothing. Mom was lifting boxes off the top shelf of the closet, so I helped her.

"Marcy came to help," I said.

Mom turned and gave Marcy a polite but insincere smile. "Oh. Sure."

I returned to the kitchen to help Dad.

"I thought you were going to be a priest?" He jerked his head in Marcy's direction.

"I am. She's a friend from school. Smartest kid in the class."

He stood up straight, arching his back to relieve stiffness. "It's okay if you want to go to high school here, you know. Make friends with some other girls. Plenty of time to decide on the priesthood."

It was a conundrum. If he spent the stolen money on my tuition, he'd be saddled with Gram's bills. I didn't want him to steal more money, but I couldn't stay in his house for four more years. "No, I'm ready to go."

I loaded boxes and carried them to the trunk of Dad's car. I humped trash bags to the curb. Mom and Marcy laid Gram's clothes in the backseat. It didn't take long for all traces of Gram's life to be wiped away.

Dad was about to toss Gram's wall clock in a trash bag when I stopped him. "I want to keep that."

"Why? It never worked."

"It reminds me of Gram."

"Suit yourself." He handed it to me. "Be sure to lockup when you leave."

He and Mom drove away. I wandered from room to room, remembering the good times with Gram, feeling her spirit, hearing her laugh echo in the cramped space. So sad that Gram would never return, and neither would I.

In the kitchen, Marcy was slurping water directly from the faucet.

She straightened and wiped her mouth with the back of her hand. "Let's see if we can get into the school and catch Father Mac doing something."

It felt too soon to resume our stalking, an intrusion on my grieving, but I didn't want to be alone. "I know how to get into the school. I need to use the facilities first."

I climbed the stairs to the odd commode and wished Gram had a door on the strange bathroom. As I peed, I flushed with the knowledge that

Marcy could hear what I was doing. After I zipped up, I took a peek into the attic bedroom. Decades-old dust stuck in my nostrils. It dawned on me that when Mom and Edward were young, this was likely his bedroom. A rickety bed and a chest of drawers were all that remained of his life. *It's so easy to wipe a person off the map.*

The bare floorboards creaked as I walked to the dresser and pulled out the top drawer. Empty. In the second drawer, papers stood in neat stacks, as though waiting to be discovered by an archeologist. I took them to the bed and sorted through them. On top was the property deed for the house. The names on the title were Joseph and Abigail Sachs and the date was 1919. Gram was single and still a teenager when she paid for the house. I set it aside.

The second document was Gram's life insurance policy, face value five hundred dollars.

The third document was Gram's marriage certificate, dated 1924. I caught my breath as I read the name of the groom—Klaus Jaeger. Klaus, not Bruno. She had yelled "Bruno" and then told me he was a bad man who had died long ago. I had assumed he was my grandfather, so who was Klaus?

"What is it?"

I jumped at the sound of Marcy's voice. She stood behind me, looking over my shoulder.

"You scared me."

"Had to see if you fell in."

"Look at this." I handed her the marriage certificate.

She read it. "So?"

"According to the marriage certificate, Klaus Jaeger was her husband, my grandfather, but a man named Bruno, whom I thought was my grandfather, left her with two small children and is dead."

"Maybe she divorced Klaus and Bruno was your grandfather. Are there any divorce papers in that stack?"

"There won't be. The church wouldn't grant her a divorce."

"What did the church have to do with it?"

"They threatened to excommunicate her."

"She should have let them."

The next documents were birth certificates, one for Abigail Katherine, my mom, born in 1925, and one for Edward, born in 1927. On both certificates, Klaus Jaeger was listed as the father.

"Sounds like Gram was confused about this," Marcy said. "Klaus Jaeger was your grandfather."

"Yeah, I guess so."

I turned over two fragile documents—death certificates for Charlotte Sachs in 1930 and Joseph Sachs in 1943. Joseph had been born in 1854 and Lottie in 1857. They were in their forties when Gram was born in 1901. Did people that old have babies way back then? Now people had their babies in their twenties and maybe early thirties. That's what Mom and Dad did.

I put the death certificates aside and paged through income tax filings, bank statements, and property tax notices, all dated between 1920 and 1945. There were no Baptismal certificates or records of First Communions for Mom or her brother, Edward. Maybe they had gotten lost.

"Just old junk," I said. "There should be newer records."

Marcy stepped around me and opened more drawers. When she pulled open the bottom drawer, she squealed. "Look what I found."

She handed me a stack of greeting cards, secured by a blue ribbon. I untied the stack, handed each card to Marcy after I'd read it. The cards celebrated birthdays and holidays in the 1920s and they were all signed by Bill.

"Your Gram had an affair!" Marcy's eyes sparkled. "How exciting."

"Not an affair. He was her boyfriend after the church denied her divorce."

"Well, she was still legally married, so it was an affair. Good for her."

I didn't know what to make of Marcy's excitement over an affair. It seemed tragic to me.

While Marcy waited for me on my parents' driveway, I took the papers into my house. Dad said he had handled Gram's finances ever since he married Mom in 1946. He had all the current documents. I gave him the deed and life insurance policy. The cards, the marriage certificate, and birth certificates I hid in my closet.

***

My heart wasn't in it, but I rode with Marcy to the church and we dropped our bikes on the front steps. Marcy took my camera from the storage pouch on the back of her bike and hung the lanyard around her neck.

Although the church was deserted, I spoke in hushed tones. "There are two ways into the school from the church, one through the sacristy and the other past the convent. We don't want to run into a priest in the sacristy."

She followed me to the front of the church, and I turned left. "This aisle is a dead end. Turn left to go into the convent, turn right and you're in the main school hallway. It's the route the nuns use."

"Let's go."

I grabbed an arm and stopped her from rushing ahead of me. "If a nun sees you, or Father Mac sees you, what's your excuse for being in there?"

"I want my papers from last year. I'm starting high school English in the fall, and I want to review all my work and get ready."

That sounded flimsy to me, but I could think of nothing better. *There was no stopping this girl.*

We walked to the dead end and waited a minute to see if any nuns were leaving the school or coming from the convent. The coast was clear. We took deep breaths and headed into the school. Daylight seeping through the double entry doors to our left allowed us a dim view of the rooms all the way to the rectory door. Without stinky boys and perfumed girls, an aggressively clean smell permeated the school. The hallway was deserted and silent except for the squeak of our sneakers on the waxed floor. As we advanced up the hallway, we surreptitiously tried doors and found them all locked. If Father Mac was doing something wrong behind one of these doors, he wasn't about to leave the door unlocked.

Marcy said, "We'll have to knock—" and I shushed her with a finger to my lips. I thought I heard the distinctive click of a lock. Yes, a door opened and the sounds of two male voices floated down the corridor. Marcy flattened herself in the recessed doorway of a classroom, and I skittered across the hall to the closest doorway.

Father Mac slipped into the hallway wearing his collar and a black short-sleeved shirt, black trousers, no cassock, his arm around the shoulders of a tall man whose face was in shadow but whose graceful movements were familiar. From across the hallway, I heard the whir of the camera feeding film. The two men chatted amiably, and then the priest smacked Danny on his butt. A laugh echoed in the hollow space. Click, whir, click, whir, more pictures.

Danny left through the school's side exit, and Father Mac entered the rectory. As a pair, we turned back to the door we had come through and hustled toward the church. Marcy giggled. A nun I didn't know came from the convent and gave us a quizzical look.

"Can I help you?"

"No, we have what we came for," Marcy said.

We slipped past her, hurried through the transept, down the main aisle, and out the front doors.

"Give me the camera," I said.

"Maybe I should get this developed."

"Give it here." I held my hand out.

"You can't cover this up just because it's your brother who's fooling around with Mac."

I reached for the lanyard. Marcy tried to dance away but I was quicker. I yanked the lanyard over her head. I couldn't tattle on a priest who was doing things with my own brother.

"This doesn't prove anything. We don't know what they did in that classroom."

"Mac grabbed Danny's butt!"

"No, that was a friendly pat on the butt, like coaches give baseball players when they've done something good."

"You're protecting a pedophile."

"I'm not going to expose Danny and ruin my family."

"You're not going to make much of a priest." Marcy righted her bike, hopped on, and rode away.

A smack on the butt is a supremely utilitarian form of athletic communication, right? Coaches use it to congratulate, they use it to discipline, and they use it to motivate their players. Right? Maybe Danny was being counseled by a priest who understood his affliction. Right? Danny was usually late to return home from Sunday Mass. He'd been spending time with Father Mac, trying to overcome his disease, right?

Then it dawned on me, as things often do when I give them time to percolate, that Father Mac may have had designs on me not because I was an altar boy headed for the seminary, but because I was Danny's little brother, cut from the same cloth.

Chapter Twenty-two

Marcy wasn't at the library. Marcy wasn't at the bookstore in Kimberly. Marcy wasn't at Woolworth's where her mom worked.

No one was home at my house. I stretched the kitchen phone around the corner onto the basement steps and closed the door behind me. No one answered the phone at Marcy's house. I felt as though my family was like one of those cliffside houses in California that slid down an eroded hillside into oblivion, and now I was in that house with the rest of my family. Gram was gone, and now Marcy was gone too.

Out of spite, I retrieved Mom's gin bottles from my closet and hid them in the large round planter in the living room, the one that sprouted fake fronds, courtesy of Shirley's decorating advice. In my closet, I left a note for Mom. *Hide and seek; have fun looking for your booze.*

I sulked in my room, turning over a single question and examining it from every angle, like a jeweler assaying a diamond. Should I develop the Mac and Danny pictures? Did I have a sacred obligation to report the priest's behavior no matter what it meant to Danny and our family? I already had explicit pictures of Danny and Joe. I had a boot-full of Father Bauer and Sister Mary Alice pictures I hadn't shown anyone. I had already compromised my morals to protect Danny and elicit a favor from Bauer. I concluded that I could tiptoe toward the edge of the cliff without stepping over the side—I could get the pictures of Danny and Mac developed and see if they were of any value. It had been dim in the school hallway, and the men hadn't done anything extreme.

Although I was sure the clerks were looking at my pictures, I took my film to the drugstore out on Wisconsin Avenue where they were less likely to recognize Father MacMillan. "Two copies, please," I told the clerk. We needed backup for everything, but developing film was draining all my paper route earnings.

Coming back home, I rode down Appleton Avenue, behind the College Avenue storefronts, and saw Dad exit a second-floor office. The plain white sign on the back door of the office read: Ross Berger, M.D. I stopped in a parking lot across the street and watched Dad bounce down the stairs to the parking lot like he'd just been told he would live forever. The doctor wasn't familiar to me. Our family doctor was farther west on College Avenue. If Dad was sick and hiding it from us, he certainly didn't seem worried about it. He got in his car and drove away.

By the time I got home, it looked like a party had erupted spontaneously at our house. Four cars were in the driveway—Dad's land yacht, Danny's sports car, Joe's Corvette, and the baseball coach's station wagon.

The kitchen was crowded with bodies and grins. Everybody held a drink including Mom who had her usual gin gimlet. She toasted me with her glass and winked. She must have found her bottles. Carla's glass contained a reddish liquid. Someone had mixed her a "Shirley Temple," a lemon/lime soda colored by a dash of Maraschino cherry juice.

"What are we celebrating?" I asked.

"Danny passed the tryout." Joe beamed like a backyard spotlight. "They love his speed, his ability to track fly balls, and his arm. He hit just well enough, and with plenty of power, to get through it."

"He got a professional contract." The coach smiled proudly and raised his beer bottle to me.

"Well, he doesn't have the paper in hand yet," Dad said. "But the scout let Joe know it will be here Monday or Tuesday."

"That's fantastic." It felt good to help my big brother achieve his dream.

The coach basked in the glory of coaching a future pro. Joe basked in the glory of arranging the tryout. Mom and Dad basked in the glory of raising a pro baseball player.

"Eddie helped," Danny said.

"Sure." Dad was probably thinking about my catching duties. "Celebrate with us."

Danny didn't expound on my coaching.

"What about your draft notice?" I asked.

"I'll go to the draft board and clear everything up," Dad said, as though it were as easy as taking another sip of beer.

Dad ushered Joe and the coach out of the house as it was time to dress for Gram's viewing. He asked Joe and the coach to show up as well although neither of them knew Gram.

***

Men wearing black suits and sad expressions greeted us at the door of the funeral home. What a terrible job, pretending to grieve with and over people they never knew. In the viewing room, a plain, copper-colored steel casket, flanked by sprays of flowers, lay on a pair of workhorses against the back wall. The coffin's fake-satin-lined mouth stood open. A few folding chairs were lined up in front of the coffin in case mourners needed to rest their emotions.

Mom, Dad, and Danny stood around, whispering with Joe and the coach, still reliving the moment Danny became a pro baseball player. Joe and the coach offered their condolences and left without looking in the coffin.

Carla approached the coffin, took a quick glance inside, and turned away with a wrinkled nose.

This was supposed to be family time, before friends and relatives came to see the deceased, but I was afraid to look. Beneath my sports jacket, a dress shirt, and an undershirt, my armpits were soggy. Below my shirt cuffs, my hands were sweaty. My last memory of Gram was an inert, cold body in her bed, then bouncing on a gurney as the medics carried her to the ambulance. I couldn't let that be my last vision of my favorite person, but I was afraid of replacing it with a vision of Gram in a casket.

I inched forward, looked down on the dead body, and recoiled. The body was clothed in Gram's best Sunday dress and her worn, brown rosary was wrapped in her gnarled hands, but this wasn't my grandmother. This body had sunken cheeks and a nose all too prominent in a pallid face. I didn't touch the body. I didn't get close to it. I didn't say anything to it.

"Are we sure this is Gram?" I asked my parents. "It doesn't look like her at all."

A man in black started toward me, I suppose to assure me they had the right woman in the casket. Mom stopped him with a hand gesture.

"Yes, dear," Mom said. "That's what happens when the body is embalmed."

I wouldn't want to be embalmed. I'd want to look like me in my casket. I checked the tags on the flowers. They had been donated by the funeral home, not by relatives or friends.

When the hour came for the general public to view the body, a few people trickled in—a couple of old guys who had worked with Gram and then her neighbor, Mr. Duncan. He spent a couple of minutes at the casket and then gave me a gentle hug. He left without talking to Mom and Dad. I wondered if he had been Gram's neighbor back when Mom and Dad lived at her house.

"Shouldn't there be more people?" I asked Mom.

She put a hand on my shoulder. "She was the youngest at the mill.

Her older friends are gone."

Dad's seven older brothers and sisters lived far away, in Iowa, Chicago, Maryland, and Florida so I understood why they didn't travel for the funeral of an in-law, but what about Gram's relatives?

"Did Gram have brothers and sisters, Mom?"

Mom looked at me as though I had asked what brand of sanitary napkins she used. "She has a sister who is, I think, two years older. Adeline is a nun at the Holy Hill Monastery, near Milwaukee. You might remember that we took you down there when you were very small. We'll have to find a way to let her know."

I remembered a monastery where we met a nun. I hadn't realized the nun was Gram's sister, and I never thought more about it. "So, that's it, one sister?"

"That's it."

So, Joseph and Lottie came to America and had two children late in life. That seemed odd.

Tired of waiting for people to show up, Dad took a seat and said, "Glad I paid a bunch of money for this."

I had begun to wonder how long Dad would hold out when Marcy and her mother, Judy, came into the room. Judy was still wearing her Woolworth's uniform, but I was relieved that no bruises or black eyes marred her tired face. Marcy was dressed nicely in black and her hair was solid black as well. Judy gave me a hug, and then Marcy gave me a hug. They whispered nice things about Gram and consoling words for me. My parents gawked as though they were passing a traffic accident.

Marcy and Judy had their arms around me as they led me to the coffin. We stood together, looking down, silently praying, I think. Then Marcy's chest heaved and tears rolled slowly down her cheeks. I couldn't help it; I started bawling like a baby. Mom took me by the shoulders and led me away as though bawling were undignified. Judy and Marcy followed.

Still sniveling, I introduced Judy to Mom and Dad. Mom was nice enough but not overly excited about meeting Judy. Maybe I shouldn't have mentioned that her last name was Jablonski. I walked them out of the room and out to the parking lot to their car. Judy was smart enough to give us some time alone. She lit a cigarette and moved slightly away.

"I took the film in to be developed." I wanted Marcy to like me again.

"It's okay, Eddie, I understand. We'll catch Mac with someone else." She grabbed my hand and squeezed it.

"Thank you for coming."

"I'll be at the funeral tomorrow. Mom has to work."

We waited another twenty minutes before going home. There, Mom, Dad, and Danny resumed their celebration. In my room, I carefully removed my clothes and hung them up as I'd wear them again to the funeral. Without correcting the time, I hung Gram's clock above my bed, next to Jesus on the cross. Maybe Gram could have a word with him in heaven. I needed help.

***

We dressed in yesterday's clothes and drove to the church. Father Bauer offered me the opportunity to serve him at the Mass. I declined. I never served at funeral Masses because I didn't want to validate death, and because a Mass rarely consoled the grieving parishioners.

"What was her name again?" Father Bauer asked.

"Abigail Jaeger," I said.

"And she was a member of our parish?"

"First Mass every Sunday for fifty years."

His eyebrows danced a little jig. "Oh, sorry, I didn't know her."

How can a priest not know his most dependable parishioner?

My role today was to be a pallbearer along with Dad and Danny and two men from the funeral home. We stood in the hot sun, waiting for the hearse, and once again, I became a wilting flower. Shirley and her husband, Doug, arrived for the Mass. Marcy nodded to us as she entered the church.

When the hearse finally arrived, they positioned me in the middle on one side, between the two funeral parlor men, and Dad and Danny took the other side. Although I had borne little of the weight, I was panting when we set the casket on a platform in front of the communion railing. The casket lid remained closed, and the funeral parlor men melted into the background. The five of us family members filed into the first pew on the right side of the aisle, and Marcy sat with Shirley and Doug in the first pew on the other side.

It's okay, Gram, this is all for you.

At the point in the Mass where the priest would normally deliver a sermon, Father Bauer stepped to the pulpit and read the burial service prayer. "We therefore commit this body to the ground, earth to earth, ashes to ashes, dust to dust; in sure and certain hope of the Resurrection to eternal life."

He told us what we already knew, that Abigail had been a devoted church-goer and a devout Catholic.

He paused as though trying to remember if I had told him anything else about Gram's life and looked at us for a hint or a cue. My parents sat stiffly in the pew, like the kids in class who don't know the answer.

I stood and eased past my parents, walked through the gate in the railing and up to the pulpit. Father Bauer stepped aside, relieved to relinquish the stage.

"We say goodbye to Gram today, but I'll never forget that she was a real person with a laugh and a smile and a soul. She believed in heaven and deserves to be there. Gram proved that you don't have to be educated to be kind, caring, generous and righteous. She liked to have fun, loved to dance and flirt, but she was one tough lady."

Mom gave me a bittersweet smile.

"She lived a very difficult life, caring for immigrant parents who couldn't speak English, and going to work in a paper mill at age thirteen to support her parents."

I glanced at Mom who nodded appreciatively.

"She was a single mother of two children, one of whom she lost in a tragic drowning. Later, when her daughter, my mother, married my father, she let them live with her in her small house until they could afford a house of their own."

Mom was stoney-faced now. I took a breath. No one had stopped me, so it was time to add the parts that would piss people off.

"Worn out by forty-nine years of labor, she retired as soon as she could draw Social Security and expected to enjoy many golden years. Her retirement was cut short when the hospital failed to detect a head injury after a fall down the stairs in her house."

"Eddie!" Dad hissed.

"She had three loves in her life: my grandfather Klaus, a man named Bruno, and another man named Bill. The three men preceded Gram to their final reward."

Mom gasped so loud it could have been heard in the rectory. Dad looked mortified. Danny grinned. Marcy gave me a discreet thumbs-up. Shirley leaned around her husband to gape at Mom.

"As a Catholic, she wasn't allowed to divorce the husband who abandoned her and her children, but she remained faithful to the church. Instead, she bore her sorrows with dignity, cooked all our Sunday dinners, helped raise me, watched me graduate from elementary school, befriended my friends, and helped me deliver newspapers every Sunday.

Gram was my hero."

Mom wiped tears from her eyes. Dad was red-faced and stiff.

Father Bauer gave me a cross look and swiftly finished the Mass. The funeral parlor men materialized like genies out of a bottle, and we loaded Gram's casket into the hearse. We didn't follow the hearse to the cemetery; our branch of the Catholic faith did not witness burials. The Mass was the end of things.

As we walked to our car, I told my parents to go on without me; I'd walk home. I didn't want to hear anything they had to say.

Marcy caught up to me and grabbed my arm. "You did a good job with the eulogy."

"Thanks, I owed it to her."

Marcy let my parents walk out of earshot before she said, "Your grandfather isn't dead."

"What are you talking about?"

"I looked in the phone book for Bruno and found a bunch of them. No way to know which one might be the right guy."

"Or none of them."

"So, I looked for Klaus Jaeger and found two of them, one in Little Chute and one in Appleton."

"Those listings might not get removed when someone dies. Gram's is in the book, I'm sure."

"They get deleted when you stop paying the bill," Marcy said. "Somebody is paying for those phone lines."

"Gram said he was dead. He certainly didn't show up today."

"We have to go check it out, see if one of them is your grandfather."

A nervous tingling crawled down my arms. Was I brave enough to confront a man who obviously wanted nothing to do with us? "He'd have been here if he wanted to know me."

"No, Eddie, we're going to do this. Sunday may not work for you, but we can see these guys on Monday."

"I'll think about it."

"Oh, good, you're still here." Father Bauer called from the church doors. "The Monsignor would like a word with you."

"I'll call you tomorrow." Marcy hurried away.

Father Bauer held the door for me, then grabbed both of my biceps in surprisingly strong hands. "Don't ever pull that stunt again. A pulpit isn't for your personal use, and a funeral isn't the time to accuse people of wrongdoing. Act like a priest, or you'll never become one."

"Sorry. I got overcome with emotion."

"We told you to stay away from that Jablonski girl."

"I didn't invite her. She knew Gram."

"Stay away from her."

He propelled me up the aisle and into the sacristy where the Monsignor was waiting for us.

"Time to put up or shut up, Eddie," the monsignor said. I could hear his mean side in his voice.

I wanted to get this guy off my back so I could work on Bauer without interference. Now that my parents were paying for Gram's hospital and funeral bills, I needed Bauer to work a miracle. "I'm very happy to be going to the Diocese seminary, Father. We have the money all worked out."

The Monsignor smiled, but Father Bauer tensed.

"I'm sure Father Bauer has told you that we're a little short of funds right now or we'd have given you some help. If you can get through this year, we should be able to help next year."

"That's much appreciated, Father."

"Okay, bring the tuition money as soon as possible. Don't miss out, Eddie."

"Next week, Father. I promise."

The Monsignor left, but Father Bauer blocked the door. "I'm still looking for a way to help you. Don't give up hope."

"I'm counting on you, Father."

Bauer examined my face for a minute, then stepped aside. He assumed I'd keep my mouth shut.

That was my assumption, too.

***

We ordered a pizza, with no mushrooms, which made Carla happy. Mom sat at the picnic table with Shirley, smoking and drinking one of Dad's cheap beers. Dad and I stayed inside at the kitchen table. I didn't know where Danny was, probably at Joe's house.

Dad tore a slice of pizza out of the box. "I didn't appreciate what you said from the pulpit."

"It needed to be said. She was a hero against all odds."

"We don't wash our dirty laundry in public. You gonna talk about us in all your sermons?"

"There won't be any sermons if we don't pay the first semester seminary tuition."

"Oh, have you heard back?"

I couldn't believe he was going to pretend he didn't have my acceptance letter in his nightstand. "Father Bauer gave me the news."

He grimaced, the hidden letter another of his failed tactics. "Can we wait and see what we get for Gram's house?"

I guess they had to sell her house, but the reality still came as a surprise. "No, the Monsignor was all over me after you guys left today. He's afraid I'll lose my spot. But he said they could give us some help next semester."

"Damn it, Eddie, you're like a black hole I throw money into."

Mom sashayed into the kitchen. "Give him the money, Frank, or he'll make our lives miserable." She grabbed two more bottles of Dad's cheap beer from the refrigerator.

His toothpick bobbed and his eye twitched. "I'll decide how this family's money is spent."

"You got your wish when Abby died—we don't have to put her in a home," Mom said.

"Always the smart mouth when you're around Shirley." Dad turned back to me. "I don't suppose it could be a loan that you'd repay?"

"We take a vow of poverty, Dad."

"I didn't have to take a vow to get poor. A wife and kids did the trick."

We weren't desperate poor, but we were one broken refrigerator or burst hot water heater away from bankruptcy.

He didn't move a muscle to get the money. Maybe he didn't want me to know where he had hidden it. *Silly man.* "I promised them tomorrow, Dad."

"For God's sake, let me enjoy my beer."

Chapter Twenty-three

Sunday proceeded routinely, but without Gram's spirit it seemed a chore rather than a welcome day of rest. I served at Mass, Danny went to church with Dad, Mom used cooking as an excuse to skip Mass. Dad came home with the collection money and for the second Sunday in succession, split it into a large bag and a small bag. He was still at it, still stealing, despite the priests' suspicions. I should have warned him, but I desperately wanted out of this house. That was another sin I'd have to confess.

Nothing Mom cooked tasted the way Gram made it. The food at the seminary had to be better.

After dinner, Danny disappeared again. No one wanted to play games. Dad put his transistor radio to his ear to listen to the Cubs lose another game. I went to my room. I wished Marcy had stolen a good book.

Long after dark, I watched Dad sneak out the back door with the small bag and disappear into the garage. I had allowed the day to pass without an argument about my tuition, thinking Mom would wear him down. Now I wanted to scream, "Come back here with my money!" he was in the garage a long time and I imagined him counting his hoard, like the giant in *Jack and the Beanstalk.* He'd better be careful or I'd chop that beanstalk down.

***

On Monday morning, Dad went to work, Danny went to work, and Mom and Carla walked to Gram's house to meet a realtor and put Gram's house up for sale.

I climbed onto the garage rafters and crawled to the old TV set. The pile of money had increased in size, more than enough to pay my tuition. *The idiot is going to get caught, and we'll all be sunk.* Instead of taking a Sunday off to allay suspicions, Dad had skimmed another five hundred dollars. Why am I, a sweet kid who's going to be a priest, better at theft than the supposed financial wizard I had for a father?

Depressed, I went back in the house and called Marcy. I didn't hide on the basement steps; I no longer cared what my parents thought of

Marcy. But if we were going to track down Klaus Jaeger, I wanted to get out of the house before I had to invent a story about where I was going.

Marcy answered on the second ring. "Are we going to look for my grandfather?"

"I'll meet you at the bottom of the Lawe Street hill."

I coasted down the hill and stopped beside her. "What am I supposed to say to these people?"

"If it's an old man, you tell him you're his grandson, shock him, gain the upper hand. If it's someone younger, you ask for Klaus Jaeger."

Before this excursion, I had never been afraid of the unknown or of a new adventure. I had what Dad called unwarranted self-confidence that would one day get me in trouble. I had the feeling that today could be the day.

"You have addresses?"

"Yes, let's start in Appleton. No need to go farther if he's the one."

Marcy led me past the downtown area to a house on Spring Street, between Durkee and Drew streets. The house was large and white, with a wrap-around veranda. Two nice cars were in the driveway. If this was my grandfather's house, he had done well after dumping Gram. I hated him already.

Marcy hopped right up the front steps and rang the doorbell before I could catch up. Shortly, a woman a few years younger than Mom, opened the door. She had permed blonde hair and wore a dress that looked expensive. Reading glasses hung from a chain around her neck. "Yes? Are you selling cookies or something?"

Marcy cut her eyes to me, waiting for me to speak.

"No ma'am. I'm wondering if Klaus Jaeger lives here."

"Why do ya want to know?"

"I think I'm related to him."

"You little shit! Did your parents send you? Looking for money, are ya?"

"No, no, I just wanted to meet him."

"Well, you're too late by five years. He's dead, and I'm not paying off any more people."

"Oh, okay." Gram told me he was a bad man, a dead man. With a daughter who paid people off when they came looking for him.

I turned to leave but Marcy said, "Was he married to Abigail Jaeger?"

"Don't know who that is."

"My grandmother," I explained. "She married Klaus Jaeger in 1924."

The woman cackled. "My husband wasn't born till 1926. He was a scoundrel, mind you, but he's not who you're looking for. He died young —cancer—but had enough time to piss off a whole lotta people."

Husband. Definitely not who we're looking for. "I'm sorry about that. Sorry we disturbed you."

She cocked her head and gave us a suspicious look, as though something else had dawned on her. "Leave the past alone. It can only bring heartbreak."

As we rode away, Marcy said, "She's covering up her husband's evil deeds. She thought we might be his illegitimate kids."

"Wrong guy. Gram's husband is probably buried in Utah or Wyoming."

"Don't you get it? Her husband could have been your uncle, Gram's son."

I drew a family tree in my mind. "No, there were only two birth certificates in Gram's records—my mom and uncle Edward."

"We need to know for sure. Then we can work on the Bruno's."

I followed Marcy over the College Avenue bridge and through Kimberly toward Little Chute. I was doused in sweat from my hairline to my sneakers by the time we reached the home of a second Klaus Jaeger. This house was a modest single-story home with a fake brick veneer on the front, just like my house. No cars were parked in the driveway but a detached garage was closed so maybe a car was in there.

I pushed the doorbell button but didn't hear a chime. After a minute, I opened the screen door and knocked. I was about to leave, thinking no one was home, when Marcy nudged me aside and said, "Maybe he doesn't hear well."

She pounded on the door. That did it. A man who could have been Gram's age opened the door. Wispy gray hair slid around on a polished dome of a head. He hadn't shaved in a while.

"Who are you?" he said.

"Are you Mr. Jaeger, Klaus Jaeger?"

"Who's asking?"

"Your grandson."

He didn't seem shocked. He cackled and said, "Well, look at you."

"So, you are my grandfather?"

"I wondered if you'd ever find me. You the eldest?"

"No, sir, I'm second, the middle child."

"Then you must be the smartest. What's your name?"

"Eddie, after your son, Edward."

"Oh yeah? We'll have to talk about that." He held the door open. "Come on in."

I had been taught not to enter a stranger's home or car, so I hesitated. This guy could be an axe murderer. *Bad man, dead man.* Gram had lied about his death but may have told the truth about his character. Marcy gave me a shove and I stumbled over the threshold and into a home that smelled of old people and mildew.

We followed him into the kitchen.

"I've got lemonade, not homemade but not bad. Go on out to my patio and take a load off. I'll bring the drinks."

Okay, he didn't herd us into a dank cellar or anything so maybe we'd be safe. Marcy could run as fast as me, so … we sat on ratty, folding lawn chairs. He brought us glasses of lemonade, possibly poisoned.

"I saw Abby's obituary in the paper. She was a pistol, that one. Firecracker if God ever made one. Her passing made me sad, but I didn't think your mom would want me at the funeral."

"Because you ran out on her and Gram, right?"

"Well, your mom probably thinks so." Jaeger's mouth kept moving after he was done talking, like there was something in there that he couldn't swallow.

"You married Abigail Sachs in 1924," Marcy said. "We have the marriage certificate."

"I'm sure you do." Jaeger nodded and chewed his cud.

"We have the birth certificate for your daughter, Abigail Katherine."

"I figured Abby would name me the father. Made sense." Jaeger nodded slowly.

"Because you *were* their father," Marcy said.

"This one reminds me of Abby." He pointed a gnarled finger at Marcy. "What's your name, child?"

"Marcy."

"Well, Marcy, that's where the story gets complicated." Jaeger massaged his forehead with three cigarette-stained fingers.

"What's complicated about it?" I asked.

"You sure you want to know?"

"We came all the way from Appleton on our bikes to find the truth." I sounded self-righteous.

"You mind if I smoke?"

I shrugged. He lit a Pall Mall and coughed.

"Abby got pregnant by a married man, fella who was our boss at the mill."

"Bruno!" Marcy shouted.

Jaeger jerked in his chair, as though the sound of the name was an electric shock. "That's right, Bruno Kratz. They weren't in love, mind you. Abby had the affair to keep her job."

"He raped her?" Marcy exclaimed.

"Closest thing to it. But Abby wouldn't give up the baby."

"Because of her Catholic faith," I said.

He pursed his lips. "We'll get to that part." He took a drag and coughed again. "Abby wanted the baby to have a name so we cooked up a scheme. She and me were good friends, but not, ah, boyfriend-girlfriend. So, I married Abby and agreed the baby could have my last name. Then it became a problem."

"How so?"

"She had promised to get a divorce right after the birth, but the church wouldn't let her. We were stuck married to each other."

"The Church had no right to stop you," Marcy said. "You should have gotten a divorce in the courts."

"Abby wouldn't do it. The Church would have kicked her out, and she couldn't let that happen. It would have exposed everything else."

Everything else. We sat in silence a while, digesting this news, the news that Bruno Kratz was my grandfather, at least by birth.

"Gram had a second child, Edward. Was that Bruno, too?"

"Couldn't tell ya. I was long gone. I moved to Nebraska and stayed there three years. Got married where I didn't think anyone would catch on. Came back to Appleton and went to work in a different mill so no one would bother me."

Poor record keeping back then, or lost records, or just an attitude of don't-stick-your-nose-in-other-peoples'-business, would have shielded Gram and Klaus from discovery. "So, Edward might have belonged to Bruno Kratz and he might have belonged to someone else." Saying it out loud clarified it for me.

"That's about it."

"Abby never told you?"

"I stayed away from Abby. I had committed whatchamacallit …" He touched a knotty finger to his temple. "Bigamy. That's it."

"Well, your name is on Edward's birth certificate, too."

He shrugged. "That's alright with me."

"Edward drowned when he was ten."

"Awfully sorry to hear that."

"Whatever happened to Bruno? Did Abby report him?"

"Nah, he ran off to Michigan. Or was it Minnesota? I get 'em mixed up."

"Did you ever live with Abby and her parents?"

"No one could live there with her. Old Joe wouldn't have it."

"You knew Joe, Gram's, ah, Abby's father?"

He shook his head. "Now there's more explaining to do. Don't mind me sayin' it, that man was good for nothing and sick in the head. Made Abby go to work when her sister ran away from home."

"Adeline? The nun?"

"That's what she did? Went to a convent?"

"Monastery, down near Milwaukee."

"Uh huh. Found a way to hide." Jaeger lit another cigarette from the butt of the last one.

"Joe couldn't work because he only spoke German," I said.

"Yiddish."

"Hunh?"

"He spoke Jewish German."

"Oh my God, Old Joe was Jewish?" Marcy smacked her forehead with the heel of her hand.

"Sure, Joe and Lottie, too. That's why they left Germany. Didn't you know?"

"How would I know?" I asked. "Gram went to Catholic Church every Sunday."

"You ever hear her say words like schlep and schmuck?"

"Oh, yeah. She spoke German a lot."

"Those are Yiddish words, not German. What about klutz, schlemiel, schmooze, glitch, and spiel."

"Yes, all of them. And scheisskopf."

"Shit head." He laughed. "That one is German."

I thought about Joe and Lottie being Jewish. Where would Jews fit in the Appleton class system? Bottom of the heap I figured. My history lessons gave me another thought. "Hitler didn't come to power until 1933. They must have come to America long before that, so why leave Germany?"

"Abby was maybe three or four when they came here. It was already bad for Jews in Germany, and it looked like war was coming, so Joe and Lottie took the two youngest kids and came to America.

Two youngest kids? Is that what he said?

"Then Hitler came to power, and Joe was convinced Hitler would conquer the world so he never left Abby's house. Didn't want Hitler to find him. I don't know what it was like to be Jewish around here, but Old Joe was taking no chances."

Gram was born in Germany. She never told me. "You said they came with the two youngest children. Did you mean that Abby had older siblings?"

"Two brothers, Adam and Aaron, were left with their parents in Germany. They sent Joe, Lottie, Adeline, and Abby first chance they got. The parents and the boys intended to come later."

"The *parents* and the boys? I'm confused."

Marcy had been listening closely. She reached the punch line before I did. "Joe and Lottie were Abby's grandparents."

"That's right. Guess you didn't know that, either."

"Grandparents!" I shrieked. "Joe was my great great grandfather. I thought it was strange that he and Lottie were in their late forties when Gram was born. Did the rest of the family ever come to America?"

Jaeger coughed some more. "Like I told you, Abby and I kept our distance. Neither of us wanted to get caught, but I did go to Joe's burial. 1943, I think it was. I thought enough time had passed that no one would get suspicious of me. She was with a boyfriend by the name of Bill. They seemed happy. Anyway, Abby said her parents and brothers never got out. She assumed Hitler caught them and sent them to the gas chamber."

"That's why Old Joe was so paranoid. That's what you meant by sick in the head?"

"Well, sure, paranoid as hell. But Abby kept close watch on him around her kids, thought maybe he was doing things to them."

Old Joe was a predator! I had always thought Gram's life had been filled with Job-like tribulations. Now I thought her past must have been unbearable. How could she have been so cheerful and optimistic? She was truly a saint. A Jewish saint?

"Wait, Abby's grandparents were Jewish but she was Catholic."

"Old Joe made Abby pretend to be Catholic, didn't want anyone to know there was a Jewish heritage. She hid her parents so the priests wouldn't suspect."

"Gram's whole life was a lie."

"No, Eddie," Marcy said. "It was a sacrifice, to save her grandparents here, and her parents and brothers who would come later."

"Be careful with this information," Jaeger advised us. "Some people won't want you to know. Some people won't want to remember."

Another long spell of silence engulfed us. I wasn't sure my immature brain could hold everything I'd learned, but the other Klaus Jaeger was a loose thread. "You said you got married in Nebraska. Did you stay married, have children?"

"Sure, we were very happy until Martha passed about a year ago. We had one son, named Klaus, Junior. He lived over in Appleton but died young—cancer."

***

"Where've you been? You missed dinner," Dad said.

Mom, Dad, and Danny all held beers. Carla had her chin propped on a hand, looking worried. Their plates were cleared of whatever they had eaten for dinner.

"Looks like I missed another celebration."

"This is the real celebration. Danny has his contract." Dad beamed like a spotlight.

Danny waved a wad of paper. "Rookie league team in Davenport, Iowa."

"Close to my hometown," Dad said. "It won't pay much, but the team will feed him and give him a place to sleep."

"He'll have to get a real job after the season." When it came to her children's dreams, Mom was the practical buzz-killer. At least the contract would get Danny off the family payroll.

"If I have a good rookie league season, they might want me to play winter ball in Florida or Mexico," Danny said.

It didn't seem fair that a kid who barely made it through high school, a kid I taught to hit the slider, was going to travel the world, while I was stuck in a parish on the frozen tundra of the Green Bay Diocese.

They seemed to have forgotten one huge obstacle to Danny's plan. I sidled up to the table, put a hand on Danny's shoulder. "What about the Army? The draft notice?"

"Took care of that this afternoon," Dad said. "Went down to the draft board and showed them the baseball contract. They're going to find someone to take Danny's place."

Thank God. "Oh. Bad luck for some other guy."

"Did you know that when the Continental Congress was building an army to fight England that conscripts could pay somebody else to take their place? It was perfectly okay."

"I didn't know that."

"It's always been the way in America."

I wondered where Dad had learned this historical tidbit. Certainly not in his tiny, rural Iowa high school. The oddest thing about his graduation picture was that all six graduates were boys.

I had hoped to pry my tuition money from Dad's stingy grip but it wasn't the right time. I'd have to wait for another chance to share what I'd learned about Gram's history from Klaus Jaeger, too. A dish of tuna casserole, now cold, sat on top of the stove. Rather than reheat the oven to eat dried-out noodles, I made a PB&J, poured a glass of milk, and went to my room. *Someone should invent an easier, quicker way to reheat food.*

As I climbed the stairs, I heard Mom say, "No telling where he's been today."

"I hope he's gotten attached to that girlfriend," Dad said.

"He should help us celebrate," Mom said.

Did Mom think we were some perfect TV sitcom family that materialized out of thin air with no history at all? Bruno absconded after Edward was born, when Mom was two or three. Maybe she didn't remember him and assumed that old guy in Little Chute was her father. No one at the dinner table seemed to know that we were one-quarter Jewish.

I'd never get into the seminary if Monsignor Muller found out.

Maybe Mom did know, and that's why she rarely went to Mass. What about Dad? If Mom knew, did she tell him? If Mom didn't know, he wouldn't have found out from Gram. She spent her whole life hiding her past and carrying out the ruse.

My feelings about Gram were as complicated as her history. As my protector and caregiver, I couldn't have loved her more. As a woman willing to do anything to sustain her grandparents and her children, I couldn't have had more respect. She didn't complain, she didn't shirk responsibility, she didn't run and hide like her sister. She faced life with a tenacious spirit and almost won.

But, as a woman who had allowed herself to be abused by Joe, by Bruno, by the Catholic Church, and even by my father, I had mixed feelings. I was certain Marcy would have behaved differently in Gram's shoes. Gram was a strong person, but she deferred to men. Where Gram had been compliant, maybe fatalistic, Marcy would have been defiant, would have charted her own course through life, men be damned. Was that selfish?

The bigger question was, what would I do with what I knew?

Chapter Twenty-four

After Dad and Danny left for work, I rode my bike to the northside drugstore to pick up the pictures of Danny and Father Mac cavorting in the school hallway. Mom no longer asked where I was going or with whom.

A different woman, young and busy, worked the cash register and showed no interest in who I was or what pictures I had taken. With the pictures safely tucked into a pocket, I hurried out of the store before she could remember I was the kid with the nasty pictures.

I made the mistake of taking the shortest route home, down Lawe Street to cross the river, and had to pump hard to get up the steep hill. Then I cut across Maple Street and was stymied by two dump trucks and two trucks pulling trailers on which sat yellow front loaders, one big and one huge.

I stopped next to a truck blocking Gram's driveway and asked the driver what was going on.

"Gotta clear this lot," he said. "You can watch, see if you want to drive one of these machines when you grow up."

"Clear the lot. What does that mean?"

"Knock the house down and carry the trash and rubble away. Gonna build something nice and new."

I tried to stifle my burgeoning hysteria. "Who gave you permission to knock it down? That's my Gram's house."

"I guess your gramma sold it, son. Our construction company owns it."

Not Gram. Mom. When she met the realtor. Did she know they were going to knock down her childhood home?

An operator fired up the larger machine's diesel engine with a roar, spewed plumes of black smoke. He backed it off its trailer, pivoted in the street, and headed for the house. I dropped my bike, ran past the rumbling behemoth, and blocked its path, my feet planted and arms spread. The operator stopped when the scoop was a yard from my chest.

He leaned out of the cab. "Get outta the way, kid."

"There's some kind of mistake," I yelled over the roar of the engine. "You can't knock it down."

"No mistake, kid." He revved the engine, and the machine lurched forward.

I put a hand on the gigantic steel claw inches from my chest as though I could stop it with pure guts. "Wait for me to run home and ask my parents if this is what they want."

"Too late for that." He waved a hand, and two workers in hard hats advanced on me, grabbed either arm and lifted me off the ground as easily as a rag doll. They set me down on the sidewalk.

As the front loader lowered its scoop and eased up to the corner of the house, tears bubbled and my chin quivered. The driver stepped on the gas, and the machine crashed into Gram's house with a deafening roar. I covered my ears. "No! No! No!"

The house folded inward like a cardboard box, and the attic and roof collapsed. The machine backed up, came at it from a flatter angle, and pushed the debris into the front yard. Edward's lonely bedframe slid toward the gaping hole in the roof.

My tears flowed freely.

The front loader pushed the outer wall into the downstairs bedrooms. Gram's dresser tumbled out, into the scoop, and the driver dropped it on the driveway. Another push and the commode fell out of the attic and crashed onto the driveway. The tub Dad had installed hung by the thread of a wood beam.

The truck driver came beside me and placed a hand on my shoulder. "It's called progress, son. Gotta get rid of these old eyesores."

As I watched in horror, the smaller front loader moved around the larger machine and down the driveway to the backyard. Now what? Without a pause, without slowing at all, the machine rammed Gram's apple tree and knocked it down. *Not the tree, too!* Men with chainsaws moved to the fallen tree and began cutting it into logs.

I couldn't watch any more. Gram was gone, and now the symbol of her dogged fight with fate was being demolished. She had been wiped from the earth, erased from history.

I pedaled home, part sad and part angry as hell. I stormed into the kitchen to find Mom at the table, drinking coffee.

"Do you know what they're doing to Gram's house?"

She didn't bat an eyelash. "Have they started clearing it?"

"How could you let them do that?"

"We sold it, Eddie. Had to," she said in a weary voice.

"You could have sold it to someone to live in. I could have seen it every day when I went by. Now there's nothing left of Gram."

She rose from her seat and came around the table to hug me. I backed away, didn't let her touch me.

"No one was going to live in that old thing, Eddie." Her tone had changed from consoling to stern.

"Doesn't your childhood home mean anything to you?"

"It was a terrible place, full of bad memories. You have no idea what I went through there and no right to question my choices."

I wondered if she'd been molested by Old Joe. "I want it."

"What?"

"I want the money you got for the house. For my tuition."

"We didn't get anything for the house, just eleven hundred for the lot after they deducted the cost of knocking down the house."

"You paid to demolish your childhood home?"

"Talk to your dad. We have priorities, Eddie."

"Your priority is gin."

She raised a hand to slap me.

I danced around her like Muhammad Ali dancing around Sonny Liston and went to the big planter in the living room with her on my heels. I pulled the fake fronds out but the planter hid no bottles. "Where'd you hide the bottles?"

"Don't judge me, Eddie. I've cut back so I don't have to hide the bottles."

Liar. "Everybody makes their deals, everybody gets what they want except me. Well, I know your childhood secrets, and I know this family's secrets, and I'll blow our family apart if I don't get my tuition." I started for the stairs.

"Some secrets have to remain secrets, Eddie."

"Tuition, Mom. Make it happen."

I stuffed the pictures in my winter boots. I had enough pictures to fill a photo album. I had enough pictures to blackmail everyone who stood in my way.

***

I waited for Mom to get in the shower downstairs before I gathered up the pictures of Bauer and Alice and Danny and Mac, put them in a brown lunch sack, and headed to the library. I used the public phone outside the library to call Marcy and ask her to meet me.

When she arrived, I handed her the sack of pictures. I had the crazy idea that I would confront Danny before he left to play baseball. Maybe he could work on his problem while he was away.

"Can you keep them all at your house? I don't want Danny finding any more pictures."

She dismounted, popped the kickstand, and took them. "I don't have to hide anything at my house. My mom gives me privacy."

"My parents sold Gram's house to a contractor who knocked it down today."

Sadness flickered in her eyes. "That's awful. I'm sorry, Eddie."

"My mother acts like it doesn't matter to her. She grew up in that house but she didn't shed a single tear over it."

"Adults lose their emotions when they grow old. Life beats them down until they have no feelings. I see it with my mother, too."

"Makes you want to stay a kid, doesn't it?"

She nodded. "I looked for Bruno Kratz in the phone book. Lots of Brunos and a few people named Kratz, but no one named Bruno Kratz."

"Jaeger said he moved out of state."

"One of the Kratzes could be related."

"I think I've had enough family history for a while."

"I might ask around."

She rode away, and I rode home.

Mom was waiting for me, sweating.

"Where did you go?" she asked.

"The library."

She eyed me up and down. "You didn't get any books."

"Couldn't find anything I wanted to read."

"Have you lost your camera? I haven't seen it around your neck lately."

Why does she care about my camera? "Marcy borrowed it." I shifted my weight. "To take family pictures."

I started upstairs and she stopped me. "Wait down here until your dad gets home."

This was getting creepy. "Why?"

"We have to talk."

I slumped on the couch. A chill ran down my spine and settled in my gut like an iceberg. We were finally going to have it out. Was I prepared to expose everything I knew?

***

Dad glared at me as he stormed into the living room. "What do you think you know?"

Mom was worried about my camera, but I assumed Dad was talking about his hobby of stealing church money. "All I want is my fare share, tuition for the Salvatorian Seminary."

"Nothing is fair here," Mom said.

Dad shot her a look that could kill. "We have to do what's right for the family, Eddie. You're not the most important person."

"I need to pay the tuition tonight. We're out of time."

In two long strides, he was above me. He grabbed my shirt in two fists and lifted me off the couch. I was nearly as tall but not as strong as Dad.

"You have no idea what you're doing to this family." His left eye blinked rapidly, his tick no longer a twitch or a quiver. He threw me down on the couch and turned to Mom. "He only thinks of himself."

She blew out a big sigh. "Give him Abby's money, Frank. He earned it."

I suspected that Mom capitulated because of secrets having nothing to do with money.

"We can't give that money away, Kat."

"You know how to get more."

Dad's shoulders slumped. He looked from me to Mom and left the room.

Mom and I stared at each other like enemies. "How can three children be so different?"

"Isn't it obvious? We each have different parents; Danny has Dad, Carla has you, and I had Gram. I have to look out for myself now."

When Dad returned, he was waving a check in the air, as though drying the ink.

"This won't be good till next week. Make sure they know that."

He flicked the check at me, and it landed, face up, in my lap. The amount would only pay the Diocese seminary tuition. I realized that in some ways I was no better than Dad. I, too, wanted status and a stage on which to show off.

"This isn't enough."

"Take it or leave it."

"Thank you," was all I said.

Hands on his hips, he said, "I've got to dress for the finance committee meeting."

I was afraid to move but knew I had to get out of there before Dad changed his mind. I slipped the check into my pocket and rode my bike to the rectory. The housekeeper let me in.

"They'll be glad to see you," she said.

She waved me to a seat in the small office where I had first met Father Mac. As bad luck would have it, Father Mac entered the room with the registration forms. The junior priest had been tasked with filling out the forms and collecting the tuition check because the Monsignor and Father Bauer were gathering with the finance committee in the card room across the hall.

"I'm glad it turned out this way," Mac said. "If I'm still around when you get ordained, we can spend time together."

I must have looked nonplussed because he added, "You'll be at some parish in the Diocese. Close by."

My desperation overcame my hopes. Like Marcy said, everyone has dreams that don't come true. "Of course, Father."

As we filled in contact information, family information, emergency information, and medical information on the registration forms, our door remained open to the heated and audible conversation across the hall. I wondered if Father Mac wanted me to overhear it. The Monsignor was upset by the shortfall in Sunday collections and challenged Dad to come up with ways to increase the income.

For his part, Dad was inventive. He urged the priests to be more demanding of contributions in their sermons, ushers to be more aggressive about holding the wicker baskets under the noses of parishioners who didn't contribute, taking note of those who either didn't contribute or contributed little so they could be solicited in person.

"Times are hard for people right now, but they need to make this church their priority," Dad said.

Of course, an increase in donations would be to Dad's benefit. If the donations exceeded the norm, he could skim the surplus. I thought he should have raised the flag and addressed the issue weeks ago. *There I go again with better criminal ideas than adults.*

"We're cursed with the poorest parish in the city," the Monsignor said.

The poorest Parrish in the city, and yet it generated $24,000 a month in income. I could only imagine what the Diocese total was. The Catholic Church had a license to print money.

Father Mac and I finished the registration forms, and I handed him the rubber check. "Can they wait to cash that next Monday? Times are hard for people right now," I mimicked Dad's words.

Father Mac gave me a knowing look. I was sure he knew what was going on with the Sunday collections. "We'll put this in the mail. That will take a few days. Then they'll process your paperwork before depositing the check, so you should be okay."

"I appreciate that. Thanks."

He left to take the forms and the check somewhere, and I used the opportunity to eavesdrop from the open door.

"I'd like a count after each Mass this Sunday. I want to know which ones are causing the problem." The Monsignor sounded stern, frustrated, and irate. I feared he would get to the bottom of his problem like a dogged detective.

"I think they're all just a bit short," Dad said.

Of course, he'd suggest that. His method was to skim a little cream off the top from each Mass.

"Well, we'll find out this Sunday. I'll have someone count the Masses that happen before yours. We need to get to the bottom of this issue."

That meant Dad would only be able to steal from his Mass and any later Masses.

Father Mac returned with a smile on his face. "All posted and ready to go." He stuck out a hand for me to shake. "Congratulations. You're a seminarian."

He led me past the card room to the back door. No one was smoking in the card room, no one was drinking beer, no one was playing cards.

At home in my room something didn't feel right. It looked as if someone had rummaged through my things and tried to put everything back where it belonged but didn't get it quite right. Danny was in his room, packing to join his baseball team. I supposed he had taken one last tour of my room to check for more pictures.

Chapter Twenty-five

Mom and Dad packed Danny off on a bus to Davenport, Iowa. I didn't go along to see him off; I wasn't invited. Mom was still blubbery when they got home. They had nothing to say to me, and I had nothing to say to them. I wished I was still living at Gram's house.

When I left on my bike, they didn't ask where I was going. I was looking out for myself.

I met Marcy at the library, but books weren't on my mind.

"Someone searched my room last night. Could have been Danny making sure he's in the clear while he's off playing baseball, but my things were left in different places this time. Mom acted weird and asked about my camera. She was sweating as though she'd had to exert herself. We don't have air conditioning so it gets hot in my room."

"The camera and pictures are safe at my house."

"My parents paid my Diocese seminary tuition last night, so I'm finally set."

She shrugged, maybe in defeat. "I hope you know what you're doing."

"Today I want to see Gram's grave."

"You know where it is?"

"St. Joseph's cemetery."

The oldest cemetery in the city perched on the north side of the river, a couple of miles downstream from Dad's mill. We rode under an archway into a perfectly manicured garden, with shrubbery, flower beds, and acres of green grass that would make any golf course jealous. The pastoral scene was ruined, however, by mausoleums, spires, statues, and grave markers, both upright and flat.

"Do you know where her grave is?"

"No idea. We'll have to look for it."

"It's new, so the dirt will still be fresh and in a mound on top of the grave. C'mon, we'll go this way."

She pedaled down a paved path, past a three-tiered bird bath and between pruned shrubs shaped like bullets and almost as tall as trees. Around and around the paths we rode searching for a fresh grave. We found a couple of them in an older section, but there were other peoples' names on the markers. Finally, at the outer edge of the cemetery, an area without trees for shade or flowers for decoration, a less expensive part of the cemetery, I presumed, we found a fresh grave with no marker, sitting between somebody named Walter Vander Linden and someone named William Verhoeven, a couple of Dutch guys. Vander Linden passed in 1962; Verhoeven in 1955. It was like the men had been waiting for Gram.

"Those cheap shits haven't bought her a marker," I said.

"You think this is it?"

"Has to be. It's the only fresh grave without a marker." A pang of guilt pierced my chest. I may have taken the money for tuition that had been meant for Gram's marker. If I hadn't taken the money, maybe Gram could have had a spot in the shade.

We set our bikes down and eased up to the grave.

"This is it," Marcy said. "I feel her spirit." She stood close to me and wrapped an arm around my waist. There was no one I'd rather have been with at that moment.

Leave it to Marcy to feel a spirit.

I felt anger. I'd steal the money in the garage to buy a marker if I had to. "Let's get out of here."

"We should come back with flowers," Marcy said.

"I want to come back with a marker."

"Is Edward here?"

I hadn't thought about that. We checked the nearby graves but didn't find Edward Jaeger. "He might be buried with Joe and Lottie Sachs. A family plot."

"Then why is Gram here by herself?"

"Looks like the cheapest plot they could find."

"This is a Catholic cemetery," Marcy said. "Since Joe and Lottie were Jewish, they might be buried somewhere else."

"Gram was the only one pretending to be Catholic. She shielded everyone else."

"Means that the rest of the family is buried somewhere else."

***

"I went to visit Gram's grave and it's unmarked, like she's some pauper."

Mom dropped her magazine in her lap. "We'll get to it, Eddie. First things first."

"Why is her grave in the middle of nowhere, between two strangers?"

It was written on her face: fear that divulging her secret would diminish my esteem for her, followed by the relief that comes with the disclosure of secrets that had corrupted her soul like a cancerous tumor. Secrets are like handcuffs.

"She's not with strangers. She's where she wanted to be."

"Between Walter Vander Linden and William Verhoeven?"

She looked at me the way teachers look at star students, waiting for them to figure it out for themselves.

So I worked it out. *William Verhoeven is Bill Verhoeven.* I snapped my fingers. "Uncle Bill."

"He was the love of her life."

"Who's Walter Vander Linden?"

"A friend of theirs at the mill."

I scratched my head, following elusive thoughts, unravelling mysteries like a cat pulling a loose thread from a ball of twine. "Why isn't Edward, your brother, buried with Gram?"

She lowered the footrest on the recliner like she was going to stand, then thought better of it. "He died long before Gram met Bill."

"So where is he?"

She ran a hand through her hair, buying time, thinking through possible answers. "I don't know where he's buried. I was too young to know what was happening when he drowned. You know he drowned, I guess."

She's hanging on to one last secret, as though she would lose her identity if all her secrets were no longer secrets. Or she may be protecting me from a Jewish stain that would alter my vocation. But I've been baptized, had my confirmation, my first communion. I won't be swayed. "I read his obituary at the library. I've been to the spot where he fell into the river. You and Gram never visited his grave?"

"No, it was too sad for Gram."

The Jews were literally buried in the past. "Well, I'm going to find him."

She did get out of the chair and wrapped her arms around me. "Oh, Eddie, the curious one. Live your life, not the past."

I couldn't remember the last time Mom hugged me. This was a real hug, love pouring love from her to me. "It's okay, Mom, we're almost there. Danny is off to play baseball, I'll be off to the seminary, and you'll have Carla to keep you company. The past will finally be behind you."

Mom choked back a sob. "Yes, Eddie, we're almost there."

We were nowhere close to "there," wherever "there" was.

***

When Dad got home, he slammed something down on the kitchen counter.

"The hospital is knocking our door down, the funeral home is coming after me. That check I wrote for Eddie is going to bounce higher than a kite."

"Stop payment on it. Make Eddie stay here," Mom said.

Thirty minutes ago, I was her precious son, and now I'm the least important thing on her list. Screw it. I'll climb into that garage attic and steal what I need.

"I have until Monday before they pass the check, so I have one more Sunday to save our lives."

I sat on the stairs, listening, for a long time but I heard no more arguing. What I did hear was the drone of the evening news, so I shimmied down three steps to watch. In the nightly update on what was now openly being called a war, the Pentagon announced it would require five hundred thousand troops, fighting for five years, to defeat barefoot rebels in black pajamas. The chill of fear made me shiver; In four years I'd be draft age. The talking head went on to show film clips of the Students for a Democratic Society chanting, "Hell, no we won't go!" "The organization attracted 25,000 protestors to a demonstration in Washington, D.C." The last film clip showed forty students at the University of California in Berkeley burning their draft cards. Opposition to the war seemed to come mostly from privileged kids with deferments while blue collar kids were doing the fighting on their behalf. The country was being ripped in two along economic class lines.

***

In the last game of the season, we played for the championship against the team that had beaten us in the opening game of the season—the loss attributed to my slow feet.

Leading by two runs in the bottom of the last inning, with two outs and a runner on second base, our coach gathered us on the mound for final instructions. Their next batter would be the kid who hit the ball over my head to win the first game of the season.

"Let's end this right here. Give him somethin' to hit, make him put the ball in play," the coach told Allen. To the rest of us, he said, "You do your jobs and we'll be champions."

As I trotted back to my place behind home plate, the batter took vicious practice swings in the on-deck circle while sneering at me. “Gonna be just like last time,” he warned.

“Nah, this time I’m behind the plate, not in the outfield.”

“You couldn’t catch your momma if she was wearing combat boots. That’s why you’re a catcher.”

I didn’t let him get into my head. I squatted behind him and signaled Allen we were ready for play. Allen did as he was told and laid a fat pitch down the middle of the plate.

The batter swung so hard his helmet flew off and he dropped to one knee in the batter’s box. The ball was struck hard, but the batter had overswung and topped it. Like a laser beam it streaked along the ground as the batter got to his feet and stumbled toward first base.

Our shortstop nearly made the play. The ball kicked off the heel of his glove and ricocheted toward the left field foul line. The runner from second base scored easily, reducing our margin to a single run. Our fielders chased the fleeing ball like cops chasing a purse snatcher. Timmy, our left fielder, finally smothered the ball in foul territory as the batter rounded third base. I tossed my mask aside and planted a foot on either side of the plate. Timmy’s throw was strong and true but a few feet short of the plate, nearly striking the runner as he began his slide.

Ignoring the sliding runner, I concentrated on the ball, caught it with two hands and dropped to my knees. The batter crashed into me, spikes first and the impact flipped me onto my back. The crowd groaned and gasped. Time stood still as we waited for the umpire’s call. When the dust cleared, the umpire reached down and turned my glove over to reveal the ball resting on my chest protector.

He punched the sky and bellowed, “He’s out!”

The crowd went wild. Lying there for a glorious second, Marcy’s screams of joy came from behind the home plate screen. One of my dreams had come true: we were champions.

The once-cocky batter skittered away. He knew what was about to happen and so did I. Before I could stand, I was mobbed by fourteen delirious teammates, crushed at the bottom of a delicious dogpile, covered in red dirt and borrowed sweat.

When my teammates pulled me to my feet, I discovered that my uniform had been ripped again, and my thigh had been sliced by the batter’s spikes.

I limped to the dugout to remove my equipment for the last time and heard a gasp from behind me. Marcy pointed to the blood on my uniform pants. "You'll need stitches."

"Let's get you to the emergency room, young man," the coach said.

"No way, Coach. I'm leaving it just like this for everyone to see."

He shook his head in the way fathers do when they disapprove of what their son is doing but are proud of it too. "I'll walk him home and explain to his dad," he said to Marcy.

The coach and I walked to my house, and Marcy walked to hers. On the way, he recounted our successful season and my game-winning play.

When Mom saw the blood on my leg, she shrieked, "What happened?"

"I blocked the plate and got spiked."

"He won the game for us and the championship on top of it," the coach said.

Mom took a step to hug me and thought better of it. She placed her hands on either side of my face, careful not to get dirt and blood on her sundress and gave me an air kiss. "I'll fix you up."

I guess I was her precious little boy again.

Dad shuffled up to the coach. "What's going on?"

As Mom and I headed to the bathroom for some surgery, the coach said, "I feel pretty smart now. He was the best dang catcher in the league. He wasn't afraid of the bat, foul tips, or sliding runners. No wild pitches got past him and no runner ever stole a base. Made the All-Star team."

Dad made a sound that betrayed a combination of disbelief and confusion. "I'll be darned. Has he learned to hit?"

"He got a couple hits, a lot of walks. Good eye on the kid. Every team needs someone to do the dirty work."

"Baseball must run in the family genes." Clearly, Dad was shocked.

"Just had to find the right spot for him," the coach said.

"Will we have to pay for the uniform?"

"Nah. We'll get new uniforms next season."

As Mom swabbed mercurochrome on my cut, I sulked. Even after winning a championship and making the all-star team, Dad was unimpressed with me. "He hates me."

"He doesn't hate you."

"Well, he doesn't love me like he loves Danny."

Mom wrapped an arm around me. "Danny is like him, but you're different is all."

"I'm not like anybody."

"Danny will never have a life of his own; he'll always be Dad's boy, doing what Dad wants. But you'll have your own life to live."

Chapter Twenty-six

"Wear a jacket today," Dad said.

"Why? It's going to be warm." I had chosen dress slacks and a short-sleeved shirt to wear under my cassock as usual for summer Sundays.

"Just obey me once in your life, Eddie."

I took a light spring jacket from the coat closet downstairs.

"Good. Let's go." Dad was dressed in his navy-blue suit, ready to usher at Mass.

As we walked to church, I thought about how today was different. I had heard the Monsignor say during the contentious finance committee meeting that a priest would watch, Dad count the collections. Something was up with this father-and-son-walk-to-church-together game plan.

Before I went into the sacristy, Dad stopped me and placed his hands on my shoulders. "Meet me at the counting room as soon as Mass is over. Don't waste time jaw jacking with the priest. Understand?"

I did understand. He was going to enlist me in his criminal scheme. Throughout the Mass I thought about how wrong it was for an altar boy to help his father steal collection money to pay seminary tuition and become a priest. I was no better than a priest who dated a nun or a priest who fooled around with young boys. I was already one of them. I could rationalize my behavior with the single thought that what Dad had already stolen would pay Gram's hospital bills and burial expenses, maybe get her a headstone.

Father Bauer was in his usual hurry to disrobe, so I rushed to beat him out of the sacristy and to the counting room.

When I slipped inside, Dad said, "Put your jacket on."

He came around the table with the small collection bag in his hands. He pulled my jacket open and stuffed the money into my armpit. "Clamp down on it." He pulled my jacket shut and zipped it up.

I felt foolish in a zipped-up jacket in the middle of summer. "There's got to be another way, Dad."

"There isn't. This is to cover your tuition check."

"We're going to get caught, Dad."

"Get out of here before a priest shows up. Go out the front with the crowd and don't talk to anybody. Keep your head down and walk fast.

Hide the money in your room until I get home." He made the backhanded shooing motion.

I did as I was told. As I passed the rectory, Father Bauer stood on the front steps, smiled, and waved. I had to remember to wave with my right arm, my free arm, so I didn't drop the money.

At home, the money went onto the top shelf in my closet. I delivered the Sunday papers as though life were normal. Dad didn't get home until mid-afternoon. Father Bauer had helped him count the money from the rest of the Masses and kept it to make the deposit himself. Dad's skimming had come to an end. He never mentioned the money we had stolen that day although Mom knew he was going to do it. Maybe he didn't want her to know he had use me as the getaway driver. I was certain the priests knew what we had done, and it ruined the rest of my day. I couldn't eat, I couldn't read, I couldn't sleep.

***

Dad came into my room before I had even gotten out of bed.

"Where is it?"

I pointed to the closet. "Top shelf."

He found the bag and said, "Good job."

So, the first time Dad complimented me was when I had gotten away with what he had stolen.

A call from Marcy roused me from my stupor. "Let's find Edward."

We met at the bottom of the Lawe Street hill. "Riverside cemetery is huge and public," she said. "Anyone can be buried there."

It wasn't easy to get there because Peabody Park sits between the downtown area and the cemetery on Appleton's east side. We had to ride all the way to Wisconsin Avenue and come around the north side of the park to get to the cemetery even though the cemetery was just across the river from Marcy's neighborhood.

Unlike the spiritual feel of St. Joseph's cemetery, Riverside cemetery had a military ambience. A long brick building with archways over driving paths stood at the front, like a gateway to a Civil War-era Army fort. A brick tower, like a perch for lookouts, rose from the center of the building. We rode through an arch and stopped to get our bearings. Unlike the park-like appearance of St. Joseph's cemetery, Riverside cemetery seemed in need of grooming. The grass was sparse and pockmarked with bald spots. The grave markers were covered in mold and mildew.

“Must be where poor people are buried,” I mused.

“That makes sense for Old Joe and Lottie and Edward, doesn’t it?” Marcy said.

It did make sense, but how would we find three graves among the thousands spread out before us on a hillside? Marcy turned a circle, looking for a hint or plotting a strategy.

“There are windows in that entrance building.” She pointed. “Maybe there’s an office where someone can help us.”

We rode back to the building and found a door to the interior. An elderly man wiped dust from a countertop. In Appleton, all the clerks seemed to be old.

I stepped forward. “Hi, we’re looking for our family plots but don’t know where to start.”

He pointed to a large book, like a photo album, lying on a table off to the side. “That book is pretty near up to date. How long ago were they interred?”

“1930s and ‘40s,” I said.

“Then we’ll have ‘em in that book.”

We went to the book, turned the pages, and ran our fingers down the lists of names. With every turn of a page, I was certain we’d find the right names, but we never did. After twenty minutes I gave up.

“If they’re not here, where would they be?” I asked the old guy.

“St. Joseph’s?”

“Tried that.”

“Were they Catholic? There’s the little one, St. Mary’s.”

“No, uh, not Catholic.”

“Lutheran? They’ve got one of their own.”

“No, not Lutheran, either.”

The man pulled on his chin, as though stroking a goatee although he was clean shaven. “Mind me asking, were they Jewish?”

I was ashamed of how hesitant I was to admit that my relatives were Jewish. “They might have been. We’re trying to figure that out.”

“Uh huh. There’s an old Jewish cemetery out on Roosevelt, offa Meade. It’s called Moses Montefiore. Immigrant Jews came here from Germany before the war. Most of them left for Chicago or other big cities after the war. But the cemetery is still out there.”

“Were they hiding here?” Marcy said.

“I suppose you could call it that. Looking for a better life same as the rest of us.”

We thanked the man and headed to the Jewish cemetery.

Moses Montefiore cemetery was a small place, tucked behind two enormous trees in a residential neighborhood. Maybe the Jews were hiding even after death. A worker was clearing fallen tree debris when we rode through stone pillars and onto the property. He nodded to us and went about his work. We dropped our bikes and walked the rows out of respect for the dead.

A few rows deep in the property, we found what we were looking for —the graves of Joseph and Charlotte Sachs, side-by-side, and two empty plots over, the grave of Edward Jaeger.

"Two empty plots," Marcy said. "For Gram and your mom, right?"

"Maybe. But Gram hid a different way, and Mom is like some neuter gender animal."

"A religion is just a label, Eddie. Ever since Abraham, people have believed in a single God, so who cares how they do it?"

"Catholics care."

"Yeah, that's the problem."

I understood that Mom and Gram never visited these graves because they were in the Jewish cemetery. I squatted beside Edward's grave and said a prayer. I only knew how to say Catholic prayers. I hoped he didn't mind. The grave markers for Old Joe and Lottie had the Star of David carved into the stone, but Edward's marker was devoid of any religious identifier. Old Joe and Lottie weren't hiding anymore.

***

Mom was preparing dinner and Dad was reading the newspaper when the doorbell rang.

"What the hell?" Dad said.

No one ever came to our front door. He levered himself out of Gram's recliner and went to the door. I stood to the side, looking past him. When he opened the door, I was terrified to see Monsignor Muller and Father Bauer standing on our porch, wearing their black suits and white collars. There could only be one explanation for why they had come to our house.

"Come on in. Come on in." If Dad was quaking in his boots, he wasn't showing it.

The priests came into the living room and stood stock still with hands clasped in front of their crotches, like the men at the funeral home.

Mom appeared. "Can I get you something to drink?" She was the one who looked scared.

"No, thank you," Father Bauer said.

"How about a beer?" Dad manufactured a fake smile.

"This isn't a social call." The Monsignor's tone was all business. "We need somewhere to talk."

"Just have a seat in the living room." Dad gestured to the couch. "Gail is cooking in the kitchen."

The priests glanced at me, perhaps wanting to exclude me or protect me, but they moved to the couch and sat.

"Go see about dinner, Kat, and keep Carla in her bedroom." Dad turned to me. "Go on upstairs."

Dad may not have anticipated a home visit, but he seemed prepared to duel with the priests. I climbed the stairs to my usual listening post and waited for the fireworks to begin.

Father Bauer was the leadoff hitter for the priest team. "The collections at the Masses you and I counted yesterday were normal, what we expect during the summer."

"Good. A lot of people are back from vacations," Dad said.

"But the collections at the two early Masses, the ones you counted by yourself, were way off. We barely got any money from those Masses."

"Hardly anybody at those Masses."

"That's not what Father Mac said."

Dad shrugged. "They all looked down and out to me."

"The shortfall from those Masses was exactly what it cost for your kid's seminary tuition." Monsignor Muller had run out of patience with Bauer's softball approach.

"Really?" Dad sounded genuinely surprised. "That's quite a coincidence."

The Monsignor slid to the edge of his seat. "Why don't you just admit you took it, Frank?"

"Because I didn't. I don't need your money to take care of my family." Dad wasn't giving an inch.

"We've had shortfalls in collections for more than a month now," Bauer said, "ever since you started bringing the money home to make Monday morning deposits."

"You've been getting rich off the church, Frank," Muller said.

"That's an outrageous accusation," Dad sounded genuinely offended. "I've made you money for years. Without me, you wouldn't have new Pontiacs to drive around, fancy vestments for Mass, or a new floor for the gym."

"Corporate donations you arranged. Maybe you've been skimming money off the top." The Monsignor wasn't going to let Dad go in that direction. "We'll check with the donors and find out."

"You ungrateful people should be ashamed of yourselves." Dad's volume had risen.

"We're grateful for what you've done, Frank." Bauer sounded conciliatory, the good cop to Muller's bad cop. "But we've had to discontinue the food bank. If school were in session right now, we wouldn't be able to pay the electric bill."

"We're going to subpoena your bank records," Muller said.

"You're really making me angry now." Dad was red in the face.

"We'll report it to the police, and they'll come with a search warrant," Muller threatened.

"Send all the cops you want." Dad bared his teeth like a rabid dog. "They won't find a thing."

I gasped. Cops would find plenty.

Bauer heard me and glanced up before I could slip behind the wall. I gave him a look—watch what you're doing here, Father. Don't want it to come back and bite you.

He couldn't know that we had pictures of him kissing a nun, but he didn't want me to accuse him of misbehavior in front of his pastor. "We don't want it to come to that, Frank." Bauer said it as he watched me. Then his gaze went back to Dad. "We just need the money back. Think about it overnight and come to us tomorrow. Confession will be good for your soul."

"I have nothing to confess." Dad stood, a sure sign he was kicking them out.

"You're no longer the treasurer," Muller said. "I've asked Gil Barton to take over and examine all our records."

"That guy couldn't fog a mirror. He'll give you all kinds of wrong information."

"I trust him. You're no longer a member of our church, Frank. You can try to find another place to defraud, but no church in Appleton will have you."

Bauer stood, having gotten the hint. "Consider your son's future. His attendance at the seminary is on the line here."

"You're barking up the wrong tree," Dad said. "I'm offended you would come to my home and say these things. I think it's time you left now."

"Let's give Frank some time to think about this," Father Bauer said.

The Monsignor rose, and Dad opened the front door.

Muller stepped onto the porch. "I can have you excommunicated, you know."

There it was, Muller misusing the church's power again.

"I don't care anymore," Dad said to their backs.

I had to give Dad credit; he stood up to the priests. That took balls. But now my future was in jeopardy again, just when I thought I had nailed it down.

"The next visit will be from the police," Muller yelled as he walked to his car.

Dad closed the door, and Mom rushed into the room.

"Oh, my God, Frank. What are we going to do?"

"Nothing to worry about, Kat. I have it under control. In a day or two it'll be over."

I didn't think Dad had much of anything under control. The shopping bag in the garage attic would be easy for cops to find. The check he wrote for my tuition was from his personal account. Once again, I felt that Dad wasn't a very good crook.

***

I wasn't the only reason Dad had stolen money but I thought I could fix my part. Call me Raskolnikov. When I was certain Mom and Dad were asleep, I snuck out of the house and into the garage. With a flashlight as my only illumination, I climbed into the attic, crawled to the stash of cash, and counted out one thousand dollars, the amount of my seminary tuition. I put it in a brown lunch bag. The rest of it was Dad's problem.

When I crept back into the house, Carla was standing at the end of the hallway, in front of her bedroom door, like a specter in a horror film. She had a question on her face.

"I'm giving my tuition back so I can stay here with you."

She smiled.

Chapter Twenty-seven

I knelt beside Gram's grave, the paper sack of money at my side. The mound of dirt had begun to subside. I hoped that grass would find its way over the top of her.

"You've always given me the best advice, Gram. Now I need to know what to do about the money Dad stole."

I looked up at the clouds, fluffy, white and moving slowly across the pale blue sky. I wondered if heaven was truly in the heavens.

"I helped Dad steal it. My conscience is bothering me, and the priests are onto him, so I need to do something, you know?"

I sat back, rested my butt on my heels. If there were aliens in some other solar systems, I figured heaven would have to be in some far-off galaxy.

"The money missing from Sunday's collections is exactly the amount of my tuition, and Dad paid the tuition with a check from his own account, which wasn't very smart. If they subpoena his bank records, that check will be right there for the detective to see. You'd call Dad a *dummkopf*. They don't seem as sure about the earlier shortfall, which is for your bills and a grave marker. but it's all in the garage attic where the cops are sure to find it if they get a search warrant. *Dummkopf*!"

No insight came from Gram, no little voice in my head. Maybe I should have brought Marcy with me to feel Gram's spirit.

"What I'm thinking is that I give the priests one thousand dollars, the amount missing from Sunday's collections, and the priests will stop looking for the other money they can't prove was stolen." *And Dad will be impressed with how I fixed the family problem.* "Dad said my tuition check will bounce without the money we stole on Sunday. That means I can't go to the seminary and I can't become a priest. But he has plenty of cash in the attic to cover your medical and funeral bills and a grave marker."

I stopped because Gram would know where this conversation was headed. She said nothing.

"You're right, Gram, I want to use some of your money to pay my tuition and then Dad won't be able to pay your hospital and funeral bills and won't be able to get you a marker for a while. So, I need your blessing to use your money for the seminary."

I waited but felt nothing. No saint appeared; no thunder rocked the benign sky; no bolt of lightning struck me. I figured Gram saw through my scheme and was frowning at me in disappointment. I wanted to play the hero by returning the money I stole without suffering any consequences for my sin.

Gram left it up to me. I wish she had said something.

***

The housekeeper let me in and led me to the same small room I'd been in twice before. I'd begun to think of the room as my prison cell.

When he finally appeared, the Monsignor had Father Bauer and Father MacMillan in tow. Muller took the seat Father Mac had been in when he tried to fool around with me while Bauer and Mac leaned against the wall and folded their arms across their chests.

I choked back a gob of sorrow. "I came to return the money I stole." My eyes downcast, I handed the bag to the Monsignor.

He unfolded the top, peeked inside, and handed it over his shoulder to Bauer. "Count it," the Monsignor said. "Does your father know you're here?"

"No, he'd kill me if he knew." I was pretty sure that was an accurate statement.

"But you stole it, not him?" He cocked his head like the nuns did when they didn't believe your excuse for not doing your homework.

I did help steal this money and I'm sorry I helped. "Yes, Father, I stole it. He told me the tuition check was going to bounce higher than a kite, so I stole it."

Bauer finished counting. "It's a thousand. Exactly what we're missing from Sunday's early Mass collections."

"Your father was the only one in the counting room." The Monsignor needed convincing.

"He had to use the bathroom, and while he was gone, the ushers dropped the money off, and I took what I needed." I looked at Bauer. "You saw me leave, Father. I had it under my coat and I thought you were going to stop me."

"I did see him," Bauer said. "He was wearing a jacket even though it was hot outside."

The Monsignor sat back and sighed. "Is that all you stole?"

"Yes, that's all of it. Just what I needed for the seminary."

"That takes care of it, doesn't it?" I had the feeling Bauer didn't want me to open any cans of worms.

"The tuition check cleared and yet you have this money to return today." That was MacMillan adding his two-cents worth.

I had to act surprised at this revelation although I guessed Dad deposited some of the stolen money to cover the check. My mouth flopped open and my eyes tried to pop out of their sockets.

Bauer looked nervous. "I'll check with the bank to be sure—"

MacMillan cut him off. "Frank's been stealing for weeks. We've been short every Sunday. That's how he covered the check."

I had an impulse to shoot the little weasel down with my information about his homosexuality, but I didn't have the pictures with me, and it would mean ratting on Danny, too.

I had an inspiration that may have come from Gram. "No! They sold my grandmother's house. That's how he paid my tuition. He should have told me. I wouldn't have stolen more money."

The priests exchanged glances, a silent conversation.

"So, your father didn't steal any other money?" Bauer asked.

"No, Father, he'd never do that."

"He's always been good with the money," Bauer said.

The Monsignor gave him a cross look. "Afraid I don't believe that." He slapped his knees and stood. "You're saved by the bell, Kovacs. We're going to keep that tuition money so we'll have most of our money back. No need for the police."

"You have no right to that money. It was Gram's."

Father Bauer frowned a warning at me and gave me a slight shake of his head. *Don't go there.*

The monsignor flicked a hand, unperturbed by my protest. "We'll revoke your registration at the seminary because we can't have a liar and a thief becoming a priest. Not in this diocese."

My blood froze. This was not how it was supposed to go. I was supposed to confess my sin like a good Catholic and get absolution from a compassionate priest. "But I only stole because I want to be a priest. I made a mistake because I didn't need it and I'm sorry."

"Maybe God will forgive you, but I won't," the monsignor said. "You'd be a disgrace to the priesthood."

A disgrace? What about Bauer and Mac? "Fine. I don't want to be like you people anyway."

"We made the mistake by supporting you, Mr. Kovacs, but now it's rectified. Unless you have more to tell us."

God help me, I thought about ratting on Dad. But Gram had made sacrifices for her family and I could make one for mine. "There's nothing more to say, Father."

"Then we're done here." The Monsignor stood to leave.

"Wait! What about my Dad? He did nothing wrong."

"He did nothing wrong," Bauer echoed.

"The Kovacs family isn't welcome in our parish," the monsignor said. He left and Mac followed him like a puppy trailing its master. Bauer paused and tilted his head: Was I going to rat on him?

I gave him a sad shake of my head. He could make his own deal with God.

From the age of nine, when I had become an altar boy, I had wanted to wear the priests' frocks and lead the solemn, complex, awe-inspiring services. I had wanted to be important, and thus I understood my dad's compulsions. I had never imagined myself as a lay person, had adopted the church, or had been adopted by the church, as my real family. Now I'd been set adrift, like a life raft on the ocean.

Bauer left with the paper sack of money I'd returned.

***

Mom was struggling to cook dinner, and I'd have been amused by her clumsy and inept efforts if I hadn't been waiting nervously for Dad to get home from work.

He came in the door and made his dismissive shooing motion again, as though I were a fly buzzing the picnic food. "I need to talk to Mom."

"I need to talk to both of you," I said.

"Out, Eddie."

I gave them a loud sigh and moved around the corner into the living room, but I did not go upstairs. I quieted my breathing so they couldn't hear me listening to them and leaned toward the doorway as though the sound waves would be stronger if I were a foot closer.

Something made a soft plop on the kitchen table.

"Is that all you could get?" Mom asked.

"Two hundred," Dad said. "I needed one more Sunday."

"No more Sundays now."

I thought they were done because neither of them spoke for a couple of minutes as Mom stirred pots and grunted over the challenge of cooking. She tapped a spatula on a pot. "Sell Danny's car."

"What's he going to drive when he comes home after the season? He'll need to drive to a job."

"We'd have enough if you hadn't bought that car."

"We'd have more than enough if you hadn't made me pay Eddie's tuition."

"Well, get that money out of the garage before the cops turn up or you'll be in jail, and I'll be in the poor house."

That was my cue. I came around the corner into the kitchen. "The cops aren't coming." I thought they'd be happy to hear that.

"Not now, Eddie." Mom wasn't happy.

"I fixed our problem with the priests."

"You talked to them?" Dad started toward me, his jaws clenched. "Don't meddle in my business, Eddie."

Mom placed a hand on Dad's arm, holding him back. "How did you fix it, Eddie?" She seemed to want to know but was afraid to find out.

"I gave them back the money we took last Sunday. I told them I stole it for my tuition and then it turned out you were able to cover the check."

"What?!" That was Dad.

"Oh my God, Eddie, you have no idea what you've done." Mom wrung her hands.

"I got you off the hook is what I did. I thought you'd be proud of me."

Dad grabbed his head in two hands and squeezed. He growled something that sounded like "Awrgghefgaw."

"It's okay. They're going to keep the tuition money so they won't call the cops or subpoena your bank records."

Dad released his head and stood still as a cemetery statue, staring at me. He held his eyelid still with his fingers.

Mom was animated, her arms flailing around. "We needed that money, Eddie," she screeched. "We needed that money."

I thought they were thinking of me and my future. "They revoked my registration at the seminary, but that's a sacrifice I'm willing to make for the family. Like Gram did. I'll stay here for high school like you wanted me to do. Danny and I can help with Gram's bills."

Dad sank onto a kitchen chair, propped his elbows on the table, leaned his head against folded hands.

"The money wasn't for Gram's bills," Mom whispered.

"Her marker can wait a while. I know how to find her grave."

Mom looked at Dad and seemed to fold into herself like a cheap cardboard box.

"Sit down, Eddie," Dad said.

I took a seat across from him.

He drew a deep breath. "You know that Danny was drafted by the Army, right?"

"Sure. You got him out of it because he was playing baseball. No wait, someone took his place."

"Baseball didn't get him a deferment and there wasn't anyone to take his place." He pursed his lips, seeming to summon the courage to continue. "A doctor was going to give him a medical deferment—a 4-F classification—for a heart murmur. But the doctor costs money, a lot of money."

Danny has a heart murmur? "Why does a doctor's visit and a physical cost a ton of money?"

Mom and Dad traded looks. I guess Mom got elected.

"Because Danny doesn't have a heart murmur."

They let that sink in. When I figured it out, I got mad. "You bribed the doctor."

"We will if we can come up with the money," Mom said. "You've screwed that up now."

This sounded like another of Dad's hare-brained schemes. "You think the draft board will believe that a professional baseball player has a bad heart?"

"The doctor knows how to make it work," Mom said. "It's something he does for good families."

Good families? "You risked going to jail for Danny but you made me steal my tuition. You made me risk getting caught to protect yourself. I know where I fit in this *good* family."

"You weren't going to die if you didn't go to the seminary, Eddie." Dad spat the words at me. "But Danny could die in Vietnam."

"Doing his duty, as you did. Fighting to spread democracy, you said."

"You want to play high-and-mighty with me? Poor people are just pawns in the government's hands. The only kids fighting over there are poor kids. Why should rich kids live and poor kids die? We aren't the only poor family the doctor is helping."

I understood his logic, Marcy had made the same point about *Animal Farm*, but the nuns had taught me that the end doesn't justify the means. "You stole from a church to pay a bribe. What kind of people are you?"

"We've been making contributions to that church for years so your father could be a big wig." Mom's voice had a sharp edge. "We just wanted some of it back." She jutted out her chin and tilted her head back, a haughty gesture. "I'm not even Catholic, for Christ's sake. Abby never had me Baptized."

So Mom gave Dad the idea to steal the bribe money. "I know you're Jewish, that we're all part Jewish because of Old Joe and Lottie. I found their graves and Edward's too."

"You're a sneaky little shit, you know that?"

"Oh, you have no idea."

"You've got a mouth on you, kid." Dad turned to Mom. "What's he saying?"

"I'll talk to you later," Mom said.

The dufus doesn't even know his wife is Jewish. "Gram was born a Jew, faked being a Catholic to protect her family but didn't bother to have Mom baptized."

"There you go. I'm nothing." Mom raised her hands and let them fall into her lap.

"Jesus Christ, you never thought to tell me?" Dad pointed to himself.

"What does it matter? It's just a religion my grandparents belonged to."

Mom apparently knew part of the secret, knew that Old Joe and Lottie were Jewish but didn't know they were her *great* grandparents. I wondered if she knew she was the product of rape.

Dad looked at Mom as though he didn't know who he had married. Poor Dad: the war got in the way of his baseball career, and then Mom got in the way of his Navy career, and then kids got in the way of a good life. He may have started to steal church money to pay Gram's bills and my tuition, but when Danny passed his tryout, the temptation to relive his life was too much to resist.

I had time to think about the bribe, and I remembered the day Marcy and I were riding bikes behind the College Avenue storefronts. I had forgotten about Dad's visit to an unfamiliar doctor because he never seemed sick and no one mentioned it. "Berger."

Mom was about to say something, but Dad stopped her. "The less you know the better."

"It's not my fault that you got caught."

"Sunday's take would have been enough if your mother hadn't made me pay your tuition."

"Up yours, Frank," Mom said.

"They were already onto you, Dad. They had a priest guarding the money. Then you wrote that stupid check from your own account. Don't blame this on me or Mom."

"You always think you're smarter than everyone else but you're not. If you have to know, I put half the Sunday money in Gram's account, along with the proceeds from her house sale and moved the whole amount into my account. It looked like the money for the tuition check came from Gram."

So, he's not a total *dummkopf*. He had it rigged, and that's why he was so brash with the priests. And his scheme lined up with the story I told the priests. I am to blame after all, and Danny is going to die in Vietnam.

Mom moaned. "We're so short now, we'll never make it up, Frank. What are we going to do?"

"We're out of time." Dad ran a hand through his hair. "I'll register Danny for the local community college."

"He'll hate that," Mom said. "Will the team take him back next season?"

"We can only hope," Dad said.

"Married men are exempt. He could marry one of his girlfriends." The devil made me say that.

Mom laughed so hard she had to brace herself against the table to keep from falling over.

***

Mom didn't laugh when Dad came home from work the next day.

"I couldn't get him into the community college." Dad grabbed a beer from the refrigerator, drained half of it, and slumped onto his usual chair at the kitchen table.

"I thought Fox Valley Community College would take anyone," Mom said.

"He's not dumb, Kat," Dad said. "We're too late to register for the fall semester. The classes are full up." Dad drained the rest of his beer.

"Community college should have been our backup plan all along. He could always have dropped out later."

"It was a last resort, Gail," Dad said.

"Gail," not "Kat."

"It was Eddie's idea a long time ago. You should have listened."

I could have said, "I told you so," but I leaned against the wall and bit my tongue. Mom pulled her bottle of Beefeater's Gin out of the cabinet and made herself a cocktail.

"Is it too much to ask what we do now?" Mom asked.

"I'll have to go back to the doctor and see if we can get some kind of payment terms," Dad said.

"Or find a doctor in Milwaukee or Madison who does it cheaper." Mom capped the gin bottle and put it back.

"How would I find somebody in those places? We don't live there."

"Sell Danny's car. He doesn't need it to play ball."

"The car's not in great shape, and it still wouldn't be enough."

Danny's car! I hadn't included the cost of Danny's car when I added up what Dad had stolen. If he hadn't bought the car, Dad would have been able to pay the doctor. It wasn't all my fault.

The numbers spun in my mind like the three wheels on a slot machine and when they stopped, they were a three-way match and I had won the jackpot—Dad had begun stealing before Danny's draft notice dropped in his lap. The scheme to bring the money home and deposit first thing Monday morning had been his way to scam the priests for a car. If he had only stolen money for Danny's car and my tuition, he might have gotten away with it. But Mom nagged him, Danny got drafted, and Gram died, and he was overwhelmed with money crises.

Chapter Twenty-eight

"I really messed up this time," I said to Marcy. So far, I had only had the guts to tell her that Dad and I had stolen my tuition money, and in a fit of remorse, I had returned it.

"You did the right thing." Marcy sat beside me at the end of the Woolworth's counter, sucking strawberry float ice cream through her straw. "The priests are hypocrites. Use the pictures to blackmail Mac and Bauer and they'll get you back in the seminary."

I hadn't touched my float although I was sure her mother, Judy, had made them especially good for us. Judy was at the other end of the counter serving customers, and empty stools flanked us, so we could talk without being overheard.

"That won't work, because Monsignor Muller will block me."

"I know you had a dream, Eddie, but maybe this is a sign. It's not normal for men to deny their attraction to women, which is why priests are all queer. I know you like girls because I know you like me."

If I were going to make it through life, whether as a priest or as a layman, I would have to find a way to prevent blushing at every provocative remark. This time the temperature of my entire body rose to fever heights. "I do like you, and we know Bauer likes Alice, so all priests aren't gay."

"Bauer and Alice are exceptions. You have other flaws, Eddie—you are mean, vengeful, and far from modest and humble. You aren't priest material, and that's a good thing."

When you live to achieve a singular dream, you are fragile and in danger of total collapse. "Well, I'll have four years of high school to figure it out, and then I can be a Jesuit if I still want to be."

"If that's what you want." Marcy said it breezily, sure that I wouldn't waste my life as a priest.

Her doubt stuck in my craw like curdled cheese.

"I'm not our only problem." I told her that at first, I thought the money was to get Gram a place and the care she needed. Then Gram died and I thought the money was for her bills and my tuition. "He wasn't stealing for any of those things."

"He bought Danny a car."

"He stole a lot more than that." If I couldn't tell Marcy, I couldn't tell anyone. "I'm sorry I haven't told you our whole story. Danny has been drafted by the Army."

"Oh, no. I remember how bad I felt when Ray got drafted."

"Your brother got drafted, too?"

"Yeah, I guess they ran out of men and started drafting kids."

"Is he in the Army? I thought he was working at the lumber supply store."

"He is. He got out of the draft because he's the head of household."

"What's a head of household?"

She gave me another of her sad looks. "I didn't tell you our whole story, either. My parents are divorced, but I don't tell anyone."

"I thought your dad came around and stayed with you sometimes."

"He shows up and they try to get back together, but they fight and he knocks her around. Then he gets drunk and forgets I'm his daughter, not a bar girl, and she kicks him out again." She sounded as though she had delivered that speech many times and now considered her situation to be normal for a poor family.

I had felt a bond with Marcy because we both suffered some parental abuse, but sexual abuse at the hands of her father put Marcy in a completely different category. A priest was the only predator in my life. Gram had been abused by her grandfather and her boss and Marcy had been stalked by her father. What was wrong with these men?

"I'm so sorry, Marcy. You said there were other men around, too."

"Mom calls them auditions but no one ever gets the part, so Ray is the head of our household."

"How did that get Ray out of the Army?"

"Mom found a lawyer who knew how to work around the draft rules. He told Dad to pay support in cash and Mom to spend the cash, never deposit it in a bank, so it would look like Ray's income was our primary means of support. That meant that Mom and I are Ray's dependents. Heads of households with dependents are exempt from the draft."

"Dad thought he had found a way to save Danny from the draft. He intended to bribe a doctor to say Danny has a heart murmur for a 4-F medical deferment. Now he can't pay the bribe and he can't keep stealing from the church."

"Eddie!" She grabbed my arm and shook me. "Danny doesn't need a heart murmur; he's a homo."

Confusion seemed to be my normal state around Marcy. "So?"

"So the Army doesn't take homos. They can't have homos in the barracks or in foxholes, for crying out loud."

I didn't know whether to laugh or cry. "Are you sure? How do you know?"

"The lawyer explained all the ways to get out of the draft. If you aren't brave enough to defect to Canada or Sweden, there's 4-F, conscientious objector—that one's really hard to get—head of household, or, voila, you're a homo."

My euphoria faded as I thought about what it would mean if Danny admitted he was a homo. Dad would never believe it, would never allow it.

"It won't work," I said. "We can't have a homo in our family."

"Don't tell your parents. Get Danny to do it himself."

"Is it moral to evade the draft and make some other schmuck go to Vietnam and get killed?"

Marcy scoffed. "A homo would never survive basic training. Is that moral?"

I paced in a circle, thinking it through. "Do you know this lawyer? Where his office is?"

"Sure, we went there a couple of times, to do all sorts of paperwork and signatures and everything like that."

"How much did it cost?"

"I don't know; I think he let us pay over time."

Last I knew, there was a bundle of cash in the garage attic. Maybe my screw-up could be fixed. "Okay, let's go."

Marcy led me to a wood frame storefront on Superior Street that had once been an ice cream parlor.

"If we were brave kids at dentist's appointments, Dad would bring us here for an ice cream cone," I said.

"That was year's ago," Marcy said.

The peeling white exterior paint had faded to a sickly gray. A wooden plaque announced the offices of J. Peter Klein, Esq. Family Law. When we opened the door, a bell rang over our heads and a heavyset woman came out of a back room.

"We don't need no Girl Scout cookies," she said.

Everybody thinks we're selling cookies since we're not old enough to be doing anything important.

"We're not selling anything," Marcy said. "We'd like to see the lawyer."

"I don't suppose you two have an appointment since you're still in diapers."

No one was waiting in the two hard-backed visitors' chairs. "Doesn't look like you're all that busy," I said.

"Hush, Eddie." Marcy elbowed me and turned to the woman. "The lawyer did some work for my family, Jablonski. He'll remember me."

The woman propped her hands on her hips. "I remember now. That one was tricky. What would this visit be about?"

"Draft dodging is what the lawyer called it when I was here before."

The woman looked at me and frowned. "You get a draft notice? That's got to be a mistake."

"No, ma'am," I said. "This is about my brother, my older brother."

"Is he with you?" She craned her head to see around us and peered through the front windows, which wasn't easy for her given the thickness of her neck.

"Danny, that's his name, had to work today, but he's hoping we can get some information for him."

"Uh huh, and why does he think he can evade the draft?"

"Danny is a homosexual."

"Ah." A sympathetic smile replaced the woman's stern façade. "That one's tricky, too. The big brother was too embarrassed to come down here himself so he sent his little brother to get the scoop."

"I guess you could say that," I said.

The woman turned toward the back room and shouted, "Pete! Get your ass out here and talk to these kids."

"Bring those chairs over to the table." She pointed.

We carried the two visitors' chairs to a folding card table along the wall. She opened two folding chairs and sat in one.

A moment later a man emerged carrying a sandwich and a glass of soda which he set on the table. He wiped his hands on a napkin and shook our hands with old world formality.

"Peter Klein at your service." A trace of Germany lingered in his accent and reminded me of Gram. "You've met Dolores." He indicated the woman.

"I'm his wife, his clerk, his office manager—"

"And ball buster," Pete added.

Pete shoved horn-rimmed glasses up a narrow nose in the craggy face of a man who should already be retired in Florida. He smoothed thinning black hair with a liver-spotted hand and took a seat. "What can I do for you?"

Pete ate his sandwich as I talked. "Danny is nineteen and a pro baseball player who has a bachelor boyfriend in our neighborhood. He's been drafted by the Army and has a reporting date coming up fast. We're hoping you can get him a deferment for being homosexual."

"The smart kids who saw this coming enlisted in the Navy or Air Force. Those branches of service are full up now, so the kids began to declare themselves gay—that's what they call it these days—gay. A few months ago, all a kid had to do was walk up and say, 'I'm queer' and he'd be excused. But a lot of them were fakers so now you have to prove it."

"We have pictures," Marcy said.

Pete recoiled like he'd been slapped. "Does your brother know you have pictures?"

"Yes, and they're irrefutable evidence." I sounded like Perry Mason.

"Will his, uh, boyfriend, submit a statement in support of Danny's claim?"

"We have pictures of the two … doing things," Marcy said. "And pictures of Danny fooling around with a queer priest, too."

Pete scratched a spot above his ear, maybe the location of a switch to turn on his brain.

"Being a baseball player is a complication. The Army doubts that gay men can be professional athletes."

"Danny is handsome and well-built and in great shape, so I think his boyfriend went after him the same way a girl might chase a good-looking guy," I said.

"Like you and your girlfriend here," Pete smiled sweetly. He sat back and finished his soda. "Maybe Danny isn't gay but fell into a relationship with a predator. It's easier to get kids a deferment if they're flamers."

"What's a flamer?" Marcy and I said simultaneously.

"A flamer is a gay man who flaunts his sexuality, exaggerates his female nature."

"That's not Danny." I was certain of that.

"Our best hope is for Danny to get a statement from his boyfriend, and a statement from the priest would be icing on the cake. The Army generally trusts priests."

Marcy snorted. "What else?"

"He'll have to make a statement of his own and see a psychiatrist. The American Psychological Society has classified homosexuality as a mental disorder, like schizophrenia. The condition has to be diagnosed and treated by a shrink so the Army doesn't end up with sick people."

"Wow." I didn't realize Danny had a mental illness.

Pete nodded. "You might be surprised to know that various homosexual acts are illegal in Wisconsin."

"Would Danny get arrested if he admits to being gay?"

"Doubtful. Homosexuals are criminals, but the law is rarely enforced. Getting caught could result in a fine rather than incarceration."

"Can you set him up with a psychiatrist? We don't know one."

"Sure, I have a guy who will be helpful. Bring the witnesses to me and I'll depose them."

"We'll bring the pictures, too," Marcy blurted.

Pete cleared his throat. "The pictures aren't enough. If Danny can convince the shrink, I'll fill out all the paperwork for him. Then he'll take the package of documents to the entrance station in Milwaukee and he'll have to convince the Army doctors that he's not faking it."

Danny would have to run a perilous gauntlet and endure pain at every step in the process. "What does all this cost?" I asked.

Pete looked at Dolores. "What do you think, honey? Three depositions, a psychiatrist appointment, paperwork, coaching."

Dolores squinted at us with the cunning eyes of a rabid fox. "Give the kids a break. Twelve hundred fifty dollars."

A break? Are they ripping us off because we're desperate kids? I hoped the money in the garage attic hadn't been spent on anything foolish like burial and hospital bills. "Okay. We'll bring the witnesses and your fee."

"Bring Danny," Dolores said.

***

"Joe Morada and Father MacMillan are never going to admit they're homos," I said as we pedaled down Appleton Street toward Oneida Street. "We may as well ask them to confess to murder."

"With Danny's deposition and the pictures you can twist their arms to cooperate."

Thinking out loud, I said, "Joe has some kind of white-collar job at the Fox Cities paper company he won't want to lose, and Father Mac could be defrocked."

"But you have to choose between saving your brother or stopping Joe and Mac from abusing other boys."

I remembered a catechism lesson during which we discussed the moral quandary of the individual good versus the collective good. The collective good was supposedly more important, and I felt that Marcy, the social justice revolutionary, was leaning in that direction, but a parallel occurred to me, and I hit my brakes. "Danny is the Mockingbird.

I can't let anyone kill the Mockingbird."

A flush of excitement spread from my face to my chest. I could do what Dad couldn't do and get redemption for screwing up Dad's scheme to get Danny out of the draft. Could I save the mockingbird without Mom or Dad learning how I did it? It didn't take a genius to realize that I had to act fast or my parents would do stupid, crazy things to save their kid from Vietnam.

***

After dinner, I sat in my bedroom chair beside the window with WABC in New York blaring in my headphones, trying to stay awake until everyone was deep asleep. I kept nodding off and was roused hours later by the DJ's exuberant voice. I had no idea what time it was but the sky was dark and cloudy with no moon and no promise of dawn. *Now or never.*

I tiptoed down the stairs, through the living room and the kitchen, and out the back door. I smelled the rain that was on the way, entered the garage through the side door, and inhaled the oil and gas fumes in the creepy space. My heart raced for fear that Dad had spent the stolen money as I climbed the ladder to the attic and crawled to the deteriorating TV. To my relief, two sacks of cash huddled inside. Either he hadn't gotten around to paying Gram's bills, or he hadn't given up on the fantasy of buying Danny a medical deferment.

By the light of my plastic flashlight, I counted the money and arrived at a total of seventeen hundred dollars. Dad had brought the last two hundred home from work, probably borrowed from buddies, so he had stolen two thousand before we stole the one thousand that I returned to the priests. How in the world did he think he could steal that much without the priests noticing?

I sat back on my heels and ran the numbers one more time. I had forgotten to include the eleven hundred for Gram's lot, so he stole three thousand from the church and borrowed two hundred at work. Gram's house sale money covered my tuition, and I thought that ironic or apropos or something. Maybe that's why she had nothing to say at the graveyard. Mom said that if I hadn't returned the thousand I helped Dad steal, he would have been two hundred short, so the doctor had asked Dad for thirty-five hundred dollars, an obscene amount given Dad's modest income. But if he hadn't paid my tuition, he'd have been able to pay the crooked doctor, so it *was* all my fault.

I had one last chance to make this right. I felt self-righteous as I carried twelve hundred fifty dollars to my room.

Chapter Twenty-nine

While Dad went to pick Danny up at the bus depot, I slipped away to my room and stuffed the lunch bag of bills down the front of my shorts. No one paid any attention as I pulled the phone around the corner and down the basement stairs to call Marcy. No one stopped me when I left the house.

Marcy met me at the top of the Lawe Street hill and I handed her the money to hold for me.

Dad and Danny arrived home in time for dinner. Dad grabbed a beer from the refrigerator, drained half of it, and slumped onto his usual chair at the kitchen table. Danny's usual cockiness was replaced by slumped shoulders and downturned lips. Danny grabbed a beer and wandered around the kitchen. "A week! A week is all the playing time I got. I was just settling in."

Mom stepped next to Danny and wrapped an arm around his waist. Dad tried to pump him up with lies about how there were still options to get him out of the draft but I don't think Danny believed him. He picked at his food, the way Carla does when she's pouting.

***

I rapped courteously on Danny's bedroom door.

"Nobody home."

"You need to talk to me, Danny. I can save you from the draft."

I heard rustling and then the door cracked. "What are you talking about?"

"Let me in. You don't want Dad to hear what I have to say."

Mom and Dad had the sound up on the living room TV. Danny's brow furrowed as he thought about the things I might possibly have to say. After straining a few hundred brain cells, he relented and let me in.

Danny had a desk in the corner, intended for homework but rarely used, and I sat in its chair.

He plopped on his bed. "What do you know about the draft?"

"Remember the night you and Joe heard noise in his backyard and you scrambled around to see who it was? You came into my room all hopped up about it."

Danny bounced to his feet, tensed for violence. "I knew it was you!"

"That was me. I saw what you did."

"You don't know what you saw." His fists curled into tight balls.

"I had seen you and Joe once before in his driveway after one of your visits to him."

"You a pervert, a peeping Tom, creeping around the neighborhood?"

"It's okay, Danny, I'm not going to tell Dad."

"There's nothing to tell. Get out of here." He took a menacing step toward me.

"You think you destroyed the evidence, but I have more."

"Evidence? What are you talking about?"

I reached for the pictures, then thought better of it; I didn't have to throw them in his face just yet. Instead, I held up two hands, signaling him to be calm. "Danny, homosexuals don't have to serve in the Army."

"You calling me a faggot? I'm no faggot!" He grabbed the front of my shirt with both hands and lifted me out of the chair. Snarling through clenched teeth, he dragged me to the door, my heels off the floor, my toes bent backwards and scraping the pile carpeting. He tossed me into the hall. I landed on my butt like a bag of discarded garbage; my head swung back and collided noisily with the wall. "I'm no faggot," he hissed.

"What's going on up there?" Mom called.

Danny slammed his door shut.

"Nothing, Mom," I said.

I got to my feet and trudged to my room, castigating myself for being naïve. How could I expect a star athlete to admit he's a homo? The sore spot on the back of my head was proof that Danny was no flaming queer. He was big, strong, handsome, and athletic, so why choose to be gay, why adopt a lifestyle you have to hide? Maybe I had been too subtle when I implied I had another copy of the pictures he pretended to know nothing about.

I had to find a different way to broach the subject of a 4-F homosexual deferment, a person other than me to convince Danny to come out of hiding and save his life. Father Mac was the obvious first choice; whether he was another of Danny's boyfriends or merely counseling him about being gay, Father Mac might be able to gain Danny's trust and guide him through the deferment process.

Downstairs, the late local news droned in a deserted living room. "The president signed the Voting Rights Act which made southerners' attempts to quash black voting illegal," the news anchor informed viewers. To me, this meant more National Guardsmen would be deployed in our own country to keep the peace, and that meant more fresh draftees would be needed for Vietnam. As though to confirm my thinking, the next story was about the revocation of draft deferments for recently married young men.

The war would now produce young widows and babies who would never meet their fathers.

Chapter Thirty

When the early workers' Masses were over the next morning—the Masses at which my family and I were no longer welcome—I met Marcy and we rode to the rectory. She gave me one set of the pictures of Danny and Mac and waited out of sight around the corner as I knocked on the door and asked for Father Mac. The housekeeper made me wait on the front porch. Several minutes later, Father Mac came to the door but didn't offer to let me in.

"Have you come to give back the rest of the money?"

"Uh, no, there's nothing to give you."

He didn't look like he believed me. "You came to grovel and ask for another chance at the seminary?"

"No, Father, I'm not interested in being like you."

He crossed his arms and gave me a harrumph. "What then?"

"I want to talk about my brother Danny."

His eyebrows shot up and he tried to hide his surprise. "What about him?"

"He's gay."

"Gay." He guffawed. "You mean homosexual?"

"Yes."

"No, he's not."

"I've seen him with other men. I have pictures. I thought maybe you've been counseling him about it."

"You don't know what you're talking about." He didn't have room to pace so he took tiny dance steps on the porch, left, right, left again, nervous steps.

"I've seen you two together, acting very, ah, too friendly."

His head wagged back and forth on his neck like a flower blown hither and yon on its stem. "I have spoken to Danny from time to time, but never about homosexuality."

"What about then?"

"You know I can't divulge what I talk with a parishioner about."

Apparently, I would have to go nuclear to get people to cooperate. I pulled the envelope of incriminating photos from my pocket. "Have a look at these, Father."

He flipped through pictures of him with his arm around Danny in the school hallway and stopped at a photo of his hand on Danny's butt. In real life, that motion looked like a friendly pat on the butt, but in the still photo it was the priest fondling Danny's backside.

"You're the worst kind of sinner," he snarled. He ripped the photos to shreds and stuffed the pieces into his pants pocket. "You and your whole family are going to hell."

"We'll meet you there."

He gave me a shove, and I stumbled off the stoop onto the sidewalk. "Don't ever come back here, Kovacs."

"You're going to wish you had cooperated." With as much derision I could muster, I added, "Mac."

***

Marcy and I rode to Telulah Park to commiserate under shade trees.

"I've swung and missed twice. Once more and I'll strike out. How can I get a hit?"

"We take the pictures of Mac to the monsignor," Marcy said. "He'll make him help us."

"No, he'll just cover it up. The Catholic Church isn't going to admit its priests are homos."

"Then show the pictures to Danny so he can't deny it. It's one or the other."

"I don't want to antagonize him again. He has to give a deposition, see a shrink, and convince an Army doctor. He needs support to get through all that, not threats."

Tension drained from Marcy's face. "We can be gentle with Danny, but we have to force Joe to help his boyfriend."

"Joe terrifies me. What if he's just picking on Danny the way Mac wanted to lure me into something?"

Marcy pulled a dandelion from the lawn and blew its seeds into the breeze. "Then it's back to Danny. Maybe he faked confusion about your *evidence*."

"His confusion seemed genuine."

"Let's come at it from the other direction then. If he's telling the truth, who could know about those pictures other than you and me?"

I was stumped. "No one else knew."

"Think about what you told me, Eddie. Before Danny left for Iowa, someone searched your room. What if someone else searched your room?"

I leaned against the tree, the bark stabbing my back, and gazed at the sky through gaps in the limbs and leaves. The sun snuck through in places and lighted small patches of lawn. The lawn was dappled with sunlight, I thought, *dappled* being a word I had read in a poem. Walt Whitman, maybe.

I remembered the night someone searched my room. Mom was sweating when I came home, but she wouldn't let me go upstairs. We had no air conditioning in our house because Wisconsin was only warm for three months of the year. Mine and Danny's rooms became saunas from June through August. She could have gotten sweaty upstairs. She wanted to know where my camera was. But how could she have known to look for pictures and my camera?

A dastardly thought wormed its way into my brain and wouldn't go away. The clerk at the neighborhood drug store left a note on a picture of Danny and Joe kissing. She was the only person who had seen the picture other than Marcy and me. She told Mom!

"She called Mom!" I said. "Mom knows!"

"She who?"

"The clerk at the drugstore. She put that note on the picture, but that wasn't enough for her. She told Mom."

"That slut couldn't keep her nose out of your business. Your mom knows Danny is queer and she covered it up, threw the pictures away."

I put a hand on Marcy's shoulder and shook her. I couldn't help it; I was on a roll. "She knew before that ever happened. Dad wanted to invite you and Danny's girlfriend to dinner and Mom shot him down. After I followed Danny, she and Dad had a date night but she told Gram not to let me outside. She didn't want me following Danny again. Another time, she said it was strange that I had a girlfriend but shouldn't, and Danny didn't have one but should."

"You let her call me your girlfriend?" She batted her eyelashes and gave me a coquettish rocking of the shoulders.

I chuckled but I pushed on. "She laughed her head off when I suggested Danny could get married to evade the draft. She made Dad pay my seminary tuition so she could get rid of me and save Dad from finding out about Danny."

"Make her help you."

"Will she help me or hate me?"

I raced home, fearing Mom would find and destroy the last pictures of Danny and Joe, but I needn't have worried. She sat at the picnic table, still in her bathrobe, drinking coffee, smoking a cigarette, and staring into the distance.

"You know." I eased up to her.

"Huh?" Her movements were slow, laconic, all the fight siphoned from her emotion-wracked body.

I sat across from her, grabbed her free hand, and gave her my most sincere look. "You know that I know about Danny and that's why you destroyed the pictures and searched for more of them last week."

She pulled her hand away and fiddled with her bathrobe collar. "I don't know what you're talking about."

"I have another copy of the pictures. You can't deny what we both know."

Her hooded eyes, snake eyes, opened just enough to betray her surprise. "Don't do this to us, Eddie."

"This is good news, Mom, because the Army doesn't take gay men."

Mom wasn't the sharpest pencil in the drawer, but I could see in her eyes that she knew where I was headed. She stubbed out her cigarette. "You want him to tell the draft board he's gay so the whole town will know?"

"Not the draft board—a lawyer and a doctor. They have to keep the secret."

"No one can know we have a gay boy. Frank couldn't handle it. We have a pro baseball player for a son."

"And in ten days you'll have an Army Private."

"That's our fate. We're an ill-fated family. You know that."

"We can't let it happen. We have a lawyer to do all the paperwork and depositions. Dad doesn't have to know."

"Who's we?" She lit a new cigarette.

"Marcy's brother used a lawyer to get out of the draft, got himself declared head of his household. The lawyer knows how to do this kind of thing."

She blew smoke at the sky. "Lawyers cost money."

"We have enough."

She stilled and blinked at me. "You found the money? I should have kept a better watch on you."

"I've moved the money we need for the lawyer. We can't let Dad discover it's gone."

"Jesus, Eddie, that girl has turned you into a conniving little shit. I suppose I should be thankful I have one kid who's normal, likes girls."

"Danny can't go into the Army. He's big, but he'll be bullied. The other guys won't let him into their foxhole. He could get killed in

Vietnam. Best case, he'll go into the Army, and then get a dishonorable discharge. Dad wouldn't like that very much, would he?"

She pinched her eyes closed to stop tears from falling. "How did you find out?"

"I thought he was fooling around with Shirley, so I followed him to blackmail him into hiring me at the club. Instead, I caught him making out with Joe. Twice."

She choked back a cry. "I knew there was a problem because Shirley tried to get Danny in bed and he wouldn't do it. If Shirley can't get you in bed, there's something wrong."

"You were going to let him sleep with your friend?"

She laughed mirthlessly. "Would have been good for both of them."

Mom's lax attitude toward infidelity was troubling, but I understood. If Danny had slept with Shirley, he'd have put Mom's mind at ease. I returned her mirthless smile. "There were other clues, Mom."

"Which I ignored. So, how does this work, with the lawyer and everything like that?"

"Danny has to give a deposition to the lawyer and then have a session with a psychiatrist, arranged by the lawyer. He has to, uh, admit that he's gay." Shame on me for soft-pedaling the process, but after Danny's first reaction, I needed to make this seem as easy as possible.

"That's it?"

"Almost. The lawyer puts the paperwork together and Danny takes it to Milwaukee on his reporting date." I intentionally left out the parts where we'd coerce Joe and Father Mac to give depositions. That was for me to worry about. If Danny wouldn't cooperate, those depositions wouldn't matter.

"Oh, God, Eddie, that's so hard for Danny to do."

"It's that or get shot at by Commies in Vietnam, Mom."

She jerked back and flicked her cigarette away. "What do you want from me?"

"Help me convince Danny to save himself."

"Okay." She drew a breath. "I'll talk to him."

I walked to her side of the table and took her hand to encourage her to get up.

"Right now?" she said.

"We're out of time, Mom."

"God help me." She stood unsteadily, and we walked into the house and climbed the stairs.

She rapped on Danny's door.

"Go away."

"It's Mom, Danny."

He cracked his door and saw me behind Mom. "Not him."

Mom gave me a forlorn look and slipped into Danny's room. Through the door I heard snippets of unintelligible conversation mixed with snivels and sobs, whether Danny's or Mom's I couldn't be sure. When Mom emerged, her eyes were red and her cheeks moist.

"I tried, Eddie, but he denies everything."

"That's no surprise." Through the cracked door, I yelled, "I have pictures, Danny."

"Go away!" He pushed the door closed.

"He's always been the marked child, like my brother, marked for an early death. I can feel it." She patted my shoulder and left me stranded in the hallway.

Danny's refusal to cooperate left me one last option: I'd have to twist Joe's arm to corroborate Danny's homosexuality, and I wanted Marcy with me to do it because Joe would be less prone to violence if I had a witness.

Chapter Thirty-one

I was about to fall off a railroad trestle and into the Fox River.

"Hey."

Someone nudged my shoulder and woke me from my dream.

"Wha? Wha?" I shook off visions of rushing water.

"Tell me how I dodge the draft."

"Now?" I rubbed the sleep from my eyes and recognized Danny's curly head hovering over me. "In the morning, dingleberry."

"Now, goober. Mom and Dad can't know."

I swung my legs out from under the covers, sat upright, and yawned.

Danny sat in my chair. He did not turn on my lamp. "How does it work?"

I shook the cobwebs out of my head. I'd only get one chance to convince Danny to make this perilous journey. "We hire a lawyer who takes your statement—he calls it a deposition—and he gets you an appointment with a psychiatrist."

"A shrink? Why?"

"Homosexuality is a mental defect."

"I'll say, but I'm no homo, Eddie. I let Joe do things so I could get a baseball tryout. It worked."

I might have fallen for Danny's denial if weren't for all the clues. He never had a girlfriend. He didn't take advantage of Shirley's advances. Mom covered up for him. He displayed a degree of passion with Joe that couldn't be faked.

"To get out of the draft, you have to convince the lawyer and the shrink that you're a homo. You have to tell them about your experiences with Joe."

"Jesus, I didn't like it."

"It's that or you'll be slogging through the jungle, sidestepping booby traps"

"Christ Almighty, I don't want to talk about this stuff with strangers."

"No one will ever know what you tell them. Attorney-client privilege and doctor-patient confidentiality conceal your statements."

He was nearly invisible in the darkness, but the sound of air rushing from his lungs reached me. "You talked to the lawyer?"

"Yes, that's why I know how it works. He's ready to help."

"Lawyers are expensive."

"I stole the money from Dad. He was saving up to bribe a doctor for a 4-F."

"Dad bribed a doctor?"

"He arranged it but didn't have enough money to pull it off."

Danny didn't speak for a minute or two. "All he told me was that he had fixed it."

"This way is safer and not a crime. The lawyer and shrink are just doing their jobs, and you really did have homosexual encounters. I have the pictures."

"You're a creep, Eddie. When this is over, the pictures get shit-canned forever. Got it?"

"Got it."

"That's it? I talk to a lawyer and a shrink?"

"That's it." I didn't think that was a lie. I intended to take care of Joe and Father Mac myself.

***

We did lie to Mom. Danny said he was taking me to the golf club to get a job. With the top up under threatening skies, Danny and I rode in his claustrophobic little sports car to Mr. Peter Klein's law office. He didn't drive fast and he didn't take sharp corners. At every stop sign and traffic light he seemed tempted to turn around, but he stayed the course.

Marcy was already there. With a sly grin, she handed me the paper sack of pictures.

Dolores let us in, giving Danny a thorough once-over as she called for her husband. She accepted payment from Marcy, gave us a smile, and stuffed the wad of bills in a pocket of her dress. Pete came out wiping his lips with a napkin—he seemed always to be eating—and examined Danny as though he were a prize bull up for auction.

"Gonna be a tricky one." The lawyer grinned, as though relishing the challenge.

"Looks more like a movie star than a queer," Dolores said.

Danny stiffened. "I'm not—"

"I brought the pictures as evidence," I said.

"Jesus, Eddie," Danny slumped and ran a hand over his face.

I pulled a copy of the pictures of Danny with Joe and Mac from the bag and handed them to Pete. I wrapped the sack around the remaining copies and put it in my pocket.

Dolores peeked over the lawyer's shoulder as he flipped through the prints. Pete stroked his five o'clock shadow—already prominent at 9:00 a.m.—and whistled.

"Such a waste." Dolores shook her head.

"Okay, Danny, let's you and me get started." Pete rose and started toward the back room.

Danny didn't follow. Pete turned back and grasped Danny's arm, tugging him out of his seat. Danny dug in his heels like a recalcitrant horse.

"I can't do this." Danny shook his head.

"Listen, son," the lawyer said, "you don't want to go to war. Korea was my war, and it haunts me to this day. I saw things I can't forget and I experienced terror that crippled my nerves. The Army will train you to kill and tell you that if you're good at killing, you'll survive. It's a lie. I survived only because I was luckier than the guys who died. Or, worse, got maimed. The lucky ones come home and wear their souvenirs and march in their parades and act like they had something to do with it, but they didn't. They were just lucky. Don't test your luck, son."

Danny's face tightened, the flesh in his cheeks crawling back to his ears. He looked like he was about to be sick.

"You have to do it, Danny," I said. "You can't be a soldier in this war."

"All wars are started by egomaniacs but they're fought by the poor," Dolores said. "Draft dodging is the privilege of the wealthy, but you have a legitimate claim. Don't waste it."

Danny gave me a forlorn look and I returned a slight nod.

The lawyer gently pulled Danny's arm and led him to his office.

Dolores brought Marcy and me Cokes in the distinctive glass bottles and we took seats in visitors' chairs. I wished I could be with Danny to help him give the right answers.

Dolores said, "I'm the witness and have to swear to what your brother says."

She left us alone in the outer office to consider whether we were doing the right thing. Whether Danny's claim was legitimate or not, I concluded that morality was a luxury the poor couldn't afford. I had to prevent Mom's premonition from coming true. I had to save the Mockingbird.

After more than an hour, the three of them emerged. Dolores was stone-faced, Pete stern, Danny bedraggled and exhausted.

"What the doctors expect to hear," Pete explained, "is that a gay guy felt different than others from an early age—say seven or eight—and looked actively for other kids who seemed the same. A gay boy is attracted to other gay boys and forms relationships with them, and they all keep the secret until they're old enough to act on it." He placed a comforting hand on Danny's shoulder. "That's not Danny's case. He was the same as normal kids, played sports and so forth, but never felt comfortable around girls, never had the urge to pursue them, ah, romantically. An older man recognized his, uh, queerness, and awakened his, ah, condition. Right, Danny?"

"I guess so." Danny shrugged.

"You'd better be sure when you talk to the psychiatrist," Dolores said. "Would be easier if you'd admit to returning the favor when your boyfriend did things to you."

"I didn't do anything," Danny insisted.

"Then you'll need a statement from the boyfriend." Pete was adamant.

"What about Father Mac?" Marcy asked.

"He just gives me advice." Danny didn't make eye contact with anyone.

To Pete, Marcy said, "The priest is queer, went after Eddie, too."

"The important thing to tell the psychiatrist," Pete said, "is that Danny enjoyed his homosexual experience and willingly repeated the experience several times. To the Army doctor Danny will say he wanted more of those experiences and intended to look for a more age-appropriate partner than his neighbor. The Army does not want gay guys seducing other soldiers."

Danny made a choking sound like he was about to puke.

Pete flashed Danny's sworn statement. "Took a while to get it right but this a good one."

"Made a movie of it, too," Dolores said. "He looks like he's in pain and that should help."

"When he speaks to the psychiatrist, his mantra is, 'I can't help who I am. I like boys,'" Pete said.

Danny groaned.

"You're gonna need depositions from the neighbor and the priest to have a chance at this." Dolores placed a hand on his shoulder.

"They won't agree to depositions." Danny was worn down to the nub, like a pencil that had been sharpened too many times.

"Don't worry, we'll make those guys play ball," Marcy said.

Outside, Marcy gave Danny a hug and told him it was going to be all right. I felt a twinge of jealousy; Danny could have had any girl he wanted, if he had wanted one.

I broke their embrace by saying, "You have to ask your friend, Joe, for help."

"Don't make me do that."

"He was your baseball mentor, took you under his wing."

"It's too embarrassing. Joe will kill me if he finds out I've told anyone about what we were doing. I'm afraid of the guy."

"Okay, we'll leave you out of it," Marcy said.

Her plan was to drop a note wrapped around pictures in Joe's mailbox.

What bothered me about the plan and the whole strategy to get Danny a 4-F deferment was the possibility that Danny was telling the truth—he was no more gay than I was.

"Do not tell Dad," Danny said as he drove us home.

"The Pope couldn't make me do that."

***

Dad was red-faced, waiting for us.

"Where's the money, Eddie?"

Danny stayed near the back door, poised to flee. He looked as though a bear had just popped out in front of him.

Mom sat frozen at the kitchen table, her finger laced through the handle of a coffee cup. Her head and eyes and shoulders moved in jerky motions, an attempt to communicate with me, but I didn't know what her body language meant.

"What money?"

"Don't mess with me, Eddie. You were the only one who knew where it was."

A slight shake of the head from Mom. "I don't know what you're talking about."

"Did you give it back to the priests so they know now that I stole it? Am I about to be arrested?"

My plan had been to say that I took the blame so they wouldn't involve the police, but Mom's signal meant I should deny everything. "No, I only gave them what you made me steal. I took the blame for you."

"You lied to me," Danny snarled at Dad. "You bribed a doctor so I could cheat my way out of the draft."

Dad lunged toward Danny. “I tried to save your baseball career.”

Danny gave Dad a smart aleck look. “*My* career or *yours*?”

“Are you as ungrateful as Eddie and your mother?” He turned to me. “Where is it, Eddie?”

I was trying to think up a new answer when Mom blurted, “I gave it back.”

Dad slammed his hands on the table. “How stupid could you be? Now they know.”

“They don’t know. I slid the envelope through the mail slot at the rectory. They were coming for you, Frank, and I didn’t want it here when the cops showed up.”

“We needed that money, Gail.”

“You were never going to have enough for the doctor.”

“We have bills.”

“You have the money you borrowed at work.”

He scoffed. “You’ve cooked your goose. You can work the soda fountain at Woolworth’s. You’ll look real cute in the pink outfit,” Dad said.

***

My life had become a series of nocturnal forays to correct one problem or another. In the black hooded sweatshirt, I climbed into the garage attic and counted out two hundred fifty dollars, the last of the church money. The two hundred Dad had gotten at work was his problem.

Then I crept through backyards and past Joe’s dark windows before scampering between houses to the street. A rubber band secured the note around the three pictures I had taken of Joe and Danny. The note read:

Joe: Your good friend Danny is grateful for your help with the baseball tryout. Now he needs your help to avoid the Army so he can keep playing baseball. He’s been drafted but can get out of it by admitting he’s gay. All you need to do is go to the office of Peter Klein, a lawyer, and sign a statement that you had a relationship with Danny. No details required. The lawyer has to keep it confidential. If you “play ball” your boss and neighbors will never know you helped Danny. Otherwise …

The package went into Joe’s mailbox and I raised the red flag to get his attention. Trotting home, I felt like a Viet Cong terrorist setting a booby trap and waiting for the explosion that was sure to come.

Chapter Thirty-two

The explosion came when Joe Morada banged on our back door after Dad, Danny and I returned from Sunday Mass at St. Mary's uptown.

"Get out here, Danny," Joe bellowed.

Danny gave me a questioning look as he stepped through the door and faced Joe. I ran to the back door and watched Joe give Danny a one-handed push in the chest.

"What have you done, Danny?" Joe pushed Danny with two hands, moving him to the backyard. "Tell me what you've done."

"I haven't done anything." Danny must have suspected that Joe had been asked for a deposition, but he continued to play dumb. "What are you upset about?"

Joe gave Danny a third push and that lit my fire. I burst from the backdoor and jumped on Joe's back. Joe twisted around trying to throw me off. As though I were on a bucking bronco, I hung on for dear life.

Danny seized Joe's shirt and stopped his spinning momentum.

Joe grabbed my arms, pulled them apart, and with one violent twist, shook me off. I landed on my butt and my head snapped back and struck the stone façade of our house. My vision clouded, but I saw Danny get Joe in a headlock and throw him onto the ground.

"Get in the house," Danny shouted at me.

I ran straight into the bathroom.

"I told you not to go in there," Mom yelled from the living room.

I closed the door, locked it, and raised the window.

Joe sat up and swiped grass off his head and arms. He told Danny about the note and pictures in his mailbox.

Danny admitted that he had engaged a lawyer to get out of the draft. "I had nothing to do with a note or pictures. I was going to ask for your help."

"Your dad must have put the note in my mailbox."

"Couldn't have," Danny said. "He doesn't know about us or the lawyer and I don't want him to."

"Then it was the lawyer. They're all sleezy as hell."

"Could be." Danny must have known it was me. Or Marcy. "The lawyer needs your deposition to make it work so he can get his money."

"You told him my name?" Joe cursed.

"It's all confidential and protected by lawyer-client privilege. I need it to get back to baseball."

Joe stood. His feet pawed the ground like a bull preparing to charge a matador. "It will be a secret?"

"Absolutely. Otherwise, you'll never see me again."

Joe's expression softened. "You haven't been around in a while. Thought you'd forgotten about me."

Danny shrugged. "I've just had all this stuff to deal with."

Joe gave Danny a warm smile. "Come over tonight and I'll cook you dinner. Tomorrow I'll see your sleezy lawyer."

They embraced, and Joe headed home.

Was Danny willingly going on another date, or using Joe again to get what he wanted? I couldn't convince myself one way or the other.

When Danny came inside, Mom said, "What was that all about?"

"Joe heard I might have to quit baseball. He was upset. Put a lot of effort into getting me a contract."

Nice recovery, brother!

Danny took the stairs two at a time and closed his door behind him.

Poor Danny. Guilt crept into my organs like an evil virus. A lot of people had taken the blame for the things I'd done.

As I started up the stairs, I said, "I only had to pee, Mom. No stink in your bathroom."

***

On Monday, Marcy and I slumped in our pew behind three old ladies only to be disappointed when Father Mac emerged from the sacristy to say the early workers' Mass. We had to sit through that Mass and the second Mass before we could corner Father Bauer.

Marcy deserves all the credit for this plan: Since Father Mac resisted my attempt to strongarm a confession, we'd coerce Bauer to convince Mac or we'd expose Bauer's dalliance with Sister Mary Alice. It sounded like a complicated plan to me.

"Let me have the pictures," Marcy said. "I'll do this to save you the embarrassment."

I let her have the envelope with one copy of the pictures of two priests violating their vows.

As Bauer's Mass concluded, we snuck up a side aisle and into the sacristy. The handsome priest fumbled the chalice when he saw us waiting for him.

"You're not welcome here." He glared at me as he picked up the chalice.

Acting as though I was still in charge of altar boys, I told the two young altar boys to leave us and they complied.

"If you've come to blackmail me, you're wasting your time. Coming from a disgraced family, no one will believe anything you say."

Marcy waved the picture packet at him. "People will believe the pictures we have of you and Alice having a picnic. Kissy-kissy fun in Telulah park. Remember that day when Alice changed clothes in your car?"

Bauer's ruddy complexion couldn't hide a flush of embarrassment. "I've sinned and I've confessed." He disrobed and started for the door, but I blocked the exit.

"You may be right with God, but the parishioners might not be so quick to forgive you," I said.

"If you care about her, you should think about Alice," Marcy said.

His Adam's apple bobbed when he swallowed. "I tried to get you into the seminary, Kovacs, I really did, but you made it impossible. You're a sinner … just like me."

"We don't want to shame you," I said. "We want your help. Can we go somewhere to talk in private?"

He seemed resigned to listening because he led us into a classroom and locked the door behind us. I explained Danny's predicament and Father Mac's refusal to help. Marcy held the pictures of Danny and Mac for Bauer to see.

"These photos aren't proof that Mac was doing something sinful with your brother," Bauer said.

"Your parishioners might see things differently. Mac doesn't have to admit to doing anything wrong. He just needs to confirm that he was counseling Danny about being gay."

"Convince Mac to help Danny or we make your picnic pictures a public scandal." Marcy handed the picnic pictures to Bauer.

Bauer's eyebrows flicked up and down as he leafed through them. "Sister Mary Alice and I had a crisis of faith, but we've reconfirmed our vows. It would be an unnecessary tragedy to expose our sin."

"It would be a tragedy to refuse help for Danny," Marcy countered.

"I assume you have another copy of these pictures."

"You'd assume correctly," I said.

Bauer pursed his lips and nodded. Unlike Mac's crazed ripping up of his pictures, Bauer slipped his into a pocket inside his cassock. "Can I have the pictures of Father Mac and Danny?"

"Of course." Marcy handed them over.

Bauer sighed. "I'll have a talk with Father Mac."

***

I had looked up grave markers in the yellow pages. Marcy and I rode to Appleton Monuments, Inc. on Wisconsin Avenue and got help from a smarmy guy who wondered why kids were buying a gravestone.

"This isn't some kind of a prank, is it?"

"No, sir, it's for my grandmother's grave. My parents can't afford it, but I have paper route money. They'll be surprised that I bought it." What I had in my pocket was the last two hundred fifty dollars Dad had stolen from the church. I left him the two hundred dollars he had borrowed so he could pay it back.

The smarmy guy showed us several options, but the standing markers were too expensive. I picked a simple flat marker. Then he told me they charged by the word for the engraving. Symbols, like a cross, were extra.

"Okay, no cross. Just write *Abigail Sachs Jaeger* and her birthday and the day she died."

He calculated the price and I still didn't have enough money.

"I'll pay the rest," Marcy said. "Add a cross and a Star of David."

"You want both symbols?" The man was nonplussed.

"That's right. Both."

"You don't have to do this," I said to Marcy.

"I want to. I loved her."

The man calculated a new price. I handed over two hundred fifty dollars and Marcy paid the rest. It seemed appropriate that Gram had gotten a small reparation from a church that had denied a divorce.

We told the man where to install the marker.

As we stepped into the sunshine, I mumbled, "Death is big business."

***

Danny kept his appointment with the psychiatrist that day. When he returned home, his eyes were bloodshot from crying. He went straight to his room saying he didn't want to talk about it.

For two days, Marcy and I held our breath, often lolling under shade trees in Telulah Park. Then Marcy lost her patience. She went to the law offices to see if our arm-twisting had worked. She had me meet her afterward.

"Father Mac was just leaving. I had to hide around the corner so he wouldn't see me."

"Took him a while to do the right thing. I'll have to thank Bauer if I see him."

"Mac swore that Danny needed counseling for his sexual preferences. According to Dolores, Joe was candid about the times he and Danny engaged in homosexual acts."

Back home the mood was somber, so I hid the ebullient swelling in my chest; Danny was going to get through this.

On Friday, Danny boarded a train for Milwaukee with half a dozen other draftees, all of them as young and as scared as him. The sendoff was tear-soaked. When I hugged Danny, I whispered, "You know what to say. I'll see you tonight."

In the car heading home, Mom sniffled. "We'll never see our boy again."

She was wrong.

Danny called from the bus station late that night—apparently rejects didn't merit the cost of a second train ride—and said he had gotten a 4-F medical deferment.

"See," Mom said, "we didn't have to steal and cheat."

Oh yes, we did.

"I have some kind of problem with my eyes," Danny lied. "That's why I have trouble hitting breaking balls. Would have made firing a weapon difficult."

Danny woke Joe who joined us for a backyard party that lasted until the wee hours of the morning. After Joe left, Mom, Dad, and Carla went to bed, and I retrieved the nasty photos from my room, a pack of matches from a drawer in the kitchen, and two beers from the frig.

Danny and I went to the burn barrel at the back of our yard where I pretended to conduct a sacred ritual as I lit the pictures of Joe and Danny on fire. We clinked beer bottles and I toasted Danny for his courageous run through the military gauntlet.

"It's the worst thing I've ever had to do," he admitted. "At first, they screamed at me and called me a draft dodger. I kept saying what Pete told me to say. They were angry."

"But you had the legal papers."

The fire cast flickering light and streaky shadows on his tortured face. "Yeah, they read the papers and treated me like I had the plague or something. They left me alone in a room for hours. Guess they thought

I'd change my mind, but when they came back, I said it all over again, so they made me describe to three doctors exactly what Joe did to me."

"That had to be hard. Did it convince them?"

"Oh, hell, no. They threatened to call my parents if I didn't confess I was faking it, but I remembered what you told me about confidentiality. I didn't give in."

"You beat them at their game and they gave you the deferment."

"Yeah, they finally gave me the deferment and sent me home. It was all terrible."

I had to hand it to Danny. It took immense bravery to remain steadfast through that ordeal. I was ashamed of the relief I felt; my screw-up was fixed at Danny's expense. But Danny was safe and that's all that mattered.

"Well, we can go on with our lives now."

I couldn't have been more wrong.

Chapter Thirty-three

I rode along as Dad drove Danny to the bus station. Unlike the day Danny took the train to the induction station, Mom shed no tears. She was jubilant. Her boy had survived the draft and achieved his dream. Carla did cry. I didn't know she and Danny were that close.

When Danny hugged me, he whispered, "Thank you."

We waved as the bus pulled away and carried Danny back to Davenport, Iowa.

On the ride back home, I said, "I have to register for high school."

Mom twisted around in her seat. "I'll give you your birth certificate, and you can do it yourself. It's on Ballard Road. The people in the office might remember me."

The high school on Ballard Road was the public high school. I doubted anyone would remember Mom from the class of 1943. "I'm not going to that school. I'm going to Xavier, the new Catholic high school on Prospect Avenue. I'll need money for tuition."

"I'm not paying for more Catholic schools." Dad glared at me in the rearview mirror. "Not after what they did to us."

Seemed to me Dad had committed crimes against the church, not the other way around. "You don't have to support Danny. Or Gram. It's my turn."

Dad smacked his hand on the steering wheel. "No!"

"We've been kicked out of the church. They might not consider you a Catholic," Mom said.

"Fine. I'll drop out of school and go to work in a factory, like Gram did," I said.

Dad punched the steering wheel again. "No more lip, Eddie!"

***

Mom and Dad had no choice but to leave me in charge of Carla so they could have one last date night before the union election of officers on Monday.

I did my best to mimic Gram, drowning hotdogs, finding TV channels, adjusting the rabbit ears, playing silly card games. It wasn't so bad. Carla said I was more fun than Gram and that we'd have these nights together forever. She finally went to her room to sleep, but I didn't want to be upstairs if she woke in the night, so I brought my transistor radio down from my room, sprawled on the couch, and listened to Uncle Brucie on WBZ in Boston. Between rock songs, he made fun of the New York Yankees who were in sixth place in the American League. The irony was that the Boston Red Sox were in eighth place and hadn't won a pennant since they traded Babe Ruth to the Yankees about fifty years ago.

I must've nodded off because the next thing I heard was Mom and Dad hissing at each other in the kitchen like a cobra and a mongoose. They probably thought I was upstairs because they didn't temper their insults.

"No one would talk to me because you're drunk," Dad said.

"I'm sober as the Pope. You're too obvious about wanting their votes. You're like a little kid begging for candy."

"I couldn't beg because you were always in the way."

"The men like me because I have a personality, Frank, and you don't."

"I do great things for those men. They think you're a loose woman."

"They think you're a buffoon, and so do I. You can sleep on the couch tonight."

Uh oh. I scrambled to my feet and quietly hurried up the stairs.

***

No one went to Mass that Sunday. No one had anything to say to anyone else. I delivered the newspapers, then sulked in my room until Marcy called. I met her at Telulah Park although we weren't hiding from anyone any longer. I dropped my bike next to the tree she was sitting against and sat down.

"Why so glum?"

I guess I looked down in the dumps. "I should be happy that we saved Danny—"

"The Mockingbird."

"But I feel like someone let all the air out of my balloon." I was no longer an altar boy, no longer a seminary candidate, didn't even have a church.

"You spent a lot of emotion on Danny, and now it's done. You don't have the priest-thing to look forward to, so you need a new project. And I have just the thing." She looked like the cat that ate the canary.

"What's your new idea?"

"Your mother has brothers!" She grinned and punched my shoulders.

"What?"

"I told you I was going to find Bruno's relatives. His two sons live in Kaukauna with wives and kids. Let's go see them."

Half-brothers. Not all that shocking. Old man Jaeger had said that Bruno was married when he and Gram were lovers. I wondered what Mom did or didn't know about Bruno. If she knew, she had already chosen not to befriend her half-brothers or speak of them. If she didn't know, why hurt her.

"No, Marcy, I'm not going to upend any more lives."

"I thought you wanted to get to the bottom of your family's history." Her voice trailed off in disappointment.

"We hit the bottom of my family's history when Gram died. I know about Jaeger and Bruno and Old Joe and Lottie. I know who I am."

"But your mother doesn't know who she is."

"She knows the Jewish part. If she wanted to know who her father was, she'd have asked Gram long ago."

"Bruno should be punished for raping Gram."

"He's dead. His sons didn't do anything wrong."

She studied my face, as though she wanted to remember every contour. "Then what's next?"

"Tomorrow, I have to register at the public high school. Dad won't pay for the Catholic high school."

"Well, Eddie, you'll get used to fraternizing with the poor and the sinners. It won't kill you." So quickly I didn't see it coming, she lunged at me and pressed her lips to mine. My first kiss!

She held the kiss a few moments then stood, brushed grass and leaves off her backside, and straddled her bike. Over her shoulder, she said, "I guess summer is over."

Chapter Thirty-four

On Monday, I rode to the public high school and registered. It didn't kill me, but it confirmed that my life would now be very different from what I had imagined just a few months before. I understood that Marcy's kiss had been goodbye to an exciting but transitory partnership.

I rode to St. Joseph's cemetery and visited Gram's grave. It pleased me that her marker was in its place, but I wished Marcy was with me to see it.

Like a prisoner resigned to his fate, I spent the afternoon weeding the garden in the hope that Dad would appreciate my attempt at reconciliation.

Mom, Carla, and I ate TV dinners and waited for Dad's triumphant return from the union meeting at which he'd be reelected President. I grew tired of the shows Mom and Carla watched and retreated to my room to read and listen to the radio. It was very late when Dad's headlights flashed through my window. I knew something was wrong when he slammed the back door. I crept to my usual listening spot at the top of the stairs.

"Those idiots elected Bob Van Dyke! I got voted out of office," Dad shouted.

"Why would they do that? Did you mess up a contract negotiation?"

"They're never satisfied. They think the company can just spend more and more on wages and benefits. They don't understand the economics."

There was no hope now for a tranquil household. Dad had lost as much of his life as I had lost of mine.

"Oh, honey, it's not the end of the world."

A rustling of clothing was followed by a shocked grunt.

"Don't push me," Mom screeched.

I jumped to my feet. If he hits her, I'm going to beat him with my bat.

"*You're* the problem," Dad growled.

"What?"

"The members don't like you. They like Bob's wife, so he won."

"My name's not on the ballot. You just lost."

"They look at you, Gail, and they see a lush and a flirt."

"You can shove it, Frank. You're a loser."

Something smacked the wall and broke. Maybe a glass. Maybe a plate.

"Stop it!" Dad yelled.

Mom began sobbing.

"If I'm not heading up the union, I have no reason to work in that filthy mill."

"You can't quit in our condition."

"I need more from life than a mill job."

Although he worried about money every minute of the day, position, status, and prestige defined him, not his paycheck. The union is why he worked at the mill; his position as church treasurer is why he went to Mass. He had been stripped of everything he valued.

***

A taxi dropped Danny at the curb, and he humped his clothes and baseball equipment to the back door. I hustled down the stairs to meet him and Mom in the kitchen.

"What are you doing home?" Mom's face betrayed her confusion.

"The team cut me." Danny dropped luggage and equipment on the floor.

"Oh, sweetie, I'm so sorry." Mom embraced him and held on tight.

"You were hitting breaking balls so well," I said. "What happened?"

Over Mom's shoulder Danny gave me a stern look and a slight shake of his head. "It's my 4-F deferment, for my eyes, you know. The team gave me another physical to make sure I could play, and I failed the physical."

I got it. He didn't want Mom or anyone knowing that we had gotten a homosexual deferment.

"We'll get you to a doctor, fix you up so you can go back."

"Sure, Mom. Help me with Dad. He'll be disappointed."

That was an understatement. Dad was furious when he heard the news. "You have a contract! They can't just cut you."

"You have to pass the physical, Dad."

Mom, Danny, and I were sitting at the kitchen table, hoping to keep the conversation calm, but Dad paced and threw his arms around. Carla cowered in the doorway.

"You should have had him see an eye doctor before he went back to the team." Mom decided Dad was at fault.

"I had to get back or they would have cut me for being absent." Danny shook his head. "I didn't think the 4-F would matter if I could hit the ball."

"They have to honor your contract," Dad said.

"Sure, Dad."

I didn't know how Danny could get out of this jam. The doctor would say his eyes were fine, and then Dad would go off on the team.

"I need a drink," Dad said. "Don't wait up for me."

He barged out the back door, got in the car, and roared away. Dad had never gone to a bar without Mom. Danny's failure was Dad's failure. If Dad's life hadn't ended with the lost election, it was surely over now.

Chapter Thirty-five

I picked the mail off the floor under the front door mail slot and idly flipped through the envelopes as I carried them to Mom. One thick letter addressed to Mr. and Mrs. Frank Kovacs was from the Tri-Cities Hawks Baseball Team, Danny's team in Davenport, Iowa. I plopped the mail on the kitchen table where Mom was drinking coffee.

Mom picked the envelopes up one at a time and tossed them aside. "Bills, bills, bills."

Then she got to the team letter. She glanced at me with a worried look and tore it open. As she read the letter, all color drained from her face. She folded the letter and stuffed it back into the envelope. She rose and carried it into her bedroom. When she returned, she didn't have the letter.

"What was the letter about?" I asked.

"Don't play dumb. It's an official contract termination letter. For 'moral turpitude.'"

How in the world did the team find out? "The lawyer assured me it was confidential."

"Dad can never know."

"No, never. Why was the letter addressed to you and Dad instead of Danny?"

"We had to co-sign the contract for Danny because he was a minor for legal purposes."

There's always one little detail that trips you up when you try to pull a fast one.

***

First chance I got, I searched for the letter in Mom's bedroom. I found it under the mattress along with a few folded dollars she was hiding from Dad. She must have learned her hiding skills by watching TV.

The letter said the team would never have signed Danny had it known he'd already been drafted. Their lawyer said my parents were bad actors and had negotiated in bad faith. The letter went on to explain that when Danny returned to the team with a 4-F deferment, they repeated their earlier physical to confirm he was fit for baseball. They found no abnormalities, so they contacted the draft board to find out if they had missed something. That's when the team learned what kind of 4-F Danny had received. The contract was terminated for moral turpitude. That's what they called homosexuality. No homos allowed in dugouts or clubhouses.

***

Dad basically took up drinking as a hobby. Today, he was at the picnic table surrounded by empty beer bottles when the front doorbell chimed. I opened the door to a man with a purple birthmark on his cheek and an arm sawn off at the elbow.

"I'm Duke Fisher," he said.

"I remember you. Want to see Dad?"

"Yes, sir."

I led him around back to the picnic table.

"Hello, Frank. Hope ya don't mind a visitor."

"Duke?"

Dad struggled to his feet. If three sheets in the wind is drunk, Dad had two sails up and was running with a strong breeze. He was so tipsy he wavered as he waited for Duke to extend his good arm to shake Dad's hand.

"Want a beer, Duke?" I asked. "Need a refill, Dad?"

They both wanted one, so I hustled away. When I got back, I opened Duke's bottle for him.

"Thanks." He flashed me a smile. "I'm learning to live one-handed."

He wore a long-sleeved shirt with the sleeve rolled up even with the bottom of his stump, a pack of cigarettes and a lighter stuck in the neat folds. He showed his one-handed dexterity by plucking a cigarette from the pack and lighting it with his good hand.

I loitered next to the table to hear what happened after the ambulance had carried the poor man away.

"You saved my life, Frank, and I owe you for that," Duke said.

"Nah, Jake saved your life."

"I don't mean getting me out of that blasted machine. I mean getting me disability and my pension. Me and the missus would be in the poor house if it weren't for you."

"That's what the union boss is supposed to do for the members."

"Yeah, ah," he wiped his lips with the back of his good hand, "I want to talk to you about that, about the election." He waved the cigarette at me. "Don't think what I have to say should be heard by young ears."

Took Dad a second to comprehend what Duke was saying. He looked at me and said, "In the house, Eddie."

I wasted no time running inside, into the bathroom, closing and locking the door, and raising the window.

"You shouldn't have lost the election," Duke said. "You were the best damn president we've ever had."

"Well, the men didn't think so. You never know how people are going to vote."

Duke took a long drag and blew smoke at the sky. "I voted for ya. I hope you'll consider it a favor if I tell you how you lost the election."

"You don't have to tell me about Gail's behavior. I already know."

"Gail? No, everybody likes Gail." Duke sighed. "Two hundred dollars went missing from the union treasury. Some guys thought you took it."

Dad didn't borrow money at work; he stole from the union! He didn't flinch, didn't react at all. The alcohol had deadened his senses. "Why would I steal two hundred? I might steal two thousand." He grinned at Duke.

Dad had learned to dissemble. A necessary criminal trait.

Duke laughed along. "That's what I told the guys. "You wouldn't risk getting caught over a measly two hundred bucks."

"Is that why I lost the election? Because of a lie?"

"That cost you a few votes." Duke drew on his cigarette, took a pull of his beer. "Did you know that Bob Van Dyke's father-in-law is on the county draft board?"

"No, I didn't. So what?"

Dad was too inebriated to understand where this conversation was going, but I knew. I shook with fear. I wanted to stop Duke from revealing the rest. "You guys need another beer?" I shouted through the screen.

"Get away from that window, Eddie," Dad barked.

I backed away from the screen but did not leave the bathroom.

Duke lowered his voice but I could still hear him. "The father-in-law told Bob how your kid got out of the draft, and Bob whispered it to all the members."

I couldn't see Dad, but I imagined him thinking through his alcohol daze because a minute passed before he said, "Danny got a 4-F because of his eyesight. Now it's cost him his baseball contract. What does that have to do with Bob's big mouth and the election?"

"Eyesight? That's not what Bob told everybody. He says your boy got a 4-F for bein' queer."

"My son is no faggot! That ass wipe is spreading lies. He cheated his way to winning that election. We'll have a new vote."

The silence in the backyard made my skin crawl. I heard the snap of the lighter being closed as Duke lit another cigarette. I moved back to the window and watched.

"Now I feel terrible. I thought you knew about your son, Frank. I only meant to tell you how Bob found out. Some guys voted against you because your boy is queer, and some guys voted against you because he's a draft dodger. All the members served either in the big war or in Korea, you know."

"It's not true! This is some kind of trick to win an election. I'll get that man fired."

"You better check with your boy before you raise a ruckus, Frank. Bob has the papers, official from the draft board."

Dad knocked over beer bottles as he got to his feet. "I have to take care of this right now. You better go, Duke."

I burst from the bathroom yelling, "Dad knows! Dad knows!"

Mom darted out of her bedroom with Carla. Danny dashed down the stairs. We gathered in the kitchen, a string of condemned prisoners about to face a firing squad. Dad came through the back door, tripped over his own feet, and hit the floor. We did not help him. He scrambled to his feet, his eyes blazing like a rabid dog. He jabbed a finger at Danny.

"Tell me the truth, son. How did you get a 4-F?"

"Carla," Mom said, "go in the living room and turn up the TV real loud."

Looking scared, Carla did as she was told.

Mom took Dad by the arm and guided him to a seat at the table. She sat across from him. "Calm down, Frank, and let us tell you the story."

"What the hell is going on behind my back?"

Danny glanced at me, and I shook my head.

"I'm not gay," Danny said confidently.

"You *pretended* to be a homo?" In a flash, Dad's face morphed from surprise to confusion to rage.

"Yes."

"How'd you do it, Danny? Did you go to Milwaukee and prance around in front of the doctors, tell them you like boys?" Dad made a limped-wrist gesture and mimed acting like a flamer.

"Eddie fixed it," Mom said. "Got us a lawyer and a shrink to say

Danny shouldn't be drafted."

"*Eddie?* Eddie, the mistake." Pure hatred poured from his eyes.

"You were going to bribe a doctor, but you failed." I shook a fist at him. "I did what you couldn't do, old man."

He pointed a finger at me, and I was glad it wasn't a gun. "You cost me the election!"

"The election is all you care about?" Mom asked.

"What about *me*?" Danny wailed. "I got cut because of the 4-F."

"They can't cut you because you're a homo."

"Stop calling me a homo."

Mom went to her bedroom and returned with the contract termination letter. She threw it at Dad. He opened it, blinked his eyes to focus, and read it.

"Moral turpitude. What's that?"

"It means they don't allow homos on the team," I said.

Dad slammed his fist onto the table. "So, you ruined Danny's life, too."

"Want to see him in a flag-draped coffin? Want to be Gold Star parents? You only tried to save him from the draft so he could play baseball."

"We'll fight this." He tossed the paper on the table and it slid to Mom. "He has a contract."

She picked it up and read aloud the part about negotiating in bad faith. "They'll say the contract was invalid. We signed it knowing Danny had been drafted."

Dad slumped forward, two elbows on the table, a hand running through his thinning hair. "My life is ruined," he moaned. "Everybody knows,"

With the stark, honest-but-ugly revelation that Dad cared only about his destiny and reputation, our fragile family was torn asunder and time stood still like an immutable date in a history book. Our family's disintegration was a preordained certainty, born of middle-class poverty, conflicting ambitions, and internecine battles, but the astonishing weight of bigotry was "the last straw."

Chapter Thirty-six

Danny never unpacked. I helped him carry his things to the driveway. He stuffed small bags into the tiny trunk of his car, lowered the canvas top, and comically piled the rest onto the passenger seat.

Mom came running out of the house. "Where are you going?"

"You wanted me to get a job and a place of my own—I heard you say that. Well, now I have."

"How are you going to support yourself? Where can you work?"

"Joe hired me at his mill."

"Oh, my God. Am I ever going to see you again?"

"Of course, Mom, but not with Dad around."

In the bravest act I had ever witnessed, Danny started his little car and drove away. Mom was wrong; Danny would have a life of his own, and he would claim that freedom because of what I did. I was proud of him and envious, too.

Upstairs, my life seemed suddenly empty without him in the next room. I walked through his open door and was struck first by the bare spaces once occupied by the possessions that he had taken with him, and then by the things he had left behind. On the crude shelf over his bed, half-a-dozen baseball trophies stood as forlorn reminders of a life forsaken.

***

That evening, the local news broke the story about a scandal at St. Catherine's church and elementary school. The story was front-page news in the newspaper, too. Someone had sent a letter and pictures to the TV station, the newspaper, and the Bishop of the Green Bay Diocese alleging misbehavior by the priests and nuns. Specifically, it charged Father Bauer and Sister Mary Alice with fornicating, Father MacMillan with sexual assault, and Monsignor Muller with dereliction of duty in failing to manage his parish. "Out of respect for the Catholic Church, we won't show the shocking pictures on television," the TV anchorman said. "The letter was anonymous, but was signed, 'For Gram.'"

The daily newspaper had no such scruples and printed a picture of two unidentified people kissing in a park. The implication was clear that the couple were the priest and nun accused of an illicit affair. It also printed a picture of a priest wearing a collar and grabbing the ass of a young man whose face had been blacked-out. The location of the photo was reported to be St. Catherine's elementary school. The young man was obviously not a student.

In his response, the Bishop announced the Monsignor's retirement and the transfer of Father MacMillan to a parish in the rural town of Hortonville. There was no mention of Father Bauer or Sister Mary Alice. The church had covered up the scandal in its usual fashion.

Marcy had withheld a copy of the pictures and used them to get a pound of flesh for Gram.

***

On the Saturday before the start of the new school year, Dad answered a call from the new pastor at St. Catherine's, a Monsignor York. He asked that I stop by to see him. "It's rather time-critical," he said. "Come today, please."

"He knows who ratted on the priests," Dad said. "Now you'll get what's coming to you."

Nervous, but thinking there was nothing more the church could take away from me, I rode my bike to the rectory and rang the bell. The housekeeper let me in and led me to the same office Monsignor Muller had used.

I wiped sweaty palms on my pants as I waited. Shortly, a bald, plump priest with cherubic eyes and cheeks bounced into the room carrying a sheaf of papers. He could have played Friar Tuck in a Robin Hood movie.

"I'm Monsignor York. Pleased to meet you, Master Kovacs." His tone was as pleasant as his demeanor.

"Welcome to St. Catherine's, Father."

He waved me to a seat, sat himself behind what was now his desk, and leafed through his papers until he found the one he wanted.

"Why haven't you followed through on your seminary application?" He held up a paper too far away to read.

I imagined myself in a mine field, tentatively stepping here and there to avoid getting blown to bits. Surely, he must have been told that Dad and I had stolen money? "Ah, Monsignor Muller discouraged me from attending, Father."

"Nonsense." He flashed the document at me. "Your application was accepted, and the initial tuition was paid. Were you having second thoughts?"

The tuition was paid? Perhaps Muller couldn't lay his grubby hands on my tuition money since it had been paid by Dad and not the church.

It was easy to play along and tell the truth. "Yes, Father, I had doubts about my worthiness."

"Seems to me, you're the perfect candidate. Years as an altar boy, straight A student, never in trouble." He folded his hands on the desk, watched me closely.

Was this some sort of cruel game? Was he testing me? I couldn't let this come back to haunt me later. "I did get into trouble once, over missing collection money."

He canted his head, nodded, looking pleased, and gave me his cherubic smile again. The essence of the Catholic faith is confessing one's sins. "Monsignor Muller mentioned the theft. Father Bauer explained that you were covering for your father who had stolen it. You returned the money and took the blame. Is that true?"

God bless, Father Bauer. Just one last lie and I'll be a better person. I promise. "My father stole the money to pay my tuition."

"But he found another way to pay it after you returned it, Father Bauer said."

"My grandmother passed away, and Dad sold her house. But there's no more money where that came from." I sighed, I shrugged, I tapped a foot on the floor. "We won't be able to afford the tuition next year or the year after." *After what I did, Dad won't give me another penny.*

The Monsignor pursed his lips and nodded. "We can subsidize your future years at the seminary if you maintain good grades." He leaned toward me, across the desk. "Do you have any doubts about your faith?"

He obviously had not spoken to Sister Mary Frances. Play it humbly. "Yes, I've had to grapple with doubts." All the things Marcy told me about the church. All the bad behavior by the parish priests. An infatuation with a girl. A kiss.

"Ha! So did Paul. And Thomas, of course. No way to know for sure unless you give it a try."

A try? I'd kill for a try. "If there was a way to try I'd give it my best shot."

"Uh huh." He folded his hands on the green blotter on his desk. "You know why I'm here, of course."

I know all about it. I tried to act nonchalant. "I saw the news reports, Father."

"Everyone did. You have any idea where those pictures came from?" He didn't look angry but the smile had left his lips, the twinkle had faded from his eyes.

So, my lies would have to continue. "No, Father, I have no idea who would disgrace the Church that way."

"It was a terrible misunderstanding. Father Bauer was helping Sister Mary Alice with a crisis of faith and Father MacMillan was counseling your homosexual brother."

For all I knew, he could have been telling the truth about Father Mac, but he was lying about Bauer and Alice. I played along. "Yes, Father, both priests were fine role models for me."

"And the Church took care of the matter, so there's no need for any more gossip about that."

I could read his thoughts on his broad face. He was sending me away like the Church sent Bauer and Alice and Mac away, buying my silence. *Sold.* "It's a sin to speak evil of others."

"Good. We understand each other. Classes start on Monday. If you can get packed up, I'll have our driver take you to St. Nazianz tomorrow."

St. Nazianz. The Salvatorians. I suppressed my surprise. "I thought you were referring to the Diocese Seminary."

He pursed his lips and blinked his eyes in apparent confusion. "I didn't find any registration for the Diocese Seminary. The tuition was paid to the Salvatorians. That's where you want to go, isn't it?"

No registration for the Diocese Seminary. Muller pulled that one but didn't know Bauer had submitted my paperwork to the Salvatorians behind his back.

"The tuition has been paid in full?"

York frowned at me. He must have wondered why I was confused. "Yes, two thousand dollars."

Where did Bauer get two thousand dollars? I thought back to the scene in Muller's office when I returned the money I had stolen. Bauer was vague about Dad's check clearing the bank—one thousand dollars—and he walked out of the room with the cash I had returned—another thousand dollars. Bauer wanted to get rid of me and he had deceived Muller to do it. Had he known Marcy would blow the lid on the church scandal, would he have helped me? Monsignor York doesn't want me hanging around his diocese, either. He'd pay me to stay away from his diocese.

I couldn't pass up the chance to escape the gravitational pull of my family, a black hole into which I could fall like Edward fell in the river, but guilt and shame flooded my senses as I would be the only one of us to get what he wanted. Did I deserve a happy ending?

And did I want to be a priest? What I had learned from Bauer and Alice and Mac was that the clergy are human. I wouldn't have to be perfect to be a priest. Maybe I'd be worthy and maybe I wouldn't be, but there was only one way to find out. Only ten percent of Salvatorian Seminary students went on to the novitiate; if I failed, there would be no shame in getting a good education.

"I'll have to check with my family, Father."

"I spoke to your Dad about it, of course. He's very much in favor of it."

He wants to get rid of me, too. "Then I'll be ready to go tomorrow, Father."

I rode home happier than I'd been in months. I had regained my dream.

Dad was in his usual spot at the kitchen table. "Thank you for letting me do this," I said to him.

"Don't thank me. Saves me from having to look at your face."

Carla emerged from her bedroom looking sad and scared.

I gave her a hug and said, "You'll be fine now. They got rid of the mistake."

Mom watched as I scurried around my room, selecting things to pack in a cheap suitcase.

"Oh my God, Eddie. Will I ever see you again?"

Mom had been complicit in Dad's scheme, the driving force perhaps, and just as neglectful of me as Dad had been, but she had not been cruel or abusive.

"Of course, Mom. But not with Dad around."

1970

Epilogue

When he heard of my scheme to avoid the Army, Danny locked me in a bear hug. "I knew you'd find a way. You're too slick to get snagged by the Army."

How slick was it to trade two years in Army green for four years in a sky blue uniform? I was haunted by Jean de la Fontaine's ominous prophecy: "A person often meets his destiny on the road he took to avoid it." I had no idea what my destiny might be.

Danny's townhouse wasn't spacious, but he did have a spare bedroom. "Can I leave my stuff here while I'm away?"

"It's been here for four years. What's another four?"

During four years at the seminary, I left books and summer clothes, a bike, and sports equipment at Danny's place. Just stuff I couldn't store in dorm rooms but used when I spent my summers with Danny.

"What if you decide to get away from here and start fresh somewhere else? You want to schlepp all my stuff with you?"

A storm cloud formed around Danny's eyes. He knew what I was implying. "I'm not going to run away. I'm happy here."

Happiness is such an indefinable state of mind. Certainly Danny was resigned to the fact that the brass ring was just beyond his reach; resigned to work in a paper mill for our gay neighbor, Joe Morada. When we hung out with his circle of friends, he was relaxed, just an ordinary member of the group. No one mentioned his athletic exploits. I never identified a secret boyfriend or girlfriend, but I recognized his friends as a community, a mutual support group of like people. Either Danny was "in the closet," or he had pretended to be gay to get a baseball tryout and a draft deferment. I didn't ask, he didn't tell, and I didn't judge. He bore the stain of his homosexual deferment like Hester Prynne bore her scarlet letter, and I bore an equal measure of guilt for coaxing him down that path.

He was fascinated by my Marcy stories and wanted to meet her, or have me reconnect with her, but I never sought her out. I wanted to remember her as she was during that summer of 1966; the memory mine alone, unshared, and untarnished by the woman she may have become. Marcy's brother hired me as summer help driving a forklift at the lumber yard where he had become a manager, and he told me she was organizing anti-war protests, student sit-ins, and professor strikes at an elite liberal arts college in Ohio.

By chance, Danny had seen an article in the Lifestyle section of the Sunday *Milwaukee Sentinel* about the lives of former members of the Catholic clergy and had clipped it for me. Among the dozen biographical snippets, I read that Ronald Bauer and Alice Schmidt had gotten married and become teachers at a Catholic high school in a Milwaukee suburb. The article quoted Bauer as saying the couple were happy with their choices.

I was happy with mine, too. When I decided not to go to the novitiate, not to become a priest, Danny wasn't surprised. "I think the seminary was just a place to hide from Dad."

From Dad, sure, but, like Marcy, I needed to know what I believed in. Maybe I should have felt guilty about using Diocesan money to get a superior education, but I didn't. They paid for my exile until memories of the scandal had faded to irrelevance. The priests at the seminary weren't disappointed when I dropped out.

"I wanted to get an intensive education in church doctrine so I could make up my own mind and choose my own path."

"You still believe in God, don't you?"

Danny looked worried that I had fallen off the cliff, stranding him with his beliefs.

"Until someone can tell me who lit the match on the Big Bang and where that tight little ball of material came from, I'll believe in God. Don't worry about me; I'm just searching for the truth."

I don't think I put Danny at ease.

The truth is I couldn't handle a confusing and cruel world, a terrifying place formed by a tissue of lies: lies about the Vietnam war; about my religion; about racism; about homosexuality; about my family's origins; and about the mythical American Dream. In 1966 I learned that morality is a luxury the poor can't afford. So, I hid in the protective cocoon of a boarding school where life was regimented, meticulously planned and orchestrated, where everyone followed the same rules. I found tranquility but not enough answers.

Danny has been hiding, too. He admitted he hadn't made any attempt to heal his rift with Dad. Bitter over the loss of the union election and devastated by town gossip, Dad quit the mill, sold the house, and bought a dry-cleaning store in Neenah. He, Mom, and Carla live in the apartment above the store, far from our old neighborhood. Several times each summer, Danny and I met up with Mom and Carla for nostalgic, and sometimes tear-soaked, reunions. Mom says Dad likes being his own boss, a man respected by a group of regular customers. Another irony. He blames me for losing his positions of importance at the mill and the church, but now he's found the approbation he always desired. Mom's arrangement with Dad is that she's his hourly wage employee at the store and her paychecks belong exclusively to her. Carla told me things were better since Dad was happy and Mom had some money. Dad wants Danny to work for him and take over the store when he retires, but Danny refuses to relinquish the freedom to live his own life.

Maybe I have no reason to feel guilty about the disintegration of my family. Maybe my family had to be blown up before it could be reassembled more harmoniously.

This morning, Danny drove me to the train station to catch the same train he had ridden to Milwaukee four years ago.

We hugged, and Danny teared up. "I'll miss you, goober."

"Don't worry about me, dingleberry. This is a piece of cake compared to what you did."

Was it the rocking of the train or my intent to pull a fast one on the U.S. government that made my stomach queasy?

***

An Army captain in a dress unform starts a stopwatch and bellows, "Begin."

I'm relieved to find the questions simplistic. I answer the first forty questions then stop because I don't want to get more than forty right and end up in Cat III. I resist the temptation to look for easier questions. No way will I get more than nine wrong. I sit back, stretch my legs, fold my arms, and relax. A barrel-chested Army sergeant wearing starched fatigues with creases so sharp they could slice cheese, patrols the perimeter of the room. He gives me a quizzical look on his first pass and on his second pass, the kind of look a mother gives a mischievous child. Navy, Marine, and Air Force recruiters meander into the room and look us over like bidders at a stock auction. My guy is here, like he promised.

When time expires, the tests are taken away for grading. During the lull, the draftees raise a ruckus, hooting and howling, throwing pencils at one another, or using them to fake-swordfight. I remain calm and quiet. My Air Force recruiter gives me a thumbs-up, so I am completely unprepared when the Army sergeant yanks me out of my chair and drags me and two other guys out of the classroom. He sits us at a table in a smaller room where a gnarly Marine sergeant leans against a wall.

Pacing in front of us, the Army sergeant shouts, "You're cheaters and draft dodgers." Spittle sprays from his distorted mouth.

The Air Force recruiter hadn't warned me about this step in the process. My piece of cake has turned out to be gristle.

"Y'all are faking it," he screams and slaps a hand on a table. "Acting dumb so you can avoid service to your country. I'm not going to let you get away with it. You're gonna take another test, and if you don't pass this one, you'll be Marines."

He hands the three of us a second test. On this one, each question is a set of four pictures, and I'm supposed to choose the picture that doesn't belong. The first question shows pictures of a car, an engine, a tire, and a cow. The second combination is a barn, a tractor, a hay bale, and a boat. I'm unsure whether this test will secure a grade in Cat IV or leave me in the clutches of the Marine recruiter. More terrified than ever, I answer all the questions correctly.

The Army sergeant picks up our tests and leafs through them. "That's what I thought." He steps over to the Marine sergeant. "I still have business with that guy," he says, pointing to me. "These two," he indicates the other Cat V kids, "are yours."

"I'll take 'em and turn 'em into men," the Marine sergeant says.

The three Marines leave me alone with the hostile Army sergeant.

He pulls up a folding chair and sits across the table from me. The name strip above his breast pocket reads Horner. Sergeant Horner has the broken-veined cheeks of a dedicated drinker.

"You got a score of twenty on the entrance test. That made you a Cat V, only eligible for the Marines." He jerks a thumb over his shoulder. "That Air Force recruiter out there tell you how to fake it? He's an idiot, doesn't know that we count off a quarter point for each question that isn't answered and …" he leans close, "you're not going to tell him."

The idiot recruiter has doomed me to be a Marine!

"I just did my best on the test," I stammer.

"Like hell you did," Horner growls. "You got every question right that you answered and then you quit. You probably would have aced the test if you'd been honest."

Every kid the recruiter coaches fails at the subterfuge because it takes a precise combination of right answers, wrong answers, and unanswered questions to achieve a Cat IV score. The Army is smarter than I thought.

"Let me retake the test. I'll show you how smart I am."

"Hell, I know you're smart enough to be in the Army, so I'm going to make you a tank driver and ship your ass to Vietnam. We'll have a ticker tape parade for you if you make it back. How do you like that?"

I make an audible gulp. "I shouldn't have let that recruiter talk me into cheating. I'm sorry."

"Too late for sorry. I'm doing you a favor by putting you in a tank. Otherwise, you'd be an Infantryman, carrying an M-16 in the boonies, eating C-rations, pulling leeches off your face, praying you don't step on a booby trap, asking God to keep you alive for three hundred sixty-five days."

Horner's speech is scarier than the fire and brimstone diatribes Bishop Fulton J. Sheen broadcasts. I swallow hard. "I am grateful to you for saving me from the Marines and the infantry, Sergeant, but there must be a way to take advantage of my intelligence."

"Sure, if you had played it straight up and made a high score on the exam, you'd have qualified for Officer Candidate School. 'Course the life expectancy of a 2nd Lieutenant in Vietnam is about two weeks, so …" He rubs his chin, raw and red from daily shaving with a straight razor. "There is one way to avoid tank duty," he says, as though an idea has only now popped into his head. He plops a book as thick as a telephone directory on the table. "Here's a catalog of courses you could qualify for if you enlist for a third year." He pushes the thick book toward me. "See if anything looks interesting."

A third year! The Air Force recruiter's ignorance will cost me three years in the Army.

Page after disappointing page, I scan course descriptions for cooks and medics and vehicle mechanics and armorers and radiomen and heavy equipment operators and truck drivers. None of those occupations would save me from Vietnam. Depressed and weary, I recompute my life-or-death calculus—three years in a menial job in Vietnam versus two years in a tank in Vietnam—and the answer comes up in favor of two risky years rather than three wasted and equally risky years. There are no front lines and safe rear echelons in this crazy war. I'd rather die fighting in a tank than get hit by a rocket while stirring a vat of stew.

Horner returns with a document. "I'll fill in the course and have you sign the enlistment."

I take a deep breath. Dad said the Army would make a man of me and there's only one way to prove him right. "I'm not enlisting for a third year. I'm going to drive a tank."

"Let me save your ass, Kovacs." He sounded like he was pleading.

I'm pleading, too—with God. I raise my eyes to the ceiling and ask

Him to keep me safe. "I appreciate your help, Sergeant, but I've made my decision."

"I give a smart-ass cheater a chance at easy duty and you blow me off? You're an idiot."

The sergeant smacks the thick catalog. He leaves and returns with a Captain who administers the oath of service.

"What now?" I ask Horner.

"Get your ass on the bus to the train station. You'll go with the rest of the troops to Ft. Leonard Wood, Missouri for basic training. The fort is called "Little Korea" because the terrain and weather are just as nasty. Have a nice life, trooper."

I step out of the room and look down both hallways, trying to remember the way out of the building. In the room behind me, the captain is talking to Horner. I stop to listen.

"You're losing your touch, Sarge. If you can't get kids to bite, they're going to ship *your* ass to Vietnam."

"I focused on the wrong kid this time," Horner replies. "He thinks he's too good for the schools I can offer a Cat V."

"You should have told him how tankers get broiled alive when they're hit by an RPG."

They share a laugh.

I consider turning around and begging to become a cook or a mechanic, but I can't match Dad's World War II submarine duty by working in a mess hall or a motor pool. I can't be second best to that man.

I turn to the right and find the exit. On the bus, I'm greeted with catcalls and profanity.

"Sucker!"

"Coward!"

The other draftees know why the bus hasn't left the station. A big, blond kid across the aisle taunts me. "I'll be screwing your girlfriend while you're still saluting and pulling KP."

I wave my hands over my head, asking for quiet, and the jeers subside. "I didn't fall for it," I announce.

A boisterous cheer erupts. Everyone on the bus is betting their life in a colossal game of craps. Now I'm rolling the dice like the rest of these kids.

The newly minted soldiers pat me on the back as I make my way down the aisle. The "Band of Brothers" has already formed. I take my seat and close my eyes. I had always dreamed of leaving home to see the world. Ironically, the Army would be the vehicle.

My heartbeat slows as I wonder, not for the first time, if I had done the right thing in that summer of 1966. Had it been necessary to save Danny from the draft, or had I spitefully wanted to show Dad that I could do what he had failed to accomplish?

If I hadn't interceded, Danny could have died in a Vietnam rice paddy or in a testosterone-fueled, anti-gay brawl in an Army barracks. Dad couldn't save the Mockingbird, but I did.

As for me? Well, I'm no Mockingbird.

~The End~

Next

To find out what happened to Eddie, read the sequel, *The Two Lives of Eddie Kovacs*, available wherever you buy books.

Acknowledgements

How many roles can one woman fill? Editor, mentor, muse, and friend to name a few. My humble thanks to Stacey Britt Jackson for taking the entire ride with me from concept through final polishing. Chapter by chapter, Stacey corrected errors, honed prose, offered sage advice, and saved me from my wild impulses. She supplied tough love when necessary and told me what I needed to hear. Most importantly, she quelled my doubts and tolerated my compulsions. You can find her at StaceyBrittJackson.com.

Once again, my wife Angie encouraged me and gave me the room and space and time to do what I do. This novel is the result of her sacrifice.

About the Author

Mike Nemeth, a Vietnam veteran and former high-tech executive, has written four mystery novels in which ordinary people face moral dilemmas in extraordinary circumstances. *Defiled* was an Amazon bestseller in the Crime Fiction Noir category. *The Undiscovered Country* won the Beverly Hills Book Award for Southern Fiction and the Frank Yerby Prize at the Augusta Literary Festival. The book inspired singer/songwriter Mark Currey to compose *Who I Am*. *Parker's Choice,* won a Firebird Award for thrillers and American Fiction Awards for Diverse and Multicultural Mystery, and for Romantic Mystery. His latest novel, *The Two Lives of Eddie Kovacs*, was released in late 2022. Mike's short pieces have been published by *The New York Times*, *Georgia Magazine*, *Augusta Magazine*, *Southern Writers' Magazine*, *Deep South Magazine*, and the *Writers' Voices* anthology. *Creative Loafing* named him Atlanta's Best Local Author for 2018. Mike lives in suburban Atlanta with his wife, Angie, and their rescue dog, Scout.

Made in the USA
Columbia, SC
09 April 2024

34146902R00155